Deadly Intruder . . .

There was a dark pickup parked on the other side of the firehouse. A strong sense of something not being right made her quietly slip in and see what was going on.

A flashlight beam was moving around the fire engine and the pumper. There was something else happening. She grabbed an ax from its place near the door and advanced on the drifting light.

Her heartbeat accelerated as she moved through the darkness between the equipment. She held the ax close to her, hoping she wouldn't round a corner and face someone with a gun.

It probably would have been smart to call the police and let them handle it. Someone dropped something—a heavy tool perhaps—on the floor. The sound ricocheted around the vehicle bay. She dropped down and waited to see what happened next. The flashlight beam hadn't found her. It would be just as hard for her attacker to see her as it was for her to see him.

Stella heard footsteps coming closer and clutched the ax, not giving away her position by making any sound. Her plan was to catch whoever it was off guard, maybe trip the intruder with the ax. She wasn't sure she had it in her to actually use the ax on a person.

"Sweet peppers and fires and ghosts . . . oh my! J. J. Cook's Sweet Pepper Fire Brigade Mystery, featuring Fire Chief Stella Griffin, has it all: a pinch of paranormal, a dash of romance, and recipes that will leave you burning for more. Not to mention a well-crafted mystery that will keep you guessing until the smoke clears in the end."
—Kari Lee Townsend, Agatha nominee and national bestselling author of the Fortune Teller Mysteries

That Old
Flame of Mine

J. J. Cook

BERKLEY PRIME CRIME, NEW YORK

THE BERKLEY PUBLISHING GROUP
Published by the Penguin Group
Penguin Group (USA) Inc.
375 Hudson Street, New York, New York 10014, USA

USA / Canada / UK / Ireland / Australia / New Zealand / India / South Africa / China

Penguin Books Ltd., Registered Offices: 80 Strand, London WC2R 0RL, England
For more information about the Penguin Group, visit penguin.com.

THAT OLD FLAME OF MINE

A Berkley Prime Crime Book / published by arrangement with the author

Berkley Prime Crime Books are published by The Berkley Publishing Group.
BERKLEY® PRIME CRIME and the PRIME CRIME logo are trademarks of
Penguin Group (USA) Inc.

For information, address: The Berkley Publishing Group,
a division of Penguin Group (USA) Inc.,
375 Hudson Street, New York, New York 10014.

ISBN: 978-0-425-25204-8

PUBLISHING HISTORY
Berkley Prime Crime mass-market edition / April 2013

PRINTED IN THE UNITED STATES OF AMERICA

10 9 8 7 6 5 4 3 2 1

Cover illustration by Mary Ann Lasher.
Cover design by George Long.
Interior text design by Tiffany Estreicher.

ALWAYS LEARNING   **PEARSON**

For my grandfather, Henry Koch,
who fought the Our Lady of the Angels' fire in
Chicago, and my great-grandfather, Michael Sebastian,
who drove the fire wagon in the early 1900s.
I'm proud to be related to you both!

Prologue

〰〰〰

"Where's the fire?" The deputy's accent was as thick as syrup when he reached her. "You must not be from around here. We don't get much motorcycle traffic out this way."

Stella knew he'd seen her Illinois plate. "I'm headed for Sweet Pepper. I'm the new fire chief."

"Sweet Pepper, huh?" He licked his finger to draw back the top sheet in his citation book. "License and registration, ma'am. And take off that helmet, if you don't mind. Nice and easy now. I like to see the faces of the people I do business with."

Deputy Chum. His name tag was very white against his brown uniform.

Stella removed the plain, black helmet that matched her 1979 Harley touring bike. Her shoulder-length, straight red hair spilled out around her shoulders. A puff of warm, flower-scented wind caught the ends of it, dancing it around her lightly freckled oval face and stubborn chin. Her brown eyes were filled with impatience at the interruption.

Deputy Chum started to reach for her license, looked up—and stepped back from her.

"Abigail? Is that *you*?" He dropped his citation pad and pen. His eyes unfocused and his face lost all its color. He shook all over.

Stella thought she might need her CPR training. Deputy Chum looked like he was having a seizure or a heart attack. She reached a hand toward him.

He yelled and ran back to his sheriff's car, revved the engine, and left rubber on the road as he raced away.

What the—?

She waited a few seconds to see if he was coming back. When there was no sign of him, Stella put on her helmet, started her motorcycle, and went the other way down the empty road toward Sweet Pepper.

Chapter 1

~~~~~~~~

It was a fine, cool September day in Sweet Pepper when the fire alarm rang. There was already smoke in the air from countless woodstoves and fireplaces—not to mention piles of burning leaves.

"Let's go! Move out!" Fire Chief Stella Griffin shouted above the clamor of the fire alarm as her volunteers got ready for their first fire.

It was the first time in forty years that the fire alarm had rung here and the Sweet Pepper Volunteer Fire Brigade would respond to an emergency. She took out her stopwatch. Everyone, including Stella, was being tested and evaluated. This was where the training paid off—or not.

They'd been practicing for weeks. Stella watched as her seven volunteers grabbed their bunker coats, pants, boots, and breathing apparatus, then jumped on the engine and pumper truck. Four of them carried axes and pipe poles too. They were ready for anything.

She hoped.

There were a few slipups as they got ready. Petey dropped her ax on Banyin's foot. Bert Wando, the mayor's son, slid on the newly resurfaced concrete at the firehouse and appeared to have sprained his ankle. He kept going.

Stella gave him credit for that, but she made him stay behind anyway. He complained about missing their first run, but it was only practice. No point in making the injury worse when they didn't need him to be there. She took her seat in the front of the engine and gave the okay to Ricky Hutchins Jr. to head out to the fire.

The rebuilt engine sprang to life after a lot of TLC and elbow grease from Ricky, who had a gift for engine repair. Sweet Pepper couldn't afford a new vehicle, or they weren't confident enough to spend that kind of money on a new volunteer fire department. Stella wasn't sure which.

The old pumper truck followed the engine, with Kent at the wheel. They'd found the 1970s vehicle in the shed behind the firehouse and had spent hours getting it ready after years of it sitting and waiting for the next call.

Ricky, Stella's engine driver, grinned at her when the pumper had finally started after a few tries that morning. "I told you. She's got some life in her yet."

"Let's get to the fire and we'll see," she replied, pushing back her helmet.

Her customized Sweet Pepper gear was a little big, but it worked. It was only for three months, after all. By that time, the little band of firefighters she'd worked hard to train would be on their own. She'd head back to Chicago, her family, and her fire station.

They were headed to a controlled burn, supposedly to let everyone have an idea of how the fire brigade was doing. Town Councilman Nay Albert had a big farm at the outskirts of town. He'd wanted to get rid of an old henhouse that was falling down.

It seemed like a good way to introduce everyone to a real-life situation. It was one thing to excel at tests and training exercises. It was another to handle an actual fire, even if it was created for them.

The engine and the pumper flew down the two-lane

blacktop from the firehouse with sirens blaring and lights flashing. Cars moved quickly out of the way. So did a few wandering goats that had escaped to chew on some grass near the edge of the road.

Stella smiled when she thought of her first fire, more than ten years ago. Even though she was a third-generation fire-fighter, she'd still been scared. Training had been hard. She'd been the first woman at the station. The men back home, who were now her friends, had placed bets on her not making the grade.

She hadn't wanted to let down her father, uncles, and grandfather, who'd put so much time into helping her prepare for that moment. When it came, she'd been ready.

She wondered if her recruits would be ready. Would they continue on after actually fighting a fire?

She'd lost a few volunteers in the first days of training. Some people had the mistaken idea that a volunteer fire department was a social club instead of a community service organization. She'd let them go, even though she'd cringed inside at how small the remaining group was. Firefighters who wouldn't train were firefighters likely to be injured, or worse. She didn't want that happening on her watch.

The engine made a wide, fast turn onto the narrow gravel road that led to the henhouse. Stella arched one dark red brow at her driver.

Ricky shrugged and apologized. "Never lost control, Chief. This baby handles like she's brand new. Don't worry so much. You're going to get old before your time."

Stella liked Ricky. He was one of the best mechanics she'd ever known and an enthusiastic volunteer. He was a good driver too—if a little fast at times. He bragged that it came from his granddad that drove bootleg whiskey through the Smoky Mountains. Ricky said he'd gone with him on some of those adventures. She'd smiled at some of his tall tales.

"Just follow the smoke and stay on the road," she advised him. "And if you ever take a corner like that again, I'll have you back at the house cleaning toilets while we're out fighting fires. We have people holding on in back."

"I'm sorry, Chief. Really. It won't happen again." Ricky gave her his girl-chasing, boyish smile. His blond hair curled on his forehead, making him look younger than his twenty-eight years and his deep blue eyes were sincere.

Stella nodded and got ready to confront what might be either a great success or a dismal failure. When she'd first read the help wanted ad for a temporary fire chief in the station newsletter back home, she'd never guessed that she'd take someone up on it.

Then she'd injured her shoulder in a difficult fire, and the doctor said she'd be off the job for at least three more months.

What had really pushed her over the edge—the part no one knew about except those closest to her—was finding her longtime boyfriend, Doug, in bed with one of her oldest friends from high school.

Doug was a tough, good-looking cop. He'd seemed as surprised as she was when Stella had landed a lucky punch to his jaw. Before either of them realized, he was on the floor, naked, looking up at her.

It was a mess anyway. She'd broken his nose and he'd threatened to press charges against her. Her union rep had talked with his union rep and they'd come to an agreement. Lawyers got involved. Stella was still angry, but she'd cooled down a lot when she thought she might lose her job. She was still smarting from Doug's cheating, but he wasn't worth ruining her career.

Her station chief, Fred Henry, a man she knew well and trusted, suggested she get out of town for a while. That's when she thought about the opportunity she'd seen in Sweet Pepper. Three days later, she hopped on her old Harley and hit the road for Tennessee.

Ricky did an excellent job pulling the engine up to the fire but not too close. The old pumper pulled in behind. Her volunteers scrambled off the vehicles and began getting the equipment they would need to stop the burn.

They completely ignored the visitors from town who'd come to watch. Members of the town council and about fifty other interested spectators sat in lawn chairs on the other side of the field, trying to avoid the thick gray smoke as they waited for the volunteers to do their job.

Stella couldn't help but smile at the townsfolk out there with picnic baskets, dressed up in linen suits and colorful, lightweight dresses, as if they were on an outing. Everyone was smiling, already proud of their fire brigade without even having seen what they could do. That's the way they'd been from the beginning.

These people had welcomed her with open arms, totally convinced she would do a wonderful job for them. It was nice, and a little scary. She felt like she had something to prove. They seemed to feel that she had already proven herself just by being there.

She didn't join the town observers, though they'd made it clear there was an empty chair and food for her. Instead, she stood off to one side, watching and making notes as her volunteers pulled the heavy hose down from the pumper. They approached the burning henhouse with caution, not quite steady yet with the equipment.

The henhouse had been two stories high at one time. The fire had already claimed the top floor. The roof had crashed in as they'd arrived. Heavy sparks flew everywhere like remnants of fireworks. Heavy rains had made the burn possible. Stella didn't want the entire field to go up in flames. As it was, the mostly harvested, wet corn barely noticed the heat. It smoldered silently.

The old timber was partially rotten. The structure had been abandoned for years. The flames roared up through it, finding plenty of oxygen to feed on. The older pumper began spurting out water, not as much as a newer vehicle would have, but enough to put out the fire.

Stella wasn't worried about the water supply—this time anyway. They might have to consider other options later. In town, they could hook into the fire hydrants, which were fed from the big lake on the far west side. There would be times outside of Sweet Pepper, like this, when they would have to make do with a pumper.

Everything was going fine. Petey—Patricia Stanze—was in the lead, as she had been throughout training. Stella hadn't been sure if the scrawny, twenty-five-year-old waitress would make it through the rigorous tasks she'd set her. Petey was stronger and more determined than she'd imagined. She put some of the larger, stronger men to shame.

The spray from the heavy, powerful hose soaked the flames and left what remained of the henhouse smoldering. Stella was beginning to feel good about the whole operation when fifty-something barber, Allen Wise, tripped over the hose. He went down hard on his face—not really hurt— except for his pride.

What followed was much worse than his clumsiness. His weight jerked the hose from Petey. Sweet Pepper police officer John Trump lost his hold on it too. Kent Norris, a long-distance truck driver who drove the pumper, tried to step in and save the situation, but it was no use.

The hose, propelled by the high-pressure pump, was out of control. Stella's volunteers tried to fall on it and catch hold of it again. It became almost laughable as they tumbled around in the wet red clay that was rapidly becoming mud.

Not wanting to see any more of it, Stella walked over and switched off the pump. At least the fire was out. She supposed it wasn't a total disaster. But it came really close.

"You got the fire out! Good job!" Mayor Erskine Wando jumped to his feet and congratulated them in his hearty manner as he approached He was a large, tall man with a shaved head who liked to wear top hats. "Where's Bertie?"

Stella looked at the proud father of Sweet Pepper High School's star quarterback. "He was injured getting in his gear. He'll be fine. I didn't want him to make it worse by coming out here."

"Getting in his gear?" sneered sleazy town councilman Nay Albert, his greasy black hair combed over his bald spot.

"I hope he can still play football. It seems like his career as a firefighter might be over."

Councilman Bob Floyd, a short man with curly gray hair, was usually pleasant but always seemed to have ulterior motives. "Not a good sign. And not sure about what we've seen here today. Eight weeks gone, and they still can't keep hold of the hose."

Stella knew what he was talking about. They had paid her handsomely to get the group ready. There were only four weeks left. The volunteers still needed a lot of work. She had faith in them. They'd be ready.

"They aren't perfect yet," she said. "They're still learning. It takes practice and constant training."

"You could've told us they wouldn't be ready to fight *real* fires before you left Sweet Pepper, Chief Griffin." Bob glared up at her.

"Gentlemen." Victoria—Tory—Lambert's tone brooked no argument. "I think our volunteers have done very well today. They put out the fire and managed to keep from getting hurt, except for Bertie. I don't know what more we could ask at this juncture. Good work, Chief. I know the group will be ready to stand on their own in the next few weeks."

Stella acknowledged Tory's words with a smile and a nod. She was glad the other woman approved. Tory wasn't on the town council, but her opinion carried weight in Sweet Pepper.

Besides, Stella liked the older woman. She had a gift for wry humor and a sharp tongue when necessary. She'd been Stella's friend and fairy godmother since she'd arrived. When Stella needed anything, Tory had a way of finding it. Tory had been an unexpected ally and cheerleader in the struggle to make the old firehouse useable again and to train the recruits.

"I agree with Tory," said Ricky Hutchins Sr. He owned the Sweet Pepper Café with his wife, Lucille. The pair was always together. Ricky had gray hair now, but Stella had seen pictures of him and redheaded Lucille from years ago.

They were ringers for Lucy and Ricky in the old TV shows.
They were also ardent supporters of the volunteer group.

Of course, his son drove the engine.

"Well, there you have it." Tory smiled at the small group
assembled there in the harvested cornfield, the acrid smell
of smoke filling the air around them. "I suggest we all go
home, take a shower, and find some party clothes that don't
smell like smoke. I'll see you all at the celebration."

The councilmen complained a little—they would never
challenge Tory directly. Stella didn't know what gave the
other woman so much power, but she was glad of it, especially since she was on Stella's side.

"Don't let those old blowhards bother you or take away
from your triumph, Stella," Tory said when the spectators
had started packing up and heading back to their cars and
pickups. "You've done a remarkable job despite the raw
recruits and ramshackle firehouse we gave you to work with.
Enjoy the party tonight. You've earned it."

Stella thanked her. "I couldn't have done it without you."

Tory patted her slightly windblown gray hair, which was
always pulled back and pinned up tight. Her sharp blue eyes
were bright in her creamy face. Despite the smoke, she still
smelled of White Diamonds perfume.

"That's probably true enough. We make a good team,
don't we? Of course, I have an ulterior motive." She handed
Stella an old manila folder that was slightly dirty with time
and wear. "Remember me telling you that my first husband
died in a fire? Look through this. Tell me what you think.
We'll talk later at the party."

Chapter 2

~~~~~~~~

"Everyone on the trucks," Stella said to her crew. "We'll talk about this when we get back to the house."

"I'm sorry, Chief." Petey's large helmet hung off the side of her head, sooty smudges on her delicate face. "We let you down."

"Later." Stella didn't want to discuss this here. The appropriate time was back at the firehouse. "This isn't the time or the place."

Even Ricky seemed humbled by the experience as they drove back to the firehouse. Stella noted his conservative driving down the twilit roads in the long shadows of the Smoky Mountains.

"I don't know what happened," he said. "It seemed like we had it under control until Allen messed it all up. Maybe he's not right for this."

"I thought the same thing about you that first day in training," Stella said. "You couldn't climb the stairs with the hose, remember? You thought it was enough that you worked on the vehicles."

"Yeah. That's right." He smiled back at her. "Why didn't

you kick me out then? You got rid of some of the others. Did you see my excellent potential?"

She laughed. "No. I'd already lost a few volunteers. I didn't think we could afford to lose any more. Besides, if I kicked you out, your parents might have stopped letting me eat at the café."

"That wounds me deeply, Chief. I thought I was your favorite." He turned the big engine into the recently repaved parking lot outside the firehouse.

"You're a handful, Ricky. But you'll make a good fire-fighter someday. Just hold on to that for now."

Stella jumped down from her seat on the engine. She'd purposely left her clipboard, full of critiques, on the dash. When she saw the pathetic faces of her volunteers, she knew it was the right thing to do. She could point out errors later.

"What happened?" Bertie Wando hobbled out of the house wearing his Cougars high school letter jacket and jeans. He was a good-looking young man who seemed more mature than his eighteen years. He wore his hair cut close to his head to keep it from being a bother since he played every sport available. "Did you get the fire out? Was every-one impressed?"

The look on his companions' faces told its own story.

"How could it go wrong?" he demanded. "We've been over it and over it. It should've been perfect."

No one seemed to have an answer for that. They hung their heads and mumbled about the group not working out. Maybe it was too much to think they could save lives and make the town a better place. Who were they after all—certainly not the heroes Sweet Pepper was looking for.

Stella took off her helmet and studied her volunteers. She tried to think what Chief Henry would've said about this back home. His words wouldn't come to her, so she had to use her own from her years of experience.

"I think most of you know that the only reason I'm here is because I was injured in a fire." She smirked a little when she thought about punching Doug. *They didn't need to know that.* "I'm a ten-year veteran. I can show you lots of commendations and ribbons I've received for bravery and doing the right thing at the right time. I can also show you scars from times when I did the wrong thing at the wrong time. Sometimes things don't go the way they should."

"Now everyone thinks we're screwups," Petey called out. "They're never going to take us seriously."

"They will," Stella insisted. "It's going to take time. This one event doesn't make you screwups. You had a few . . . missteps."

They all laughed at Allen, who took the ribbing with a self-effacing smile. He pulled his fingers through the thick head of tobacco-colored hair he took such pride in. The middle-aged barber was good with people. He knew how to make them laugh. It had served him well in his profession and with the fire brigade. "Hey, I never said I could dance—especially not with Petey leading."

That brought more laughter and some relief to the volunteers' stress.

"I'm not going to tell you that you don't need work," Stella said. "You did okay for your first time. You put out the fire. There was no loss of life. The property couldn't have been saved anyway. There wasn't even an injury."

"Not unless you count Bertie," Ricky called out.

"We put out the fire." Kent Norris echoed Stella's words. He was a muscular, forty-year-old man who was beginning to sport a potbelly from his wife's good cooking. "We didn't get killed doing it. I think that calls for a celebration. I know where there's music, barbecue, and beer waiting. I think we should get cleaned up and head down there."

A loud cheer went up from the volunteers. They began to strip off their gear.

Stella stopped them. "I think that's a good idea—after you give the engine and pumper a wash, make sure your gear is clean and ready for the next time, and log your reports on the fire. I want to see them all on my desk first thing tomorrow."

It wasn't a popular decision. All the volunteers, except Petey, muttered and complained. Stella's orders weren't up for discussion, and they knew it.

"I think I might need a ride to the emergency room," Bertie said. "My coach is gonna raise hell about my ankle anyway. I hope it's not broken."

"I'll take him," Ricky said. "Next time, though, you better be able to get yourself dressed without getting hurt, Wando."

Stella thanked Ricky for his help. She cleaned and stowed away her gear. She wrote her report on the fire, such as it was. The engine and pumper were clean and shining again by the time she got on her Harley and headed up the steep road beside the firehouse to the cabin where she was staying.

She knew it would do all of them good to have some time to reflect on what had happened at the henhouse. They'd done all right, but the next time the fire alarm rang, someone's life might be in danger.

It was almost dark by the time she reached the cabin. She turned off the Harley and sat there, not moving.

The porch light was on again. She didn't know if it was someone's idea of a joke or what. Every time she went out, the porch light came on before she got back.

She knew the people of Sweet Pepper wanted to take care of her. They brought groceries and had someone clean the cabin every week. The counters inside were covered with offers for free meals at restaurants in town, free car washes, free dry cleaning, and even free pet grooming. There were coupons for entertainment at Dollywood and Gatlinburg.

It was great—except for the creepy stuff.

Lights came on when they weren't supposed to. Doors opened and closed. Items weren't always where she'd left them. Even the furniture didn't stay in the same place.

At first, she'd thought it was a prank, like at the station back home when she'd first started. The guys had frequently emptied her shampoo bottle and once put a dead mouse in her bunk.

This was different—more subtle. *Weird*.

She'd checked the doors and windows several times. They had been locked tight. There was an alarm, but it was never tripped. She'd even gone to Sweet Pepper and purchased a small camera from the local computer store that would send motion feed to her laptop.

There was nothing *wrong*. But things kept happening.

Stella stepped into the cabin, never quite sure what she was going to find. It looked like an old hunting lodge, made of large, smooth logs that were stained a light brown color. There were three big rooms—living room, kitchen, and bedroom—with a small area off the kitchen that had a rough-hewn table and a few chairs. There was also a second floor. It was obviously used for storage, packed tight with old furniture and other items.

There were deer antlers everywhere, used as a cup holder in the kitchen and as light fixtures throughout the cabin. The living room had a stone fireplace, a large brown leather sofa and matching chair, and colorful Native American rugs and prints. The single bedroom had an oversized log bed in it, along with two dressers and a side table.

Tall windows overlooked the deck in back and the Little Pigeon River. The Smoky Mountains rose up beyond the river, their majestic face changing with each passing hour.

Stella loved to sit out there in one of the handcrafted rocking chairs. It was so different than where she'd grown up. The trees soared above her and the river murmured. No police sirens or squabbling neighbors. Not even any barking dogs.

The town had even put in a hot tub on the deck for her after she'd arrived. It was a dream compared to her cramped apartment back home that overlooked an alley.

She walked up the stairs to the small porch. The door opened before she could touch the handle.

"But crazy things like this don't happen at home," she muttered, stepping inside.

The cabin seemed to sigh, as though her words had made

it unhappy. She knew it was only the wind—at least that's what she told herself. Unusual sounds happened frequently. There was no rational explanation for them.

Out of the corner of her eye, Stella saw something move. It almost looked like the shadowy figure of a man standing next to the hot tub outside on the deck. She shivered and looked away. Obviously she hadn't realized how tired she was.

She'd stopped undressing in the bedroom after her very first shower at the cabin. Usually, being naked didn't bother her. She'd had to get dressed and undressed with twenty men when she'd first started as a firefighter.

Here, she had the odd sensation of being watched even though there was no way anyone could see into the cabin from where it was, isolated on the side of the mountain.

In the bathroom—with the door securely closed and locked—she threw off her smoky-smelling clothes and jumped into the shower. She toweled off and dressed quickly in a different pair of jeans and a red Sweet Pepper VFD T-shirt. She'd packed light when she'd left Chicago. No reason to bring much and very little room in her motorcycle saddlebags to put it.

She'd gained some weight since coming to Sweet Pepper. People were always trying to feed her, and the food was delicious. There was no gym here to work out in either. She'd had to be content with running and training. That might have been enough when she was in her twenties, but at thirty-two, she felt like every biscuit went right to her hips.

She heard a knock at the front door as she was combing her wet hair. "Just a minute!" She slid her feet into slippers, always careful of the southern scorpions her new friends had warned her about, and rushed to the kitchen.

No one was there.

She looked around outside. No one was hiding behind the bear-proof trash cans or on the other side of the cabin. There was a steep drop-off to the river that would have made it hard to get down to the water from there without being seen.

This had to be a practical joke. Maybe Ricky Junior, or

even one of the guys she'd let go at the beginning, was responsible. She was tired of it but didn't want to complain to the police. *Yet.*

She didn't want them to think she was some stupid woman who made things up to get attention. Like Mrs. DeAngelo back home who called in fires once a month and met the firefighters at the door with chocolate chip cookies.

She'd never complained during her first months at the station back home either. Eventually the harassment had stopped. She was sure it would this time too.

There was no more time to think about it. She was missing the big party. It was both a congratulations party for the fire brigade and a fundraiser for the upcoming Sweet Pepper Festival. The festival, three days celebrating all things pepper, was in October. People in town had been out putting up signs and getting things ready for months. The excitement was contagious.

Stella had agreed to play her part during the festival filled with contests, games, and music. She didn't know yet what that part would be. The little town was famous for growing and selling the hottest, sweetest peppers in the world. Even the water tower was painted to look like a giant hot pepper.

She'd heard stories of pepper recipe contests too— chocolate-covered peppers, candied peppers, and stuffed peppers. Stella had never been much of a hot pepper eater, but some of the recipes she'd tried had been really good.

Ignoring the open door to the bedroom that she was sure she'd firmly closed, she pulled on her boots, got out of the cabin, and climbed back on her father's Harley.

The bike was like an old friend who'd come with her on the three-month working vacation. Her dad had helped her rebuild it a few years back after she'd found it in the garage hiding under a big, black tarp.

This was the bike her dad had traveled across the country on when he'd gotten out of college. It came with dozens of stories that she'd heard hundreds of times growing up. It was more than just a ride.

Stella kick-started the bike—it was one of the last Harleys made with a kick start. The motorcycle came to life, ready to run down the road. The transmission needed some work and clunked into first. The chrome was pitted in a few places, but she wouldn't have taken a million dollars for it.

She saw the porch light come on in her rearview mirror as she started back down the mountain. Whoever was doing the pranks was really good at it—she had to admit that. She let it go, like she always did, and kept riding until she reached Main Street in Sweet Pepper.

With such great weather, the party was set in the park adjacent to the old VFW meeting hall. Picnic tables were heaped high with food, and a small band of fiddlers played bluegrass music that traveled up and down the street. At least a hundred people were already at the party. Children ran freely, jumping into piles of red and green leaves, their laughter providing its own kind of music.

There were big, red, pepper-shaped donation boxes set around the park too.

Stella parked her bike and dropped some bills into one of them, then joined the group. At once, ten people offered to make her a plate of food and find her a chair. It was like being a local celebrity.

Two women brought her glasses of iced tea and lemonade, and one of the VFW members offered her a place of honor at the table with Mayor Wando and other members of the town council. There was a podium and microphone set up, which meant plenty of speeches. Stella was getting used to that. She smiled and looked around for Tory.

"I think they want to give us all a medal for putting out the henhouse fire, Chief," Ricky Junior said with a big grin. "Everyone thinks we're great!"

"If we get too many more medals," she said, "we won't be able to walk with them on. We've already gotten medals for getting the fire brigade together and starting up the fire engine."

"Maybe. But they look damn good. We're heroes, Chief. We might as well enjoy it."

Stella started to agree with him. She broke off when she noticed a thin plume of smoke rising straight up into the clear, dark sky. It was coming from the other end of Main Street where the old gingerbread houses were.

"Where's Chief Griffin?" Allen Wise could barely speak, short of breath from running. "Tory Lambert's house is on fire."

Chapter 3

All their emergency pagers went off. Allen ran back to his vehicle. Ricky wanted to go right to Tory's house. Stella had to tell him he couldn't. They needed him to drive the engine.

Stella jumped on her bike and headed after him. She wanted to go to Tory's too. She wasn't sure about leaving her recruits on their first real emergency call.

As she got closer, she heard the alarm screaming from within, and it started her heart pumping faster.

This wasn't an empty old chicken house. This was a crucial test of her volunteers. She said a fast prayer for them, and for Tory, hoping she was somewhere safe. She hadn't seen her yet at the party.

"We're going to need the pumper and the engine, just to be sure," Stella yelled as she parked her bike and raced inside to put on her gear. "We might have water and we might not. Ricky, you drive the engine. Kent, drive the pumper again. Everyone know the way to Tory Lambert's house?"

They all nodded solemnly as they grabbed their equipment and found their places on the trucks.

Ricky set a fast pace for everyone. Stella didn't complain

as he raced down the road to reach Sweet Pepper, sirens blaring. Already the thin line of white smoke had turned dark gray and black, billowing up into the star-filled sky. The smell of it filled the streets as it drifted across town.

The house was a three-story Victorian with tons of gingerbread and white lattice. She knew from her tour of Sweet Pepper that all of the houses in this area were at least a hundred years old. They'd been built by the founding fathers, graced with stately green lawns, and surrounded by large oaks.

They also had fire hydrants. Allen and Petey connected up as fast as possible. The firefighters had to wade through the crowd that had formed along the sidewalk. The spectators were a dangerous nuisance and were still increasing as more people from the neighboring houses came out to see what was going on.

Stella tried calling Tory and received no answer. She wished the police would respond. Without them, the task of clearing away spectators fell to her, even as she was busy urging her volunteers to hurry. Flames were already licking into the front turrets and the roof.

"Get the engine in closer," Stella yelled at Ricky. The old engine was still parked at the curb.

"What about the lawn?" he asked, respecting the deep green grass.

"Get it in there."

"Sure. Sorry. Wasn't thinking." He drove the engine across the front lawn to get up close to the burning house, leaving red gashes in the emerald green where the tires had broken through to the clay beneath.

"What about me?" Kent called out from the pumper window. He'd followed closely behind Ricky.

"We don't need the pumper right now," Stella yelled. "We need you to help Petey and Allen with the hose."

"Is Tory in there?" Mayor Wando jumped out of his car after leaving it parked in the middle of the street. He was breathless and a frown creased his bald head. "I hope she's not in there. What an awful thing to happen. This house is a historic landmark."

"What about Tory?" Stella demanded, no time to be pleasant or polite. "Has anyone seen her yet? Was she at the party?"

Too much silence answered her question.

"Okay—John, Ricky—come with me. You'll need your SCBA backpacks. Hurry. We don't know if Tory is inside."

Everyone scurried to obey Stella's commands. Two hoses were already aimed at the house, high-pressure water streaming to the fire. A ladder was raised to the roof to vent the fire.

Stella quickly put on her breathing apparatus, which was attached to a backpack. She was adjusting her face mask when Police Chief Don Rogers pushed his way through the crowd to reach her.

"What can I do? I want to go into the house with you."

The fifty-something man with graying blond hair in a crew-cut style had done his best to avoid all the training the other volunteers had fought through. Even though he was listed as a regular volunteer, he'd never bothered showing up.

She stared at him as she finished getting her gear on. "Are you kidding me? You're not dressed and barely trained. You don't go near the house. Do *your* job, Chief, and get everyone to back off so my people can work."

"But I know CPR. You might need me."

"We all know CPR. If you wanted to go in, you should've taken the training more seriously. I don't have time to argue with you. Get those people out of the way so no one gets hurt."

Chief Rogers bristled at being spoken to that way. He finally nodded and ran back to the crowd of spectators, who were still pressing forward toward the house.

He'd made it clear to Stella from the beginning that he'd been against bringing in an outsider—particularly a woman. Stella didn't like their confrontations, but she couldn't let him run roughshod over her.

"Ready?" Stella got her group together. There was no

time to waste. She was afraid for them. They were running into a burning house for the first time. She looked into their eyes and saw that fear reflected back at her. "Let's go."

Stella, John Trump, and Ricky ran into the old house, which was quickly being devoured by the flames despite the water being showered on it. Already the beautiful paintings, drapes, and furniture Stella recalled from her visits there were black with soot and streaming with water.

The heart of the fire seemed to be in the basement. They didn't have long to search for Tory. The flames were spreading up the stairs, igniting the other floors as they reached out toward the roof.

"Third floor," she told John. She'd purposely chosen him because he'd been a cop for a few years and she figured he could deal with a crisis better than the others. "Ricky, check the ground floor. Then get out. Understood?"

Ricky nodded.

John and Stella ran up the long winding stairway, parting at the second floor. Tory's bedroom was on this floor. She hoped to find the other woman there, but she didn't want to take any chances. If Tory wasn't in her bedroom, John or Ricky would find her elsewhere.

The door to the bedroom was locked. She knocked it in with her pryax then stood aside, waiting to be sure there was no backdraft. She pushed off the face mask and yelled for her friend. There was no response. She ran to the luxurious marble bathroom, shouting Tory's name. The bathroom was empty too.

"Any sign of her?" she called to John and Ricky on the radio.

"Found something down here. Not Ms. Lambert. It's a puppy," Ricky responded. "Should I come up there and help you all look?"

"No. Get yourself and the puppy out," Stella responded. "John, any luck?"

"Not up here. I'm on my way down."

Stella looked around the bedroom. It was starting to fill

with smoke now that the door was open. It hadn't been touched by the fire yet.

Her mind raced. Tory might be at the park. She might be outside in the crowd by now. She could be having tea with friends. There was no way to know.

Stella prayed Tory wasn't in the basement. There would be no way to get to her, if that was true. Common sense told her that she would have been getting ready for the party. She should've been in her room.

"Chief," John said over the radio. "You gotta get out of there. You won't make it back down the stairs if you don't move now."

"I'm on my way." Stella went through Tory's bedroom one last time. She was going to sweep the closets, then hope to God that Tory was already at the party.

Stella opened the closet door in the bedroom and pushed through tons of clothes and shoes. All of the clothes were neatly hung, even color-coordinated. The shoes were all in boxes or hanging in shoe racks.

Until she got to the back.

Here the clothes were thrown on the floor. Shoes were everywhere. Stella pushed everything out of the way and swore when she found her friend beneath the mess.

Tory wasn't breathing.

Stella called John and had him radio for an ambulance in case one wasn't there yet. She slung Tory across her shoulders, wincing as her healing shoulder injury complained at the abuse. She held on tight, hoping they could both make it out in time.

The stairs were beginning to burn even though there was water everywhere. Stella's experience told her this wasn't an accidental fire. There had to be an accelerant involved. Even in a house this old, the flames were burning too hot and fast.

She took the stairs as quickly as she could, jumping over the last three, which were starting to smolder. Tory was tall but felt lightweight on her shoulders. Stella burst out of the front door and raced down the stairs to the lawn, where debris had begun falling from the roof. Kent Norris was up there with an ax, trying to help the others get the water where it needed to go.

John and Ricky rushed forward to assist Stella. The three of them moved Tory away from the house and into the neighbor's yard, as far as possible from the interested crowd.

"The ambulance is on its way," John told her before he started CPR on Tory.

"Is she dead?" Don Rogers asked as he joined them. "She doesn't look burned."

"Probably smoke inhalation." Stella sat next to Tory in the wet grass. Chief Rogers was right, though. Tory looked like she was asleep.

Stella knew better. She'd found too many victims dead from breathing in the hot, toxic smoke. Her grandfather told stories of firefighters going in with no masks at all, dying in the smoke with the people they were trying to save. If they survived, they developed emphysema when they were in their early thirties.

It was still dangerous for firefighters. She'd taken off her mask to call Tory. Over the years, the toxins built up. It was a risk all her colleagues were willing to take—along with broken bones, concussions, and getting trapped in burning buildings with no way out.

This—losing someone—was always the worst. Not being able to save Tory felt like a hard blow to her chest. It hurt all over.

She knew she'd done her best. So had her volunteers. They'd all performed admirably. Even then, the fire was out, and Allen, Petey, and Ricky were going through the house looking for the inevitable hot spots that could flare up again.

Stella held Tory's cold hand. *Why were you hiding under clothes in your closet? I know you knew better. What made you panic like that?*

John looked at Stella and shook his head. "No pulse. She's gone."

The county ambulance pulled up at the curb, discharging emergency service techs with life support equipment and a stretcher. At the same time, a heavy-set man with shoulder-length blond hair and a bad spray tan ran up through the crowd. He was sobbing by the time he threw himself down beside Tory in the grass.

Stella didn't need anyone to tell her that this was Victor, Tory's son. He had her intelligent blue eyes. The resemblance ended there. He had a round face and rounder body. His lank blond hair hung down in his face. He was known in town as a scam artist, always looking for the next big score. Rumor had it that Tory was tight with the family purse strings.

"Is she . . . is she dead?" he wailed.

"I'm sorry, Vic," John replied, his steady hand on the other man's shoulder. "I think she's gone."

"No!" Victor fell on top of his mother, pushing the EMS team out of the way.

Chief Rogers pulled Victor off Tory so the EMS workers could continue their exam. It took only a few minutes for them to agree with John's assessment.

Stella stayed where she was, still holding Tory's hand. She was in no hurry to give up that connection. When it was gone, it was gone forever. She smoothed Tory's mussed gray hair back from her thin face, already missing her companionship.

"You did the best you could." John tried to console her. "We all did. Don't beat yourself up over it, Chief. She must've been in there the whole time. There was no way any of us could've known."

"Thanks. I know all that. It doesn't make any difference right now. Later, you can look back on it, and it keeps you going. Not now."

Stella smiled at him. She liked John. He was around the same age as she was, with ten years on the force. It was easy to connect with his quick wit and laid-back personality. He was a steady rock, perfect for an emergency worker. She knew she could rely on him.

He took her gloved hand. Their brown eyes met for a minute in understanding of loss and duty.

She looked down at her friend one last time as the EMS workers were getting ready to transport her. Stella knew she had to get up and let them do their job. She had to do her job too.

There were cleanup and follow-through procedures that all the volunteers needed to see to. They'd all have to write real reports for the state and county this time.

She realized that she didn't even know if the county had an arson investigator who'd come out and take a look at the house. She could probably give a close guess as to what had happened, but she wasn't trained for more than that. Besides, she needed another opinion before she said anything about her suspicions that the fire had been more than an accident.

Her volunteers shouldn't have to take care of cleanup and other after-fire procedures by themselves at their first fire. This was their first loss too. She dreaded what she was going to say to them when they got back to the firehouse.

She looked at Tory again and two things suddenly registered.

First of all, Tory's body was too cool. Stella wasn't a crime scene investigator, but something seemed off about that. And there were unusual marks, discolored bruising, on her wrists and throat.

Was it possible Tory was dead before the fire?

Chapter 4

~~~~~~~~~~

Stella didn't want to talk to Chief Rogers about her theory. He'd made it clear how he felt about her. Instead, she pulled John aside and asked him what he thought.

"They could do a liver temp right away and we'd know," she said as the EMS workers lifted Tory into the black body bag on the stretcher.

"All this heat." John glanced around uncomfortably. He looked at his boss, who stood a few yards away. "It could make her feel cooler to the touch. She probably had a stroke or heart attack up there in her closet looking for what she was going to wear to the party. She was diabetic, you know. Not necessarily foul play, Chief."

"I agree. But did you notice the marks on her wrists? There was also some kind of mark on her throat, John. Will you take a look before they leave with her? It could be ligature marks."

He was skeptical. "I know the two of you were tight. I think you might be upset. It's understandable."

She stood closer to him, not wanting to be overheard. "Will you at least look and see what you think? I'd do it for you if you asked."

He was nervous but finally agreed. "All right. We go with what I see, right?"

"Yes," she agreed. "Thanks."

"Okay." He followed the EMS workers to the ambulance.

Stella turned away to head over to her volunteers. Tory's son was staring at the charred remnants of the house he'd grown up in.

"I'm so sorry about your mother," Stella said as she reached him.

"Thank you. That means a lot." He smiled, blinked his reddened eyes, and took her hand. "You're a professional firefighter. You probably know about these things. Do you think the house can be rebuilt? Is it too far gone? Would it have that smoky smell forever—or is there something I could use to get rid of that?"

Stella was surprised by his question, but she'd learned through the years that everyone grieved in their own way. "You'd have to ask a contractor and a professional cleanup person. That's not part of what we do."

"I can afford that now." He looked at her shocked face. "What? I'm a very practical person. Mama is gone. I have to take care of my own. She'd feel the same way."

Stella walked on without commenting. She hoped he was in shock.

Tory had called him "the boy" when she'd referred to him. Victor was certainly not a boy—he was thirty, if he was a day.

Stella had heard from others in the short time she'd been in Sweet Pepper about all the trouble he'd caused his mother down through the years. Tory had made it clear that she didn't trust Victor.

"Is Ms. Lambert really dead?" Petey asked in a squeaky voice as soon as she saw Stella. "I can't believe it. We did everything you told us. Were we too slow? Did we forget something?"

"You did everything you could." Stella echoed John's words to her. "None of us will be able to save every person or every house. It has to be enough that we're here to make the effort."

"Why?" Petey threw down her helmet, her young face reflecting her terrible anguish. "What's the point if people die anyway? I don't think I can do this anymore. I'm sorry, Chief."

"Take a few days," Stella said, not wanting to lose the girl. "Give yourself some time to get through it. It's not easy, but you're all this town has now. Your friends and family need your help."

"I'll think about it," Petey reluctantly promised. "I just don't know."

They packed up the gear, rolled up the hoses, and got everything back on the vehicles. Ricky, John, and Kent seemed in good spirits despite the loss. Allen and Petey took it hard. The ride back to the firehouse was quiet and somber.

Stella had run out of words of wisdom. Her throat was raw from breathing in the hot smoke, and her injured shoulder hurt. She'd promised the department doctor before she left Chicago that she wouldn't do anything strenuous. At the time, it had seemed like a promise she could easily keep. She'd thought this would mostly be a desk position. No one had told her just how raw her recruits would be.

She didn't have to say anything about cleaning the gear and the trucks before they were put away. No one was in a hurry to go anywhere. Her volunteers finished their chores, filled out their paperwork, and slowly drifted out into the darkness.

Ricky was the last one to go. "It's been a tough day, Chief. Things will look better tomorrow. Hey! Did you take a look at the puppy I found?"

"Puppy? You brought it with you? I thought you probably gave it to the Humane Society or something."

"Petey brought him. He seems fine, Chief. We thought he could spend the night until we decide what to do with him."

Stella followed Ricky to the kitchen. The oldest member of the fire brigade, Tagger Reamis, was playing with the puppy.

Tagger was the only living member of the previous Sweet Pepper Fire Brigade. He was in his early seventies, not physically able to actually fight fires. He liked to be there with the other volunteers. They liked his stories about Vietnam and about the previous fire brigade. He mostly manned the twenty-four-hour communication station they had to maintain at the firehouse.

"Hey, Chief!" Tagger said as the puppy growled and played with an old T-shirt. "I think he likes it here."

It was ironic that the puppy was a Dalmatian. Stella knew several stations back home that had Dalmatians as mascots. This one was very young, maybe six or eight weeks, and had a big red bow around his neck.

"He seems fine," she said.

"That's what I said," Ricky reminded her. "There's no one else to take him tonight. Even the pound won't open until tomorrow morning."

"The pound?" Tagger scratched his grizzled gray head. "We can't let the pound take him."

"He doesn't really belong to us," Stella reminded him.

"Ms. Lambert's dead," Ricky said. "She can't take care of him anymore."

"Never knew Tory to have a dog or any other animal, especially in the house," Tagger added. "Wonder what she was doing with him?"

"We can keep him for now," Stella decided. "We'll have to think about this tomorrow."

"I'll take care of him tonight, Chief." Tagger smiled. "I'm sure Eric will like him too."

"Eric?"

"Eric Gamlyn." Tagger pointed to an old picture of the first fire brigade. "Our chief from back in the 1970s. His ghost haunts the firehouse. He built it, you know."

Stella hadn't known that. She looked at the grainy,

black-and-white picture of the group of men. The chief was a tall, broad-shouldered man. He had a handsome face and blond hair tied back at the nape of his neck. His deep chest showed off the red Sweet Pepper Fire Brigade T-shirt.

"Does he haunt the cabin up there too?" she asked jokingly. "Because I have a problem with odd things happening there."

"Oh sure, Chief," Ricky said from the floor where he was playing with the puppy. "Everyone knows that old cabin is haunted. That's why my mom comes up there to clean every week. She can't get anyone else to do it."

"Okay." Stella yawned. "Well, if Eric says it's okay, that's what counts. We'll talk about the puppy tomorrow."

The parking lot was empty when Stella went out. One of the lights on the outside of the building was flickering on and off. Fog was rolling down from the mountains around her. She'd learned quickly why they called them the Smokies.

She climbed on her motorcycle and headed up to the cabin on the narrow, dark road. The outside light she never turned on was flickering too, barely providing enough light to see where the parking area ended and the drop-off to the river began.

She went inside, ignoring the opening door. Out on the deck, the night sounds of crickets, frogs, and other creatures she didn't recognize, made the night come alive. She was a city girl, born and bred. She knew ambulance sirens blaring through the streets and car tires screeching at stoplights. A barking dog was as close as she came to identifying animal sounds. Ricky had told her the other sounds she was hearing were crickets and frogs.

The hot tub steamed and bubbled at the other end of the deck. Her shoulder and the rest of her aching body wanted to drop her clothes and climb in. She sat in a rocking chair instead, and stared at the blackness that surrounded her.

It wasn't like she hadn't lost people before. There had

been others she, and a company of well-trained firefighters, couldn't save. Mostly they were like Tory, dead long before the fire even reached them.

But dead was dead. It was never easy no matter how many times it happened.

This wasn't even the first time she'd lost someone she knew. Mr. Esposito, the butcher from the next street up in her neighborhood, had fallen asleep with a cigarette in his hand. She wouldn't even have known it was him if she hadn't known it was his place.

And there had been her third-grade teacher, Mrs. Ann Foley. She liked to light candles for her dead husband. One got tipped over and caught her drapes on fire. She'd climbed in the bathtub to stay safe instead of getting out of her apartment.

Stella wiped away old tears with those memories. It was funny how you thought things didn't bother you anymore until something happened that brought all the hurt back. She hadn't planned for that here. There was no one she could talk to. Everyone was back home.

She stumbled into the kitchen and made some hot chocolate. She decided to combine both therapies—chocolate and hot water—and took off her smoky clothes before she got in the hot tub.

"You're feeling sorry for yourself," she said aloud to the crickets and the little bat that liked to swoop around the deck at night. "It's stupid. It won't help Tory. You need to go home. You're in good shape now. You can go back to work. You don't have to see Doug. But you don't have to be here for this either."

"Cutting out already?" a deep, male voice asked.

Stella dropped her cup into the hot-tub bubbles. She used her foot to feel around for it. It was the only possible weapon she could think of at that moment.

"Get out now and I'll forget you've been playing all these practical jokes on me."

"I knew it! You can *hear* me!"

Great! He wasn't impressed by her threats. "Leave *now*!"

He laughed. "I wish it were that easy. And I wouldn't call turning on the light when I know you'll be home late a practical joke. You can have a bad fall if you don't get up the stairs safely."

"Look, I don't know who you are or why you've decided you're my guardian angel, but you should leave now. I'm expecting a police officer in a few minutes. I don't think he'd be too happy to find you here."

Stella finally had the cup in her hand. She was one step short of breaking it and using the jagged edge to make her point. The porch was in darkness, but she could make out the man's shadowy shape in the rocking chair she'd just left.

How did he get in?

He had to have a key. That's what gave him access whenever he wanted to move things around or try to scare her.

She didn't recognize his voice—he definitely wasn't one of her rejected recruits. She didn't know what else to do to get rid of him. She could hardly step out naked and threaten him. Even in the shadows, she could see he was a big man.

"A pretty girl like you shouldn't be out here alone, moping."

"I'm not moping." She checked herself. She didn't plan to have a conversation with him. "I'm not joking either. John Trump is with the Sweet Pepper Police Department, and he'll be here any minute. I'm sure you don't want to go to jail. Leave now. Don't come back. We'll forget this happened."

Yeah, right. Why don't I carry a gun?

Her cell phone was useless up here even if it was close enough for her to reach. She had no service until she was back at the firehouse.

She couldn't believe it—she'd never needed a gun in the city. Here she was, in the boonies of Tennessee, wishing she could at least *threaten* to shoot someone.

"Is that Ray Trump's boy?" the shadow asked. "No. It can't be. Must be his grandson. I think his son's name was

Bobby. That was a while back. I don't think he'd be court-ing you."

That almost brought Stella out of the hot tub. "He's not *courting* me, if that means what I think it means. He has valuable information about something that happened today."

"You mean the fire and Tory Lambert's death. What kind of information?"

This had gone on too far. Stella had to take control of the situation. "Look. I don't want to hurt you, but if you don't leave now—"

Before she could complete the threat, there was a loud rapping at the front door. She smiled and turned to her companion.

He was gone.

Is he waiting inside?

She couldn't sit around wondering. She jumped out of the tub and threw on her clothes, expecting to see him at any second. She clutched the cup in front of her like it was the gun she longed for. If he came at her around the corner, she'd be ready for him.

"Stella!" John began yelling her name. His polite rapping had turned into pounding. "Are you in there? Are you okay?"

She wrenched open the door and the porch light turned off. "Sorry. Someone's playing a prank on me. I was in the hot tub and he got inside." She didn't care what had brought John up there at that late hour, she was happy to see him. It was just luck that he'd come after she'd told the intruder that he would be there.

John was in his police uniform. She decided that he looked good in it. He wasn't a big man, but he was strong and capable. He took off his hat and set it on the table. His brown hair was short enough that the hat hadn't messed it up.

He drew his gun and switched on the kitchen light by the door. "That sounds like breaking and entering to me, Stella. Not a prank. Has it happened before?"

"I've had a few weird things happen, but I didn't want to

be a baby about it." She followed behind him as he searched through the other two rooms. "Sometimes people like to play tricks on the new guy."

All the lights in the cabin were on, including the one on the deck. No one else was in the house.

"You have an alarm system, right? Is this person going in and out? They must have the alarm code. I'll check into it."

"Thanks." She was surprised and flattered by the attention. "Someone broke into my apartment back home last year and took all my electronics. I didn't get this much of a reaction from the police."

He smiled and put away his gun. "No one's lived here for a long time. Except for knowing the alarm code, it could be teenagers. They like to hang out in back areas like this. Maybe you should change your code. I'll see if there have been any other disturbances up here."

"I really appreciate it. It kind of spooked me seeing him sitting there."

"Well, don't ever feel like you can't tell me if you have a problem." He cleared his throat. "I mean, the department. *The police.* That's what we're here for."

Stella smiled. She didn't know that much about John, but what she knew, she liked. "Would you like some coffee? I feel like it's the least I can do since you were ready to shoot someone for me."

"Sure. That would be great."

She threw some coffee into the coffeemaker and added water. "Cream? Sugar?"

"Both, actually." He walked into the small kitchen area. "This is really nice in here. I wasn't sure what it was like."

"You mean you thought they'd set me up in a rundown shack like the firehouse?" The whole town had helped clean up and restore the old building.

The lights in the cabin blinked on and off a few times. Eventually, they stopped and stayed on steadily again.

"I think you have a short somewhere," John said.

"Sometimes snakes get into the wiring if a house sits empty too long."

"Snakes?" She looked around and shuddered at the thought. "I don't think I like that idea."

He laughed. "You mean Chief Stella Griffin is afraid of something? I don't believe it."

"Yeah, well, there's a big difference between wildlife and fires." She moved a little closer to him. She definitely needed a gun.

"Don't worry. I'll have someone come out tomorrow and look around. It's probably nothing. This place may not look it, but it's been empty as long as I can remember. I'm amazed it's in such great shape. The firehouse was built the same year as the cabin. Eric Gamlyn built them both, mostly by himself, from what my daddy told me."

"Eric Gamlyn. Tagger mentioned him tonight."

"The old fire chief. My dad was a member of the original Sweet Pepper Fire Brigade back about forty years ago when Gamlyn was chief."

"So I'm living in the old fire chief's cabin?"

John told her a little about his father and his memories of the old fire brigade until the two-cup coffeepot was ready.

"Yep." John stirred milk and sugar into the coffee that Stella had poured for him.

"What happened to him? What happened to Eric Gamlyn?"

"He was killed in a fire right before the county took over fire services for Sweet Pepper. Dad said Chief Gamlyn fought hard not to let that happen. When he died, the whole fire brigade fell apart. The county stepped in after that. Service to this end of the county was always spotty. We've needed a new fire brigade for years."

The lights in the cabin went wild, flashing on and off for a few minutes before finally going off completely.

"You really have a problem up here. It could be that your alarm isn't working right because your electric system is messed up. Maybe you should pack a bag and stay in town for the night until someone can look at your wiring."

The lights immediately came back on—along with some bluegrass music on the stereo.

"It's okay." Stella studied the floor for movement. "I'm not really afraid of snakes."

"I hate to overrule you, Chief, but as a member of the fire brigade, I have to remind you that there could be an unsafe short in the wiring system, which could cause a fire hazard."

"You're right," she admitted, proud of her student. "Where will I stay on such short notice?"

"At Flo's bed-and-breakfast."

"I hope Flo will be all right with me showing up this late. She doesn't really know me yet." Stella could barely recall meeting Flo when she first got there.

"Flo's used to it. Besides, everyone in Sweet Pepper knows you, Stella. I'm sure you could tell that by all the attention you've gotten."

Stella went into the bedroom and grabbed one of her saddlebags. She stuffed a T-shirt, clean jeans, and underwear into it. It occurred to her that John hadn't told her why he was there.

"By the way, John, what made you come up here so late? Not that I'm complaining, since you may be saving me from snakes and other intruders," she said when she got back into the living room where he was waiting.

"Oh yeah. Sorry." He took the saddlebag from her. "I almost forgot. It looks like you were right about Tory. The coroner said she'd been dead awhile before you found her. It looks like she didn't die because of the fire."

Chapter 5

~~~~~~~~~~

Stella let John convince her to leave the Harley since she wasn't sure where Flo's bed-and-breakfast was located. He told her he'd either come back or send someone for her in the morning. She walked out of the cabin with him and it made the forlorn sighing sound that she was getting used to. Probably just the wind blowing through the eaves, she guessed. She didn't believe in ghosts.

She locked the door behind her after setting the alarm. Once the electricity issue was repaired, an alarm code change was next on her list.

Stella got in the police car with John. All the lights in the cabin were off. As John started the engine, the porch light came on again. Just the idea that a group of snakes was responsible for the craziness made her queasy.

Of course, that didn't explain the intruder who'd vanished.

"So what do we know about Tory. Are they going to do a complete autopsy?" she asked.

"The coroner said he'll have it done as soon as he can. That will give us some idea what happened. And the police department will investigate."

"What about an arson investigator?" Stella asked. "Is there one around here?"

"Well, there is one. Mac Williams. He won't be showing up anytime soon. He never made it out to investigate a suspicious house fire we had here in May."

"That's four months ago. Are you serious?"

"That's why you're here, remember? The county pretty much abandoned us. You might have to investigate this yourself."

"I'm not qualified to investigate arson," she protested.

"Don't worry. I'll help. I'm sure Don will lend a hand too."

"Maybe. He doesn't seem too happy that I'm here."

"People don't like new things—or new people. Nobody likes change. Don is a decent man. He'll come ar ound."

They drove through the quiet, dark streets of Sweet Pepper. The only lights were the quaint streetlights and the traffic light. No one seemed to be out but them.

John pulled the squad car into a wide driveway where a large, slightly crooked sign announced their destination, Flo's bed-and-breakfast. "Here we are."

"Thanks for the ride."

"Would you like me to come in with you? I could at least walk you to the door."

Stella smiled. "Thanks, but I'll be okay. I'd hate to think that there are bad guys out there that need to be caught and I'm taking up all your time."

"I already locked up Boyd Jeffries tonight." He chuckled. "He gets a little rowdy sometimes after he's had a few. He was dancing at Beau's bar with a lampshade on his head. The rest of the night should be easy."

They got out of the car, Stella wincing a little at the acrid odor of smoke still lingering from the fire. Back home, there were so many bad smells that people tended not to notice a little smoke. Here, where the stars looked close enough to touch, the air was cleaner and fresher. She could make out the smell of someone lighting up a cigarette even as she was going down the road on her bike.

Flo met them at the front door to the three-story house very similar to Tory's. The only difference Stella could see were the bright colors of the trim against the white framework of the house. There was a wide veranda with dozens of rocking chairs like the ones on the deck at the cabin.

"Well, my stars! What a surprise to see you here tonight, John. And you too, Chief Griffin. Are you here *together*—or will you need two rooms?"

Flo—if she had a last name, Stella had never heard it—was an adorably chubby middle-aged woman with teased-high blond hair. She always seemed to wear pink and had inquisitive blueberry-colored eyes. She was also one of the town's biggest gossips.

Stella could only imagine the news of her and John being here together hitting the diner and the coffee shop the next morning.

John's face reddened a little as he glanced at Stella. "We're definitely *not* here together. Except that I brought the chief. She needs a place for the night until I can get someone to check out the electric up at that old cabin."

"Not a problem in this world, honey." Flo winked at him. "She can certainly stay here, and welcome. You know they're not going to find anything wrong up there. That old place is haunted. I was surprised they even put you up there, Chief Griffin. What were they thinking?"

"Please call me Stella. I've already heard the cabin is haunted. I don't believe in ghosts."

"Flo," John cautioned. "Don't tell her those old stories. There's nothing wrong that an electrician can't fix." His radio went off. It seemed that there was more to do tonight than arrest Boyd Jeffries. "I have to go, Stella. I'll make sure someone comes back for you in the morning."

He nodded to them both, then was gone.

Flo giggled as he left, and pulled Stella into the old house. "He's sweet on you. And he's a good man. You could do a lot worse. Now, let's have some coffee and talk about Eric Gamlyn."

"You mean the old fire chief?" Stella asked as she and Flo sat down at a round table in the kitchen. There were coffee, juice, tea, and snacks at a sideboard. The cookies, muffins, and cinnamon rolls smelled like they'd just come out of the oven.

"Have a cookie." Flo put one on Stella's plate. "They're my own recipe—last year's Sweet Pepper Festival winner. Chocolate and hot peppers. You won't be able to eat just one. Sure you want soda this late? I don't mind it, but it bothers some people."

Stella tasted the cookie politely. She was surprised to find it was really good. Dark chocolate—with a bite to it.

"Eric Gamlyn was a popular man around here in the 1970s." Flo poured herself a cup of coffee and took a cinnamon roll from the glass platter. "He was a big man—strong—Viking blood, his daddy always claimed. He worked as a lumberjack for years somewhere up north. Maybe Canada. He settled down back here after his daddy passed. He made furniture. His daddy left him a cute little house on Main Street. But Eric was a builder. He sold that place and bought that property out there where the firehouse is. He built the cabin and the firehouse almost singlehandedly. Then he started the fire brigade."

Stella wondered if Eric's name should really be Paul Bunyan. As Flo rattled on about him, his exploits kept getting bigger and bigger.

"And that's why they killed him." Flo put down her coffee cup and shook her head. "What a waste."

"I think I missed something," Stella admitted. "I thought he was killed fighting a fire."

"That's what they *wanted* us to think. Oh sure, he was in a burning building when it collapsed on him, but that wouldn't have killed Eric. It was because the county wanted to take over the service, and there were those who were going to make some money on it. His ghost has rattled around in that old cabin ever since."

Stella took another cookie. Who knew peppers and

chocolate could taste so good together? She really needed to find some weights to work with at the firehouse if she was going to keep eating this way. "And that's why you think the cabin is haunted?"

"Cross my heart and hope that lightning strikes me dead." Flo sincerely crossed her heart with her fingers. Her dark blue eyes stared into Stella's. "Everyone knows it. Why do you think someone hasn't rented it or bought it after all these years? Why do you think it still looks like he just built it yesterday? I guess the council hoped you'd be a good luck charm for that. Eric left that land to the town. They haven't been able to unload it."

Stella digested the ghost story as she finished nibbling on her third cookie. She wasn't sure if Flo knew what she was talking about with her tales of the cabin being haunted— but that would certainly explain all the weird things going on up there—if she believed in that kind of thing.

It might also explain *why* they were going on. Maybe someone wanted to buy the property now. Scare the city girl and there was money to be made.

Stella changed the subject. "You're right about these cookies. I think I need to go to bed before I eat all of them."

"Have you figured out why Tory was in that house when it caught fire?" Flo asked. "I guess what I mean is, why didn't she get out? It doesn't make any sense, her being found in a closet. She was one of the smartest, calmest people I've ever known. I don't believe she panicked. If I were you, I'd check into that son of hers. He's wanted her money and that house for years. Where was *he* when she was killed?"

Stella had no answers for her. Flo kept talking as they climbed the staircase to a quaint room in one of the old turrets in front. "I hope you'll be comfortable here tonight. You're welcome back anytime. They can check out that cabin from now till doomsday. Unless they take an exorcist up there, things are always going to be strange."

Tired and glad that she was finally alone, Stella put on her nightclothes and stared out at Main Street without turning on the light. The room was much smaller than the one she slept in at the cabin, but the lights weren't turning on and off, and she didn't have that odd feeling that someone was watching her.

It was crazy. Her father and his big, Irish family had told stories about ghosts and other creatures since she'd been a child. She didn't believe those stories either. It was easier to believe there were snakes in the wiring—although she might prefer a ghost or two. She really didn't like snakes.

She finally lay back on the elaborate four-poster and stared at the ceiling. She went over and over the fire in her mind. Stella sighed. She wasn't looking forward to figuring out what had caused it. She'd helped with several investigations but had never done one alone. She hoped she was up for the challenge.

She closed her eyes and was soon dreaming about Eric Gamlyn. He was riding in the same seat she'd taken beside Ricky in the fire engine that day. He was barking out orders to his volunteers. They were fighting a fire in town. He ran into a burning building just seconds before the whole thing collapsed.

Stella woke up abruptly. She'd been crying. It was morning. Sunlight was streaming through the tower windows. The smell of coffee filled the bed-and-breakfast. She could hear the sounds of a TV, a hair dryer, and maybe an electric toothbrush coming from somewhere.

She washed her face, shaking her head at her red eyes. Too many ghost stories right before bed, not to mention hot pepper and chocolate. She didn't believe in ghosts. The man in her dreams, with his long blond hair and broad shoulders, only looked like the real Eric because she'd seen that picture of him.

Stella thought about the shadowy intruder who'd disappeared so quickly after John had arrived. She hadn't been able to see his face, but she could tell he was a tall, large man—like Eric Gamlyn.

"Stop it right there." She stared at herself in the tiny bathroom mirror. "Don't get carried away with this. Think about the snakes slithering around in the wiring instead. It's creepy, but at least that makes sense."

Her cell phone rang. It was her mother calling from Chicago. "How are things going? Is your team shaping up?"

Stella told her about the fire. "They don't have an arson investigator, Mom. They want me to do it."

She could hear her father's comments in the background as he listened to their conversation. "You've got plenty of training, Stella. Don't worry about it. Another few weeks and you'll be home. I'm sure they're happy with all you've done for them."

"Your father's right," Barbara Griffin told her daughter. "Anything else going on?"

"Just the usual. Oh yeah. Except for the ghost in my cabin."

"Ghost? What makes you think there's a ghost?"

"Not me. Local folklore. It's the ghost of the old fire chief. He doesn't want anyone living in his house." Stella laughed to take the edge off her words.

"I'm sure there's a rational explanation for it. We both know the only ghosts are the ones from our past that we can't leave behind."

"If you're saying that because you're worried about me and Doug, don't be. I haven't even thought about him in weeks."

There was silence for an extra minute on the phone. Stella was about to ask if her mother was still there. Barbara's voice came back with an odd inflection to it. "Anyone else interesting you've met?"

"Lots of characters," she said. "I'm sure I could write a book."

Stella thought she heard her mother whisper "*Thank God*," but she wasn't sure.

"We have to talk," Barbara said. "I know I should've said it before, but it never seemed to be the right time. I wish I could get away and be down there with you. Even though I promised not to try and sway you—"

Stella's radio started blurting out calls for help from the firehouse. She always had it with her, as did all the volunteers. "I have to go, Mom. I'll call you as soon as I can."

Chapter 6

~~~~~~~~

Stella threw on her clothes and ran out of the bed-and-breakfast, leaving Flo yelling after her about not eating the most important meal of the day.

She stopped when she reached the street, realizing that her bike was still at the cabin. This is what she'd been afraid of. How was she going to get out to the firehouse?

"Hey, Chief!" Ricky skidded up to her in his old black pickup. "John said you needed a ride. Hop in and let's go."

That's what John had meant about it not being a problem. She got in and slammed the door. "What's up with the squawking on the radio?"

"Don't know. I got the call and left the dishes half done at the diner. I couldn't tell who it was. Who's on duty?"

"I think Petey was supposed to be up there," Stella said. "After yesterday—"

"Someone's there, Chief. Wait and see. Petey was upset, but she wants this to work. She won't run out on you. None of us will."

Stella was surprised by his words. She knew she and the guys at the station back home felt like that about Chief Henry. Any of them would give their life for him. She hadn't expected that kind of loyalty from this job. All the volunteers knew she was leaving. Why would they attach themselves to her that way?

She grabbed at the passenger-side door as Ricky turned a corner on what felt like two wheels. She'd thought it was only the engine that he drove too fast. He was a speed demon compared to her, even though people called her reckless because she rode a bike. She was really a very practical, conservative person.

At least she thought so.

"I almost got a ticket for driving too fast out here," she hinted. It was his truck. She could tell him to slow down when he was driving the engine, but not when he was in his own vehicle.

"Old Chum, right?" Ricky laughed. "Yeah, he's gotten me a few times. He didn't ticket you because you're the fire chief, right?"

"No. He actually thought I was someone else and took off before he could give me the ticket. He called me Abigail."

"Weird." He grinned. "That's old Chum for you. He's strange and a real stickler for the rules. Abigail, huh? I don't know anyone around here by that name."

"He seemed to. I think he's afraid of her, whoever she is." Stella gave a sigh of relief as the pickup made it into the parking lot at the firehouse. Already three other volunteers were there.

Petey came running out. Her light brown hair was a mess. She had a few breakfast stains on her white Sweet Pepper T-shirt, but Ricky was right. She hadn't let Tory's death slow her down.

"I'm sorry, Chief," she said. "Old Tagger locked himself in there with the radio and the computer when I went to the bathroom. I tried to talk him out. He's just sitting in there laughing. I didn't know if you'd want me to break down the door or what."

By that time, Allen and Kent had arrived. Don Rogers came up with his sirens blaring and blue lights flashing.

"What the hell is going on out here, Ms. Griffin?" he demanded. "What kind of show are you putting on now?"

"You tell me," Stella demanded defensively. "You're the one who pleaded to have Tagger Reamis as some kind of mascot for the fire brigade. He's taken over the radio."

Don looked annoyed. "I didn't *plead* for anything. I asked to have a hero of our town doing what he knows best. As a veteran of the last fire brigade, and after fighting bravely in two wars, he's earned at least that much. A man like that doesn't deserve to be thrown out like old dishwater."

At that point, Tagger got on the loudspeaker. "All of you out there, start your engines. Let's hear 'em roar."

"He sounds like he's drunk as a skunk," Ricky said.

Allen shrugged. "What do you expect? That's what our town hero does best."

"I don't care how you do it," Stella said to Don, "but get him out of my firehouse."

"I'll take care of it," he grunted. "I wouldn't want you to get your hands dirty."

Stella ignored him. All of the volunteers stood outside with her, waiting to see if the police chief could coax the old man out without calling for help. Tagger began shouting obscenities—and what sounded like a recipe for preserving hot peppers—on the loudspeaker. There was no way to keep a straight face.

A few minutes later, true to his word, Don came out with Tagger in tow. The short, gray-haired hero was apologetic when he saw Stella. "Sorry about that last part," he said, a little unsteady on his feet. "That was too much vinegar. I need to write that down. That was the winning recipe in the 1979 festival, you know."

He smiled and Stella smiled back. He might be a little crazy and drunk to boot, but he reminded her of Jerry O'Toole back home. O'Toole had served her station proudly for many years. He'd lost it one day after a fire that had killed twin girls only three years old. Now he drank too much and hung around giving out advice to anyone who would listen. Maybe every firehouse needed someone like him.

"I'll be back," Tagger called out with a wave and a big smile as Don put him in the back of the police car.

"We have to figure out a way to keep this from happening again," Stella said. "We might have to get a door that locks automatically and everyone has a key."

"Everyone but Tagger, right, Chief?" Allen laughed.

"I think so." Stella looked at her little group. They'd worked so hard to get here. They still had a rough road ahead of them. "Since all of you are here, how about a few training exercises?"

No one was very enthusiastic about the idea. It was Saturday, and everyone had somewhere else they would rather be. But they were game for it, and it wasn't long before they were taking turns carrying the one-hundred-fifty-pound dummy across the firehouse floor, trying not to let his feet touch the concrete.

Petey was the best at this—as with everything else. They all marveled at her tenacity and the strength in her thin arms. Her victim's feet never touched the floor, despite the dummy outweighing her. Her face was a mask of grit and determination.

"How does she do that?" Ricky demanded. "Can somebody please tell me that?"

There was some good-natured teasing when Allen dropped his dummy, then stepped all over it. Kent picked it up and threw it across his shoulders, running to the stairs and throwing up his hands as though he'd made a touchdown.

"Hey! That's my job." Bertie joined them, hobbling into the firehouse on crutches, his ankle in a cast.

Training ceased as everyone gathered around him. "I guess you did a job on that ankle," Ricky teased him. "I thought you were clumsy. Now I know you break easy too."

"Tell me you're not out for the season," Kent pleaded. "The Cougars don't have a shot at the title without you."

"Nah. I'll be out about three weeks, then I can go back for training." He nodded to Stella. "I know I can't assist at any emergencies right now, but I could take some shifts on the computer. I'd like to hang around anyway, if that's okay with you, Chief."

She smiled. "I'm sure no one will argue with you taking some of the monitoring time. Just don't try sprinting across the concrete and you've got yourself a deal. It's good to have you back."

Ricky made a lunch run to the diner, bringing back barbecue pork sandwiches, pickles, chips, and drinks. Early on in the yard cleanup around the firehouse, they'd located an old picnic table. They spread everything out on it now, with someone's towel covering the holes.

They ate out in the sunshine while the Dalmatian puppy played in the little patch of green grass. The whole team seemed to be in love with the dog. They fed him scraps and tried to think of a name for him. Stella didn't know what to say about keeping the pup. She'd have to find out what Victor Lambert thought about it. Technically, she supposed the puppy was his.

As always, conversation was lively. The topic eventually turned to the fire that had killed Tory. The mood grew somber. It was different than it had been the night before. The group was sad but wanted to know what had happened to the woman they had all looked up to.

Stella told them that Tory had died before the fire had started. There were a few gasps of surprise at that as well as a few sighs of relief. It wasn't their fault. Inexperienced or not, they couldn't have saved her.

"What happened to her then?" Banyin Watts asked. She was the town librarian and a new recruit who'd just stopped by when she saw all the cars in the parking lot. She was a tall, strong woman, probably in her midthirties, with muscular arms that spoke volumes about her workout routine. "We lost a fine citizen and a great library patron yesterday."

"John said the coroner will do an autopsy," Stella replied. "We won't know anything until we get those results."

"What about the fire?" Petey asked, her young face creased with concern. "Does anyone know how it started?"

"No. Not yet. It seems Sweet Pepper doesn't have an arson investigator either."

There was a round of groans when they heard that, though no one was surprised.

"Can you teach us to investigate suspicious fires?" Petey asked with an obvious eye on becoming the arson investigator for the fire brigade.

"Not really," Stella said. "I'm not a professional arson investigator. There should be one. Maybe there's a grant for that schooling the town could apply for. Everything I know I learned on the job. I don't know if my testimony would stand up in court, if it were needed."

Everyone knew what her words implied—any chance at professional training would disappear after she was gone.

Stella broke that momentary feeling of loss by continuing on with the conversation. "I'll be glad to show all of you what I know, if you're interested. You can come with me when we investigate."

"When, Chief?" Ricky asked.

Stella called John and asked if he had any idea when they could go and look at the house. He suggested that afternoon.

Petey swore in a tone deeper than her normal speaking voice. "I have to work. Can't you do it some other time?"

"We have to get some answers right away," Stella said.

"I have a video recorder," Banyin offered. "I can record it so you can watch it later."

"Would you?" Petey squealed and got to her feet to hug the other woman. "Thank you so much. I don't want to miss a thing. I want to know what happened out there."

Everyone laughed at her unique enthusiasm.

"It's settled then," Stella said. "We'll meet at the Lambert house at three p.m. Wear your work boots and gloves. There will be debris that could be dangerous."

The group broke up after that. Petey headed to work at Scooter's Barbecue and Ice Cream beside the post office. Allen went back to the barber shop in town. Everyone else rushed off in various directions. Ricky drove Stella back to the cabin.

"That was good news about Tory," he said, then frowned. "Well, you know what I mean. She's still dead, but it wasn't our fault. That's worse, right?"

"I don't feel a lot better after hearing you say it," Stella admitted with a smile. "It's one of those things. I guess it's good for us as a group but bad in every other way."

"That's what I meant." He slapped the steering wheel as he careened around the sharp curves in the steep drive. "Why were you spending the night at Flo's anyway?"

"There was some problem with the electricity in the cabin. Maybe snakes," she explained. "John thought it might be dangerous. He wanted me to leave until it was checked out."

Ricky laughed. "Did they get the ghost busters up here to take a look at it? I was wondering if the old chief would start acting up while you were here. It's taken him a little longer than usual. There's money on it at Beau's. I win, if you're being haunted."

"I'm not saying there's a ghost in the cabin. I don't believe in ghosts."

Of course, the alternative was snakes in the wiring. She shivered when she thought about them slithering across her while she slept. Ricky was repeating exactly what Flo had said. That's how myths and legends—including ghost stories—got started. She didn't want to get caught up in that either.

Elvis Vaughn was still at the cabin when they pulled up. The sign on his old blue van read "Electrician and Varmint Removal." He had the look of a grizzled prospector from an old Western movie.

"Howdy, ma'am." He hobbled over to Stella as she was getting out of the pickup. "I'm just finishing up here."

Stella looked at Ricky and smiled. "Was it snakes in the wiring?"

"No, ma'am. Never is. I expect old Eric just got a mite riled with someone living in his house again and all. I been over here plenty of times. Nothing ever wrong with the wiring. He probably keeps the snakes away." He chuckled to himself as he wiped his hands on a dirty rag. "No one lives here for long."

"I told you." Ricky laughed and shook the other man's hand. "How have you been, Mr. Vaughn?"

"I been fine, young'un. Haven't seen you or your folks in a while. You should come over for some cooter stew."

"I'll tell Mom and Dad," Ricky promised.

"What do I owe you?" Stella asked, a little put out that there was nothing wrong that could be repaired. She couldn't keep spending the night at the bed-and-breakfast.

"Nothin'." He looked up at the cabin. "The town owns the property. They'll pay. They should've known better than to put you up here. If I was you, I'd demand some place where no one else was living already, if you get my meaning."

"I was just telling her the same thing," Ricky added.

"The two of you don't really believe this place is haunted, right?" She glanced between them. "I don't believe the ghost of the old fire chief is haunting this place."

Ricky and Elvis Vaughn burst out laughing, Vaughn guffawing so hard that tears came to his rheumy blue eyes.

Ricky recovered first. "Maybe you can make peace with him and he'll let you stay, Chief."

"Yes, sir. That's the way to do it. It ain't never happened before, but seeing as you're the new fire chief and a mighty fine-looking woman to boot, maybe that old rascal will play nice for a change."

Stella really didn't like that plan. She hoped he'd actually checked the house. Maybe she should call someone from outside Sweet Pepper for help.

"You know, I was friends with Eric for a long time."

Vaughn shook his head. "A real lady's man. At least, all the ladies loved him. He never married. Guess he never met the right woman. He always talked about settling down and having a pile of kids, like his daddy done. That's why he built this place two-story."

"Well, thanks for your help anyway." Stella shook Vaughn's hand. "I'm not sure what to do now. I hate to move somewhere else since this is so close to the firehouse."

"Just do like I said. I think Eric will give you a chance." Vaughn pulled at his cap as a sign of respect and shuffled back to his van.

"There you have it." Ricky's eyes twinkled with humor. "Where did you say you saw Eric? I bet it was before you took a shower or something, right? That's where I'd be if I was a ghost in a pretty woman's house. No disrespect, Chief. See you later at Tory's."

When she was alone at the cabin, Stella changed the code on the security system. She looked around carefully, then went to sit on the deck, leaving the door open to the sweet breezes coming off the river.

"I'm going to get a second opinion," she said. "I don't believe in ghosts. Snakes are disgusting, but at least they're real."

A deep, very real-sounding voice replied, "That's your prerogative."

Chapter 7

~~~~~~~~~~

Stella stood up and looked around. There was no shadowy figure this time. Maybe ghosts couldn't appear during the day?

No.

She wasn't going to start believing in ghost myths. She didn't know how someone was doing this, but she was going to find out.

"You won't mind if I ignore you, I hope," she said.

"No. That's fine with me. You get kind of used to it when you have my particular medical condition."

"And that is?"

"Dead."

"Oh. A ghost with a sense of humor. Nice touch."

There was a knock on the cabin door. "I hope you're not trying to distract me. You can only play this game for so long before I find out what's *really* going on."

"I'm sure everyone has been pretty explicit about me and what's going on," the voice said. "But right now, you have a bigger problem."

She braced herself. "What do you mean?"

"Elvita Quick and Theodora Mangrum are standing

outside the door. Good money says they're here to get you to judge the food at the Sweet Pepper Festival. Take the chocolate contest. You've had Flo's chocolate and pepper cookies, right?"

Stella peeped between the blinds and saw the two elaborately dressed women on the front stairs. "Maybe you should talk to them and you could judge the *invisible* foods contest."

"*Ouch.* I can tell you're a city girl. You've got some sharp edges. Don't I qualify as someone you should be kind and charitable to?"

Whoever was doing this was making fun of her. When she found out who it was, she was going to kick their ass.

She opened the door for the two ladies, each wearing an outrageous hat. "Ladies! I'm sorry to keep you waiting. Is there something I can do for you?"

Though they had different last names, they were certainly sisters or some other close relation. They were both short and stout with hazel eyes and little bow-shaped mouths. They wore almost matching purple dresses. One of them had on a red hat and the other, a blue hat. Both hats were decorated with birds and flowers.

"I'm Elvita Quick. And we're so glad to make your acquaintance, Chief Griffin. This is my sister, Theodora Mangrum. We represent the Sweet Pepper Festival food contest. We'd be delighted if you'd agree to be one of our judges. The festival is only a few days away. It's a big deal hereabouts."

"I can talk for myself, Elvita." Theodora smiled at Stella. "We'd love for you to judge one of our categories. We have ten to choose from."

"That would be fun." Stella was used to being tapped to help out at carnivals and to lead school groups touring the station house back home. "Won't you come in for a few minutes?"

Both the women's faces crumpled up a little like old apples.

"I don't think so." Elvita nervously eyed the open door.

"We're very comfortable standing out here." Theodora took a step back on the small porch.

"I have some lemonade and fig bars." Stella wondered what was wrong. Tory had told her to expect people to stop by for a visit once in a while. She'd given her the homemade fig bars—with bits of hot pepper in them.

"No. We'd like to. But no. Thank you all the same." Elvita stepped back too.

"Is something wrong?" Stella asked.

"No, nothing at all," Theodora answered quickly.

Stella had been standing in the doorway talking to them. The door suddenly slammed shut behind her, making her jump. She glared at the portal, then turned back to her visitors. Both ladies had already run down the stairs.

"I wouldn't set foot in that place for all the tea in China." Elvita righted her hat, which had flopped to one side during her flight. "*He* loves to tease us. He always did. It was fine when he was *alive* but now . . ."

Stella pushed the door open again. "Who? I'm the only one here."

"It's Eric Gamlyn. He was always a jokester. Loved to play pranks," Theodora explained. "We won't come in, but we would be glad to meet you elsewhere. And we would like to have you as a contest judge."

"Is there a chocolate part of the contest?" Stella asked.

"Why, yes, there is." Elvita stared at her sister. "It must be something to do with fire chiefs. *He* always judged that contest too."

"Maybe it's the chocolate." Stella felt a faint chill shiver down her spine no matter how many times she'd reminded herself that this was still only a practical joke. There were no ghosts.

"Yes. Maybe that's it." Theodora wrote in her notebook. "We have you down for the chocolate and pepper contest, Chief Griffin. Thank you so much."

"Please, call me Stella. I'm looking forward to it."

The door slammed behind her again, making the wind chimes on the porch jingle. Both ladies jumped and gave little shrieks before they stuffed themselves back into their small car and sped out of the drive.

Stella went back inside. "You scared them away."

"But not you," the lazy, laughing voice said back at her. "I wonder why that is."

"Maybe because I've been hazed by my buddies back home. Or maybe because thinking about what I'm going to do when I catch you makes me smile."

She went out to the deck again and read the *Sweet Pepper Gazette* as she sat in the leaf-dappled sunshine. The voice was absent for the thirty minutes she was out there. Maybe that was the end of it.

Stella ate lunch then piled her few dishes in the dishwasher and made a list of some supplies she thought she might need. The ordeal ahead of her made her frown as she sat at the kitchen table.

It wasn't like she had an arson investigator checklist or something. She was good at what she did—putting out fires and saving lives. She wasn't as sure about investigating the cause of the fire that had killed her friend.

Thinking about that, she took out the old manila folder Tory had given her. They'd talked briefly about her first husband's death. It had happened about forty years before, in a horrific fire. He'd fallen asleep while smoking and burned to death in his chair.

Tory believed her first husband, Adam Presley, had been murdered. The report said that it was an accident. No large-scale inquiry was ever made into the incident. Tory had investigated it herself for years. She had admitted to Stella that she was obsessed with it.

"I don't know what you could do, if anything," Tory had said one day at lunch. "I'd appreciate it if you'd take a look at the information I've collected."

One thing at a time. Stella put down the folder and tried to focus on what she needed to do at Tory's house.

She scribbled a few notes on scene investigation that she remembered from the last time she'd walked through what was left of a house with Chief Henry. She also made a list of things she was going to need.

"You're investigating Tory's house fire for arson." The disembodied voice made her jump a little.

"Aren't we done with this?" she asked in irritation. "I have things to do that you probably wouldn't even understand."

"I investigated a few fires in my day. We didn't have an arson investigator then either."

"Yeah?" She stood up and walked around the room. "And what exactly did you do? Be specific."

"I took notes and some photographs. I looked for the fire pattern to see where it started."

"You could get that from *CSI* or any other cop show on TV."

Laughter breezed through the cabin. "I've learned a few things that way. I found I can manipulate electrical devices." To show off, he turned on the TV, stereo, and microwave at the same time. "It's useful to scare people away."

"Why would you want to scare people away?"

"This is *my* house. Why would I want strangers living here? At least you can hear me. This is the first time in forty years I've been able to talk to anyone."

The voice was defiant, angry. Stella could feel the emotions running through her.

You're getting sucked into this fantasy.

"Enough is enough." She stamped her foot on the hardwood floor. "If you're still here when I get back, I swear I'll buy this place that nobody wants and let my volunteers use it for practice when we burn it down. Put that in your pipe and smoke it."

There was no response—not that she'd expected one. He had to know that she was serious. It was one thing to bandy words with this joker and another to let him make her life miserable.

Stella picked up her notes, grabbed her helmet and

saddlebags, then stalked out of the cabin. She knew she'd never make good on the threat. Maybe it would be enough to end the prank anyway.

Outside, she put on her helmet and started her bike. The sound of the engine startled some birds out of the tree next to her. Only a few more weeks and she'd be going home. She might have to stay at Flo's bed-and-breakfast so she wouldn't drive herself crazy if the harassment didn't stop.

She rode into town and stopped at Potter's Hardware on Main Street next to the Daily Grind Coffee Shop. She'd had coffee there a few times with different members of the town council, but mostly she was a morning Coke girl.

Valery Reynosa waved to her as she was writing daily specials on her white board outside the coffee shop. "How are you doing?" she called out. "I hope you're settling in."

Stella talked to her for a few minutes—she'd learned right away that people here thought it was rude to just wave and keep going.

Valery confessed that she was working on a coffee drink with hot pepper in it for the festival. "Don't tell anyone," she cautioned. "I don't want anyone else to compete in that category. I've won the prize two years in a row because I'm the only one doing coffee."

"I know this is important to the town." Stella told her that she'd been recruited as a judge for the chocolate and pepper recipe contest.

"Maybe I should make chocolate coffee with peppers. We're friends, right?"

"Are you trying to influence the outcome of the contest?" Stella asked with a smile. "I have a feeling that isn't allowed."

"No, of course not. I just like to win. It's good publicity."

Stella agreed and excused herself. She'd started toward the hardware store when Valery called out, "I hear you're going to investigate Tory Lambert's death."

"Yes." Stella went closer to her. Word got around quickly. She might not be able to ignore Valery, but she didn't want to add to the rumor mill. "It's a requirement when someone dies during a fire."

Valery nodded, her pretty face turning sinister as she whispered, "I heard her son already filed for her life insurance. Can you imagine? She hasn't even been buried yet."

It was a harsh criticism but not one she hadn't considered. "I have to go."

"Good luck," Valery called out. "I hope Vic didn't kill his mother."

Stella ducked into the hardware store. She didn't want to get involved in a discussion that could be said to prejudice her findings.

She walked around the narrow aisles on the squeaky old wood floors and added to her shopping basket. The place smelled like paint, tool oil, and sawdust. She needed reflective tape, plastic containers, labels, a few flashlights, and some gloves. She had Tommy Potter add the cost to the account set up for her and paid for by the town.

Tommy glanced at her from behind the old-fashioned cash register that looked like it had been there since the store opened in 1939. "Going out to see what happened at the Lambert place?"

"Yes. It's routine." Stella signed her name on the credit voucher.

He snorted as he laughed. "If that's what you want to call it. Around here, we don't consider it routine when you kill your own kin."

Obviously this was the accepted explanation for what had happened to Tory. "We really don't know what caused the fire, Mr. Potter. That's why we're investigating."

"Some investigation. Drag that sorry excuse for a son of hers down to the police station and beat the crap out of him. There's your investigation."

Stella nodded and smiled. "Thanks for your input. I'll see you later."

As she left the uncomfortable atmosphere of the old

hardware store, Stella noticed she still had a little time before she had to go to Tory's house. She got on her bike and drove down to the end of the shopping area and stopped again at the security and computer service company whose logo was on the system at the cabin.

"Chief Griffin!" Charlie Johnson, the owner of the company, greeted her. He was a tall, large man with close-cropped gray hair and glasses. He was good with computers, and he was friendly. The two didn't always go hand in hand, in her experience. She'd had some trouble with her laptop when she'd first arrived in Sweet Pepper, and he'd taken care of it for her. "How is the world treating you this fine day?"

Stella chitchatted with him a little, glad he didn't mention the fire. "Is there any way you could do a sweep of the cabin I'm staying in on Firehouse Road? This may sound silly, but I'm hearing voices up there. I was wondering if you could do some kind of electronic monitoring that could help me find out who's responsible."

Charlie nodded as though it was a request he heard all the time. "So what are you thinking? The house is wired? Satellite feed? Maybe you left the radio or TV on without realizing it? Ghosts?"

She could tell from the way he'd said it that he knew about the ghost of the fire chief. "I'm wondering if you can monitor and record what goes on in the house, that's all. That way I'll know if I'm crazy. Mr. Vaughn checked it for snakes. I'm still hearing some things that shouldn't be there."

"I'm guessing you've heard about the ghost but you don't believe it?" He smiled as he looked at her over the top of his glasses. "You know, I've lived other places too. No one likes their haunts like Sweet Pepper. And Eric Gamlyn is the best. Why I've heard stories—"

"Please don't tell me there's a ghost in the cabin," she said. "I'm glad it's not snakes, but a ghost? Really?"

He chuckled to himself, which Stella found a little annoying. "Certainly, we can monitor and record what goes on in the house as part of your security system—for a slightly higher fee. When would you like to start?"

"Right now." Stella put her credit card on the desk between them. "I'd appreciate it if you'd add the additional charges to this card for me, instead of billing the town."

"Sure. How long?"

"Let's say the next forty-eight hours. When can I listen to it or see it?"

"We can set you up with an online account. You can sit and listen to it all the time, if that's what you want. We've already got cameras and audio up there as part of our security package. I'll need you to bring your computer in, though, so we can check it and make sure it can access the security feeds."

"I'll bring it in later. Thanks." Stella wasn't sure if this was the answer to her problem, but since her next step seemed to be an exorcist, it seemed like a good idea.

Chapter 8

~~~~~~~~~~~~~~~

With that settled, Stella rode down to where the Victorian houses seemed to bend toward each other as though they were old ladies gossiping. The burned remains of Tory's house no doubt gave them plenty to talk about.

Stella laughed at herself. She wasn't a fanciful or overly imaginative person by nature, certainly not prone to giving personalities to old houses. She blamed it on the people and this town. Sweet Pepper was rich with legends of the mountains. Since the day she arrived, she'd realized that locals kept the tradition alive by telling and retelling old tales—like those of Eric Gamlyn's ghost and his many exploits in life.

Maybe once she'd proved to herself what was really going on at the cabin, she could prove it to everyone else and they could let go of the old chief. Then the town could sell the cabin. It was too nice to stay empty all the time.

She appreciated that the local lore was beautiful and important to the people of Sweet Pepper. But it was important to honor Gamlyn's achievements in life rather than believe he was still hanging around haunting the cabin. Maybe the town could put up a statue or plaque to him.

By the time she reached Tory's house, her core volunteer group was already waiting on the scorched and mangled grass—even Petey. Stella was surprised and pleased that learning a little about arson investigation meant so much to them. The town needed a few more volunteers as dedicated and hardworking as they were, but they were a great start.

Chief Rogers was also waiting. He was there with John, both of them in uniform. A third man she didn't recognize was wearing an orange jumpsuit and goggles. He had to be the insurance investigator since he was holding a large clipboard.

Goggles!

Stella pulled the bike in toward the curb to park with the other vehicles. She'd totally forgotten goggles or safety glasses. That was careless and stupid. It had to be a product of too much imagination and not enough focus on her job.

It was especially bad since Chief Rogers was there to rub it in her face. Their antagonistic relationship assured her that he would take great pleasure in doing so.

Her grim but welcoming volunteers walked toward her. She removed her helmet and clipped it to her bike. She handed out the tape, plastic containers, and other items she'd purchased at the hardware store and promised to explain why they needed all of it as they went along.

"Give me a minute and we'll get started." Stella saw Chief Rogers approaching, looking angry as usual.

Her volunteers refused to move out of his way, angrily staring at him with their arms crossed on their chests. They finally parted when he growled out an order to step aside. They didn't go far. Stella noticed that John had stayed where he was, with the man in the orange jumpsuit.

"Ms. Griffin—could I have a word in private?" Chief Rogers yanked his head toward the same area where they'd taken Tory after bringing her out of the house, under the spreading oak branches.

"Sure." It was the polite response. She could hear Chief Henry in her head telling her to play nice.

Chief Rogers wasted no time with pleasantries. "I won't have you going around my back again like this. When there's something that involves my department, I expect a written request for assistance on whatever it is. Officer Trump is not the chief of police. You come to *me*. Get it?"

Out of the corner of her eye, Stella saw John shrug and shake his head apologetically. She understood all right. He didn't like his men taking on any task that might undermine his position in town.

Her first impulse was to tell him what he could do with his written request. She reconsidered, realizing that John's job could be on the line. She certainly had nothing better to offer him with a volunteer department.

So she astounded herself and Chief Rogers by agreeing with him. "Of course. I'm sorry I didn't think of it."

He stared at her until she thought his eyes would bulge out of his head.

She added, "I think it's very important for the police and fire departments to work together, don't you?"

He leaned closer to her, the smell of his aftershave overpowering the odor from the fire. His blue eyes had narrowed to slits. "Sister, I don't know what game you're playing, but whatever it is, let me assure you that I've been around longer and I'm better at it."

With that cryptic statement, he stalked away, yelling, "I don't have all day. Let's get started."

Stella followed behind him and introduced herself to the man in the orange jumpsuit.

"I'm Maurie Graff." He adjusted his glasses before he offered her his hand. "I'm the insurance investigator assigned to this case."

"Nice to meet you." Stella shook his hand. "I'm the acting fire chief for Sweet Pepper."

"I noticed none of your people are wearing safety glasses. I have a few extra pair in my van, if you'd like to use them."

Stella's face felt a little hot with embarrassment, but she didn't hesitate to accept his offer. "Thanks. We can use them.

It will save me from sending someone back to the hardware store."

"You've got quite a crowd," he remarked. "Students?"

She explained the situation while Allen and Ricky, who'd walked up there with her, went to get the extra safety glasses from the van parked beside her bike.

"This should be a good learning experience," Graff said. "Even though there's probably nothing out of the ordinary."

"Really?" Stella was surprised to hear him already categorizing the fire as ordinary. Most investigators were more objective than that—or they were actively hoping the fire was arson so they could deny the claim. "I was here during the fire. It seemed a little hot to me. Something wasn't right."

"These old houses are lovely, but they're fire hazards, Chief. Bad wiring, most of the time. And they're all tinderboxes ready to go up in flame. Things happen."

It was hard for Stella to imagine Tory not being as scrupulous about safety as she was with everything else. It was always possible. Everyone occasionally got careless.

"Sometime today, Ms. Griffin." Chief Rogers looked impatiently at his watch. "Next time, try to come prepared, huh?"

She gritted her teeth but managed not to return the gibe. Having him for an enemy wasn't good for the department. She was the fire chief. She shouldn't antagonize him.

"Ready, Chief." Allen handed her a pair of safety glasses.

Stella realized when she looked into the eager faces of her volunteers that this might be the only chance they'd have to learn something about fire scene investigation. At least she *hoped* it was the only fire they would face before she left. It was important to focus on what they needed to learn.

"One of the most important things you'll do after a fire," she told them as they stood outside the house, "is to talk with eyewitnesses, if there are any. In this case, Chief Rogers collected that testimony already, I believe."

"That's right," he snarled in reply.

"And we'd appreciate a copy of that report, if you don't mind," Stella continued.

"My pleasure. Can we go inside now?" he demanded.

It was hard for everyone to go into the house. Knowing Tory had died here made the blackened rubble even harder to look at. Banyin hesitated at the front stairs, but Ricky smiled at her and encouraged her to go on.

The group walked carefully through the front door behind Chief Rogers and John, who stayed close to his side. The first floor was badly burned, some spots unsafe for them to walk across. The stairs to the second floor were damaged, charred in a few spots. Chief Rogers declared them safe after stepping hard on each stair.

"We'll start in the least damaged part of the house," Stella explained as Ricky snapped digital pictures. "The second and third floors are probably only smoke damaged. You guys kept the fire from going up above the first floor. In general, fire spreads sideways and up. Fire rises and burns in a V pattern. We'll find the point of the V at the origin of the fire."

Stella didn't realize Banyin was videotaping everything she said until she looked up. Everyone was diligently taking notes. She smiled, pleased, and looked away.

"We can see some cracking and flaking from the heat on the walls and floors up here," Stella continued. John and Chief Rogers stayed in the lead. The insurance investigator stayed beside her, furiously scribbling on his clipboard. "You can see the smoke damage throughout this floor."

"I don't see any smoke detectors." Graff made a note of it. "Having those in place might've saved the victim's life. Perhaps the new fire department could give out information on how important these are. Maybe even conduct a few door-to-door inquiries."

"A smoke detector wouldn't have saved your client's life," she replied. "Tory had been dead for a while before the fire started."

"I didn't know that." Graff looked at his clipboard and twitched a few papers without writing anything. "There was no memo about that. I just assumed she died from smoke inhalation."

"You probably wouldn't have had a chance to receive that information before you came here. We only just found out."

"I see." He jotted down a few words and started looking around again.

The group made their way up to the third floor, where Ricky took plenty of pictures of the smoke-damaged upholstery, drapes, and clothing. They discussed ways to examine the smoke damage and pinpoint the most heavily affected areas.

"Does anyone know yet what killed Mrs. Lambert?" Graff asked as they went back down to the second floor.

"Not yet." Chief Rogers jumped in (apparently listening the whole time). "But my department is working on that issue as we speak. The coroner is conducting an autopsy. We'll know soon enough."

"An autopsy?" Graff seemed surprised and uneasy about that discovery.

"We're not expecting foul play, but there were some anomalies," Chief Rogers said. "We think there was a stroke or some other medical emergency. She probably was unable to call for help." He pointed out the closet, closed off with police tape, where Stella had found Tory.

They headed down to the main floor after that sobering moment. All the volunteers had stared at the walk-in closet as though it were an evil portal from a horror movie.

"We can see some glass melting here at the foyer area." Stella tried to redirect their focus away from Tory's death. "That happens at about fifteen hundred degrees. You notice there was nothing like that upstairs. The real heat was coming from the basement. That's where we'll see the most damage and find the cause of the fire."

"I'm sure you're right, Chief Griffin." Graff seemed a little subdued and a lot more nervous.

Stella was more than a little curious about that.

"The stairs to the basement are toast," Chief Rogers said. "We'll have to go out and come in from the back."

They followed his direction, walking around the side of

the house, inspecting places where the paint had blistered
and the siding had buckled. The grass was like a swamp
from the amount of water it had taken to put out the fire.
Their feet squelched in the patches of red mud.

The basement was definitely more badly burned than any
other spot in the house. Black ash was everywhere. Nothing
had been left untouched by the flames.

"That area over there looks the worst." Allen pointed
toward the far wall in what was the center of the house. They
picked their way carefully through the damage to get there.

"Yes." Graff was suddenly in front of them, walking
immediately from the outside basement door to a spot where
an electrical outlet was located above a metal table. "This
looks like wiring to me. As I thought."

What was left of a large worktable was melted in spots. It
was one of the only large objects with enough shape remaining to easily define it. There were melted bits of glass, metal
and plastic scattered around the area, fused to the tabletop.

"You can see it here." Stella pointed to the deep burns in
the wall with pieces of wiring still hanging behind it. "The
fire probably began here. It looks like some type of accelerant here too."

"Maybe these were kerosene lamps," Graff suggested
almost cheerfully. "People keep them around for storms.
The wiring had a short and caught on fire—it caught the
kerosene and there's your accelerant, Chief Griffin. I've seen
it happen before. I'm sure you have too."

"What makes you say kerosene?" Stella asked. Graff
wasn't close enough to look at the burn pattern in the dark
basement, let alone smell it. "People keep whiskey in their
basements too. And paint thinner. It could've been any of
those things."

Stella leaned down and sniffed the glass shapes on the
table. He was right. They smelled of kerosene. A greasy black
film covered the heavy steel tools around them. She had each
volunteer come forward and sniff the area as she had.

"When you've seen as many fires as I have," Graff darkly

joked, "you know what to look for. It's an instinct after a while." He continued writing on his clipboard.

It was hard to say. Graff *was* older than her. Stella still found it hard to believe he had more experience. She could have fit this whole county into the area back home that her station handled.

His attitude had changed too. It seemed as though the cause of the fire was less important to him now and he was eager to get the whole thing over with.

Stella shone her flashlight up into the burned area above the table. It was right below the stairs on the main floor. She didn't disagree with Graff's assessment of the fire—she was very curious as to how he'd made that decision so quickly and without a more thorough investigation of the components.

"Does that jibe with what you see, Ms. Griffin?" Chief Rogers asked.

"Yes, though it seems unusual that there would be so many kerosene lamps so close together on the table."

"Maybe Mrs. Lambert was filling them," Graff said.

"If so, where is the can she was using to fill them?" Stella asked. "She had to have something close by for the main source. We can see there were only small amounts of kerosene in each lantern. Nothing here shows evidence of a large amount."

"Maybe she filled the lanterns, then took the can out to the storage shed in the backyard," Allen said. "Well, Tory didn't do it, obviously. Maybe her handyman did. I cut the grass here when I was in high school. She kept the gas can out there. Maybe the kerosene is out there too."

"Who is her handyman?" Petey demanded, her tiny pink notebook ready for his name. "Do we know him?"

"I think I saw old Tagger out here, doing some odd jobs and such," Allen said.

Ricky shrugged. "Maybe that's why he was so surprised Ms. Lambert had a puppy in her house. Guess he knew her better than most of us."

Chapter 9

"**A**re you saying you think Tagger was involved in this?" Chief Rogers demanded.

"I'm not saying anything," Ricky replied, looking at Stella for help.

"We're investigating a possible arson," she reminded the police chief, taking up for her recruit like a mother hen. "We need all the facts."

She sent Petey and Ricky to look for a kerosene can in the storage building.

"I think my job is done here," Graff said. "I can conclude from the evidence that this was an accidental fire caused by bad wiring and a poor choice of places to leave combustibles."

"You're entitled to your opinion," Stella said. "I'd like to look around a little more. I don't want to be rushed to that judgment."

Graff stared at Chief Rogers as though the officer might be able to convince Stella to change her mind. Rogers held his hands up in a gesture of surrender and shook his head.

"I understand your need to teach your new volunteers," Graff finally said. "But I'm a busy man. I need you to sign this form before I go." He handed her the clipboard.

Stella read through the form. "I can't sign this. It says I'm satisfied with your conclusions. I don't know that yet."

"Some skepticism is healthy, Chief Griffin," Graff said. "I think we both know I'm right and you're only trying to make points with your new bosses. Trying to get a raise in the near future from this unfortunate incident?"

Stella pushed his clipboard back into his hands hard enough that he made a small grunting sound. "First of all, my friend died in this fire. Second, I'm not going to be here long enough to bother trying to make points with my bosses. And third, why are you so eager to get this over with? Ever since we came in here, you've acted like you knew what to expect and where to expect it. No one is that good."

"Chief!" Ricky and Petey returned at the same time, as though they'd been racing to see who could get there first.

"There's no kerosene can in the shed," Petey said.

Ricky frowned. "It should've been easy to find. Ms. Lambert even had her shed items color-coded and alphabetical."

"Maybe she put all the kerosene in the lanterns on the table and threw away the can," Chief Rogers suggested. "This doesn't seem like a big deal to me."

"Should be easy enough to find out." Petey nudged Ricky out of the way. "We can look in the trash for the can. We can find Tagger and talk to him. Somebody can go to Potter's Hardware and ask if Tory ever bought kerosene there. We all know she didn't shop outside of town."

"That sounds like a plan." Stella approved Petey's ideas. "Ricky, you see if you can round up Tagger. Petey, you go down to Potter's."

Petey's pale pink face turned scarlet red. She bit her lip. "I'm sorry, Chief. I could only get two hours off. I could do it tomorrow."

"That's fine," Stella said. "You can leave if you need to. I'm glad you could be here this long."

"Thanks." Petey stepped toward Stella as if to hug her, then shook her head and left the basement.

"I don't have time for all of that," Graff said. "And I sure don't have to stand around being ridiculed by some fire chief temp. Good day, Chief Griffin."

Chief Rogers was laughing as the insurance investigator left. "It's a good thing you won't be around much longer, Ms. Griffin. You don't make friends too easy, do you? You might wake up some morning with a lynch mob at your door."

Stella turned and faced him. "The town didn't hire me for my sparkling personality. They hired me for my experience as a firefighter. Don't you find anything suspicious about the way Graff was acting?"

He shook his head. "The man wants to finish the job. I can empathize."

"The insurance investigators I've known would almost rather cut off an arm than admit their company was going to have to pay up. I didn't notice Graff looking that hard, did you?"

"I don't know all that many insurance people, I guess. You tell me what you think is going on here."

"I think someone may have paid him off to hide the truth."

Chief Rogers chuckled. "This ain't the big city, ma'am. Tell her, John. I believe she has the wrong impression of Sweet Pepper."

Stella couldn't help but feel the tension between the two men. Chief Rogers treated John like a lapdog, there to do his bidding. The only time he'd invited him to speak was to belittle her.

"I think Chief Griffin is right," John finally said. "Mr. Graff was in an awful big hurry to get in and out of here. There might be something else to this."

Chief Rogers glared at him and seemed ready to cut him down in front of them. He finally put his hands into his pockets and said, "Fine. Prove me wrong then. Next you'll be telling me Tory was murdered. You stay on this, John. It's your funeral with the town when it goes bad. Don't forget—*she's* leaving."

He nodded at Stella and left the basement.

Ricky let out a long sigh of relief. "Wow. That was intense."

"I don't think anyone, man or woman, has ever talked to Chief Rogers that way." Banyin looked at Stella with great respect. "Do we have to wait for Petey to go to the hardware store tomorrow? Couldn't we go now?"

"Ricky is going to find Tagger right now," Stella said. "Maybe you could go with him. Petey can go to the hardware store tomorrow. Otherwise we're going to continue to sift through what we can find down here. I didn't bring all these plastic containers for nothing."

Banyin and the other volunteers stayed with her, while Ricky left, reluctantly. Once he'd heard they were actually looking for evidence, he tried to get Allen to go in his place. No one wanted to leave the scene—at least not while Stella was looking for clues to what had happened.

Several hours later, the small group crawled out of the dark basement. They were either hunched over or trying to straighten their spines after having spent so much time looking through everything in the cramped basement. They were covered in black soot, but Stella had plenty of evidence in her containers.

"All I want is a long hot shower." Banyin limped across the wet grass.

"I want a cold beer," Allen announced, and Kent agreed with him.

It was nearly dark. The streetlights had come on around Main Street. The smell of grilling steaks wafted around them. Curious neighbors watched the weary band of volunteers leave the black husk of the grand old house.

"What about you, Chief?" Banyin asked.

"I think I need a hot shower *and* a beer," Stella said. "You guys did a good job today. I think our insurance investigator might have a few surprises coming his way."

They all laughed and traded jokes as they took off the plastic safety glasses Graff had left there and got ready to leave.

A small lady with a kerchief on her head that matched her red-and-white-checkered apron met them at the curb where their vehicles were parked. "I know you all must be starving. We've been watching you work all afternoon. Why don't you come over for supper? Bill and I have more food than we can eat, and it's already on the grill. You don't want it to go to waste, do you?"

Kent looked at Allen. "I don't want it to go to waste, do you?"

Allen laughed. "No way."

Banyin hung back. "We appreciate your offer, Mrs. Waxman. But we are such a mess. We couldn't come inside like this and eat."

Lucinda Waxman laughed. "Who said anything about inside, darlin'? I've got patio furniture that hoses off just fine. Come on now. The food's getting cold, and the tea is getting warm."

"Okay," Banyin said with a smile. "Chief?"

Stella was already on her bike, snapping on her helmet. She wanted to go back and see how things were going at the cabin. "Thanks, but I just want to go home. The rest of you go. No point in good food not getting eaten."

Banyin, Kent, and Allen didn't wait for another invitation before they walked across the street to the Waxmans' house.

John stayed behind with her. "I'm sorry about all that stuff with the chief."

"I'm used to it by now." She smiled at him. "You were kind of quiet all afternoon. I'm sorry he treated you that way."

"Yeah, well, I'm used to that by now too. It's just his way. He's a good man, Stella. I'm sorry you probably won't be here to find that out."

"I guess that's one of the bad things about the job."

He ran his hand along the handlebar of the bike, close to

where her hand rested but not quite touching. "You could come out with us sometimes, you know—me and the other volunteers. Just because you aren't permanent doesn't mean you have to be a stranger."

Stella felt his gaze resting on her face. She enjoyed the feeling. He smiled, and she leaned a little closer to him.

But she was covered in soot, and they were out in the middle of the street with everyone watching. It was awkward.

"I have a new security camera to monitor," she finally said. "I know it sounds crazy, but I have to know what's going on up at the cabin."

John touched a spot of soot on her cheek. "You'd rather be with the ghost than us, huh?"

"I'm about to debunk that old legend," she told him. "I think it may be time to let the old chief rest in peace. I'll see you tomorrow."

He waved back, then crossed the street to join the other volunteers.

Her stomach grumbled as she headed back toward her cabin. The food had smelled really good. She was starving— they all were—they'd worked right through dinner.

Her volunteers were dedicated—she had to give them that. There might not be many of them, but they were the best. She was surprised to realize how proud she was of them.

The cool night air felt good after the heat of the day. Back home in Chicago, she'd be wearing a light jacket or sweater. Even though they were in the mountains, September had still been sunny and warm.

There were signs up everywhere for the Sweet Pepper Festival in October. She'd be here long enough for that. Everyone had talked about it so much that she was starting to feel the excitement. She wasn't sure about the recipe contest judging, but there was a first time for everything.

The firehouse was only a few miles outside the main part of town. The road leading to it was empty most of the time. Stella glanced at the light that was on in the computer room at the station, wondering who was on duty tonight. She needed to import the volunteer schedule to her phone so she could keep up with it.

She had started into the turn that would take her up to the cabin when she ran into something. Or something ran into her—she wasn't sure which. It was another vehicle, no lights. It slammed into the Harley, causing it to fly off the road and into a deep ditch.

Stella tried to control the bike. In the seconds it took for the slide into the ditch, she realized the front tire had blown out. She was careening down into the darkness. Heavy brush scratched her face, and cold water splashed up at her.

She managed to stay on the bike until it hit a large stump in the bottom of the ditch. She wasn't sure what happened after that as she let go of the handle grips and everything went black.

Chapter 10

$\sim\sim\sim\sim\sim\sim\sim$

She was dreaming about a large man whose long blond hair was tied back with a leather thong. He was making coffee in the cabin's kitchen. He smiled at her, his bright blue eyes crinkling at the corners, and offered her a cup of the strong-smelling brew.

"Oh, that's right. You don't really like coffee, do you? It's better for you than that artificial cola stuff you drink."

Stella wasn't sure who he was, but she suspected he was Eric Gamlyn. She didn't know why she was dreaming about him. Her head hurt. She put her hand up to it and felt moisture there. When she pulled her fingers away and looked at them, she saw blood.

"You're okay," Eric said in her dream. "You'll have a heck of a headache, but you'll live to ride again. Do yourself a favor—get a pickup."

She opened her eyes, not sure if she was still dreaming. She was alone in a dark room, the only light coming from a small lamp on the bedside table. She put her hand up to her throbbing head and found a large bandage there. She was wearing an old-fashioned nightgown that went to her feet.

What is going on? Where am I?

Stella got up and looked around the room. She'd never been here before.

The wreck. I wrecked my bike. Dad is going to kill me.

She might have expected to be in a hospital, but if that's where she was, it was the swankiest hospital in the world.

Everything was burgundy and gold. The huge bed looked like it had been made for a king. The carpet was thick underfoot, and a chandelier hung from the ceiling. The room seemed huge. She realized it might be that her perception was off.

She walked over to a large window that overlooked millions of lights below it. Wherever she was, she had to be high up in the mountains to get this kind of view. That had to be Pigeon Forge and Sevierville down there. She could still make out the dark peaks of the Smokies on the horizon.

The double door to the room opened and a woman in a nurse's uniform came briskly into the room. "You should not be up yet. No one in your condition should be wandering around."

"Where am I?" Stella asked. "Who are you?"

"I am Mrs. Waverly. Mr. Benton Carson brought me here to take care of you after your terrible accident." The pretty cocoa-faced nurse scooted her back into bed, then immediately put a thermometer in her mouth and checked her pulse.

"And who's Benton Carson?" Stella asked around the thermometer. The name sounded familiar, but her brain felt like scrambled eggs. Not to mention that she'd met a lot of people in the past few weeks.

"Why, honey, Benton Carson owns most of the land around here, including most of Sweet Pepper. His great-grandfather started the pepper factory. As you can imagine, he is pretty wealthy. You know what I mean?"

The thermometer beeped, and Mrs. Waverly checked it. "Well, you don't have a fever. You probably have a mild concussion. The doctor put a few stitches in your forehead to close that big cut. I'm surprised you don't have any broken bones. You are one lucky girl."

Stella wasn't feeling very lucky. She remembered the accident and wondered what kind of condition her Harley was in. Had anyone even towed it out of the ditch?

"Thanks for everything. I need a ride back to the place where I'm staying." She started to get up again, looking around for her clothes. It was too dark to see much.

"Mr. Carson isn't going to take too kindly to you refusing his hospitality, especially since he paid me and the doctor to take care of you. Just lay back there and be glad his step-son found you."

"Stepson?" Stella really wasn't happy with the situation, and was getting less so with every piece of information that came out of Mrs. Waverly's mouth. "Where are my clothes and my cell phone?"

"I don't think you're in any condition to leave yet." A man's deep voice came out of the shadows. He came closer and peered down at her. "You were banged up badly on the road. Who in the world told you it was safe to ride a motorcycle?"

Benton Carson—Stella guessed by his slightly annoyed, authoritative tone—was tall and thin, his shoulders stooped a little, his gray hair thinning.

She hadn't met him before, but she recognized the name. He was the owner of the pepper-packing company that had put Sweet Pepper on the culinary map. The city council had been apologetic when she'd first got there because he was out of town and she couldn't meet him. Everyone else she'd met talked about him like he was a dark overlord.

There was something oddly familiar about him. Something about the eyes. It made her uneasy.

"I don't think you're in a position to decide if I should leave or not or if it's safe for me to ride a bike. You must be my host. Thanks for the stitches and the hospitality. I think I should go home now."

"Don't be ridiculous." He dismissed Mrs. Waverly with

a motion of his hand. "It's the middle of the night. Go back to sleep and I'll have someone take you home in the morning."

Stella got to her feet. The old pink flannel nightgown only made it down to her shins. "That's okay. I don't think someone will mind coming to get me now."

He laughed. "You mean John Trump or wild Ricky Hutchins? Yes. I know all about you and your little fire brigade. I'm sorry I was unavoidably detained on business all this time. Believe me, it wasn't my intention to be gone so long. I've waited a long time to finally meet you, Stella."

"Thanks. I really need to go."

He sat down in a chair near the bed and leaned back, crossing one long leg over the other as he looked at her. "You're a little firebrand, aren't you? I'm surprised you didn't do more than slug that cheating boyfriend of yours back in Chicago."

"*What?* How do you know about that?" She had been leaning heavily against the side of the bed and finally just sat down. Her head hurt, and the pummeling her body had taken in the wreck was catching up with her.

"I told you. I know all about you."

Stella heard her distinctive cell phone ring somewhere in the room. It was her mother's ring—"Tomorrow" from *Annie.*

She got up slowly and went to look for it. Her mother had called her a lot since Stella had left Chicago. Most of the time she worried over nothing. At least this time she had something to worry about.

"That's probably your mother," Carson said, as if reading Stella's thoughts. "She's been calling all evening. I don't think she finds your mode of transportation safe either. Why do you want to worry her that way?"

Stella was torn between letting her mother know she was okay and getting the hell out of there. She could always talk to her mother later. This place—this room and this man—were really starting to creep her out. She didn't want to be in the company of Sweet Pepper's dark overlord any longer than she had to be.

She finally located her clothes when she found her cell phone. They were damp and smelly, probably torn in a few places, but wearable. She had to get Carson out of the room so she could change.

"I really appreciate your kindness, sir. But I'm well enough to leave tonight. You can take me home yourself, or I can call someone."

He leaned forward in his chair. "Aren't you even a little curious as to why I'm so interested in you, Stella?"

This had taken a bad turn somewhere, even worse than the wreck. Stella didn't like the way he looked at her or how he sounded. Was he threatening her?

She *was* curious why he wanted to know about her and how he'd learned about her life in Chicago. She didn't think this was the time or place to find out. Even her poor brain knew such questions would be better asked and answered later—when she was somewhere safe.

"I'm going to get dressed. If you know anything about me, you'll know I'm used to changing clothes at the station back home with a bunch of men hanging around. Whatever your reason for checking up on me, I think we should discuss it later. Right now, I'm going back to my haunted cabin. It was nice meeting you."

He came and stood close to her. "Stubborn, like your mother."

"What about my mother?" She didn't care what kind of hotshot he was here in Sweet Pepper—he didn't have the right to investigate her family.

"I'm assuming your mother honored my wishes to the extreme. She didn't tell you *anything* about me, did she?"

The phone rang again, and this time, Stella answered it. "Mom? Who is Benton Carson? Why does he know so much about me?"

"Take it easy, Stella. Don't get upset. He's your grandfa-ther. *My father.* I would've told you, but I promised not to prejudice you one way or the other." Her mother's voice was gently apologetic and nervous at the same time.

"You knew I was coming here and you didn't tell me?" She glanced at the old man who apparently was a relative. Stella stalked away from him to continue her conversation.

"I'm sorry," her mom was saying. "He and I haven't always been on good terms, but that was a long time ago. He contacted me before you left Chicago, about wanting to meet you. I couldn't see any harm in it. I thought you should be able to decide for yourself."

Stella gritted her teeth. "So you got together and created a job so you could lure me down here? The whole thing was a trick?"

"Of course not! You make it sound like it was a conspiracy or something."

"That's what it sounds like. You could've told me the truth."

"I felt silly after hiding who I was for so long."

"I can't believe this." Stella looked at her grandfather, sitting in the chair across the room.

"As for the job, it just happened that way," her mother continued in a rush. "They really needed someone with your experience. It seemed like a good time for you to realize that you had other family besides your dad's."

Stella's head hurt worse. She felt a little queasy— probably from shock. It didn't help that she hadn't eaten anything since lunch and it was almost midnight. She couldn't handle this conversation. "I'm sorry, Mom. I have to go. I can't do this right now."

"Stella—"

She turned off the phone for good measure.

"You see?" Carson asked. "I had good reason to keep tabs on you. I take it you don't want to hear why your mother left home?"

"Not right now." She slid her long legs into the dirty wet jeans and pulled her mangled sweater over the nightgown. "I need my boots."

"I'm sure they're here somewhere." He glanced around on the floor without moving. "If you're that determined, I'll call someone to drive you home."

"I'm that determined." She caught sight of her boots near the door and went to get them. As she bent down, a wave of dizziness overtook her. She ended up on the floor beside them. Her legs refused to support her when she tried to get up again.

She heard her grandfather call for help. He came close and patted her arm. "Don't worry, Stella Ann. I'll take care of you."

Chapter 11

<hr/>

*"What do you think?" she whispered, looking down at
the unconscious woman.*

*"Not bad. I've had worse." He slid his hand over her
body.*

"Can you do it?"

"For fifty million dollars? Piece of cake."

When Stella woke up again, it was morning. Her head
felt clearer. She'd had some strange dreams. She
hadn't made it home, despite her attempt at a dramatic exit.
Instead, she was back in bed with a blanket tucked around
her and her ruined clothes missing again.

Mrs. Waverly was gone. So was her grandfather.

Benton Carson. Her grandfather.

The idea of this place being a part of her family background made everything seem surrealistic again. She wasn't
sure if what she'd heard was true.

If it was, how could her mother have kept something like
this from her? Thinking back, she recalled wondering many
times why her mother never spoke about relatives from her
side. There were never pictures or heirlooms, as her father's

big Irish family had. She sort of assumed her mother's family was dead.

Why had her mother allowed her, *encouraged* her, to come here and not tell her? Surely it had occurred to her that not saying anything was worse than giving her some kind of heads-up.

She got out of bed. The dizziness and nausea were gone. Her legs didn't feel shaky. Her ribs and head still hurt, but the discomfort was tolerable.

In the bright sunlight, the room was even more impressive. Stella tried to remember everything she'd heard about the owners of the pepper company. She had to admit to not being particularly interested. All that came back to her was that they had a big house on a mountain outside of town and they were rich. *Filthy rich.* Almost everyone hated them.

Tory hadn't hated them. She'd been one of those who'd apologized for Ben Carson being out of town at her arrival. "I know he wanted to be here. Something came up. He'll be back soon," she'd told Stella.

Did everyone else know that Benton Carson was her grandfather? She already understood about everyone in town being in everyone else's business. People knew the intimate details of everyone else's life. Was it possible they had all kept it from her?

Why had Mom left?

She'd probably been treated like a royal princess. People in town hated the Carson family, but they also put them on a pedestal. Why would her mother leave the family pepper empire and estate behind and struggle on the streets of Chicago?

Not that her father didn't earn a good living. Her mother worked too, as an accountant. Their little house was nothing compared to this. Stella could remember times in her childhood when things were tight for them.

She looked out of the big windows again, admiring the daytime view. The Smoky Mountains seemed to roll on forever in the distance, the flawless blue sky above them.

She was less confused, better prepared to deal with the situation today. Her clothes, boots, and cell phone were gone again. Her grandfather and Mrs. Waverly must have been afraid she'd wake up again and leave without them knowing.

Clearly she wasn't going anywhere in the old nightgown. She also had to admit to a little curiosity about this new side of her family. She took the time to look around the huge bedroom, finding pictures of her much younger mother with her grandfather and another woman who had to be her grandmother. She was amazed at how much she looked like the other two women.

There were tons of notebooks with drawings and writing in them—all of them signed "Barbara" in a swirly girlish hand. Stella realized that this had been her mother's child-hood bedroom.

She went through the old party dresses and skirt and sweater sets she found in the closet, which was the size of her whole room back home in Chicago. Her mother had such tiny feet. None of the hundreds of pairs of shoes would fit her.

Stella found a blue sweater and a pair of jeans that were a little snug but wearable. She went into the eye-popping bath-room, which had a pool-sized marble bathtub and a separate shower. There were mirrors everywhere and a small chande-lier in the ceiling. All of the fixtures looked gold-plated, and the press of a button made the floor warm beneath her feet.

Now, this was the life.

She put aside all of her questions, along with what she believed to be her mother's nightgown, and took a long hot shower. She was careful not to scrub her head too hard even though she was worried that there might be blood caked in her hair. A look in the mirror when she got out told her it was clean. Her face was a little bruised on the same side as the cut. Otherwise, she seemed to be fine.

Stella smiled at her mother's underwear, each pair of which was embroidered with her name. She had to do without the bra she'd found—that was a little too snug. She was hungry and feeling more benevolent toward her new family when she walked out of the bathroom.

Her grandfather was waiting for her. "You look so much like Barbara, which is to say you look like your grandmother, Abigail."

The name immediately jogged her memory of the encounter she'd had when she'd first reached Sweet Pepper. "I've heard that before." She explained her meeting with Deputy Chum.

He crossed his arms over his chest. "That seems a little melodramatic. Chum's a fine officer, but has that problem sometimes. I don't know why he'd act that way."

"Maybe you should've clued him in on the plan too."

"I apologize, but not everyone in Sweet Pepper knows you're my granddaughter, if that's what you're thinking. You're angry about being kept in the dark on this. Your mother told me she'd never even mentioned to you that she had a family. I wanted you to meet us and decide for yourself whether you want to be part of the family. I didn't know if she might color your opinion."

"Why? Were you afraid she was still angry?"

He stopped smiling at her. "You're a quick study."

Her observation seemed to bother him. "You said I was stubborn like her. Mom and I think alike many times." She shrugged. "It made sense. Why was she angry?"

"Let's talk over breakfast. I'd like to show you the house and grounds."

"Impress me with your pepper wealth?"

"Exactly. Maybe you'd like to stay around for a while."

"I need shoes. I can wear Mom's old clothes but not her shoes. I think her feet have grown. We wear the same size back home. When did she leave?"

"She was only seventeen." He opened the door and called out to a young woman in the hall. "Get me a pair of shoes, Felicity."

"What size?" the woman asked without looking at Stella.

"Eight." Stella wondered how often this woman had to find shoes for people.

Felicity nodded and headed down the hall.

"Why did my mom leave?" Stella continued as though their conversation hadn't been interrupted.

"I think you should ask her that. I've never really understood. It came at a very bad time in both our lives. Her mother had recently died—"

"Died?"

"Yes. She was young. It was tragic."

Stella didn't hear any longing or leftover grief in his voice. In all fairness, it *had* been a long time. Apparently he had moved on.

They passed several doors in the long hallway, plush gray carpet underfoot. She felt like she was in a hotel. The hall ended in a large stairway that swept down into an impressive foyer.

"Wow! You must sell a *lot* of peppers."

Felicity reached them with four pairs of shoes in her hands. "I hope these will work for you."

"Thanks." Stella chose the new black tennis shoes. She smiled awkwardly as she put them on.

"Box up the other pairs, and she can take them with her," her grandfather said.

"No. That's okay. I have shoes at the cabin."

"Nonsense. You might as well have the others too."

Before Stella could protest again, an attractive woman in a fashionable white suit walked to the bottom of the stairway. "Ben, are you bringing her down for breakfast? I have to leave in a few minutes for church. I wanted to meet her before I go."

"We're on our way, sweetheart. We had a shoe emergency that I'm sure you can appreciate." He held out his arm to Stella. She took it, smiling at his old-fashioned charm, and they walked down the wide, carpeted stairs together.

The woman was blond, very elegant, and chic in a way Stella couldn't imagine being. Up close, she looked like she was in her fifties—a lot younger than Benton Carson. Maybe closer in age to Stella's mother.

Everything on her seemed to sparkle with gold and diamonds, from the clasp in her upswept hair to the necklace and earrings she wore. Her makeup was flawless. She was poised and self-assured as she held out her hand to Stella. "Hello. I'm Vivian Carson. It's so nice to finally meet you, even though the circumstances are terrible. I hope you're feeling better this morning."

"Yes. I'm fine. Thanks." Stella barely touched her cool, delicate hand. "It's nice to meet you too."

There was something familiar about Vivian's voice. It felt as though she'd heard it in a dream. *"What do you think?"*

Stella shook her head to clear it. She was probably imagining things.

There was no doubt that Vivian was the mistress of the house. The way she'd emphasized her last name made it clear that she was Stella's grandfather's wife now. It was a friendly, subtle reminder. Stella felt sure future reminders would be less friendly.

She wished she could assure Vivian that she had no desire to interrupt their lives. She still wasn't really clear on why she was there after her mother had left her family behind so long ago. Obviously, a conversation on that subject was long past due.

They walked into a sunny room where breakfast was laid out on a small white wicker table. Vivian had taken hold of her husband's arm as they'd left the foyer. Stella took the hint and walked alone. She didn't understand the gesture. It was hard to believe that the older woman felt threatened by her, but that was the way she was acting.

"Eat up." Her grandfather pointed out the large buffet of several types of eggs, fruits, jams, and pastries. "The cook always makes enough to feed an army. Vivian and I are usually the only ones up this early."

Stella was about to ask how many other people lived with

them when they were joined by another man—clearly Vivian's son. He had to be in his late thirties, very good-looking in a cosmopolitan way. He had sun-bleached brown hair and his mother's blue eyes. He was dressed casually in jeans and a white sweater.

"This is my son, Martin Lawrence." Vivian introduced them. "Martin is my son from my first marriage."

"Vivian and I have only been married a few years," her grandfather wryly added.

"Call me Marty." The younger man shook her hand warmly and smiled down into her eyes. "That's a nasty cut. Does it hurt much?"

"You're the one who found me after the wreck." Stella recalled the nurse telling her.

His voice was familiar too—"*Piece of cake.*"

"That's right. It was pretty bad. I was worried about you for a while there."

"Thanks. It doesn't hurt much now. Any idea what happened to my bike?"

"I'm afraid not." Marty took the seat beside hers. "I was in a hurry to get you out of there and make sure you were all right."

"Did you see what hit you?" Her grandfather buttered his toast.

"Not really." Stella thought back on the moment. "It was dark. Someone was driving down the road without their lights on."

"I understand you're a member of the family." Marty sipped his coffee. "Ben didn't even tell us about you until the day we got back from Switzerland."

"There was no reason for anyone to know besides me," her grandfather said. "I didn't tell you because I planned to approach Stella and tell her who I was. I didn't want you to screw it up like you always do."

"Really, Ben, that's a little harsh considering that Martin saved Stella's life," Vivian protested.

"That's okay." Marty smiled. "I'm glad I could play the

Good Samaritan anyway and save my . . . I guess we're not really related, are we?"

"I don't think so," Stella said.

"Don't get any ideas either," Ben warned his stepson. "She's got better prospects!"

Vivian protested again. Marty drank his coffee and seemed to ignore their bickering.

It was a relief for Stella when her cell phone rang. She walked out of the breakfast room, leaving them to argue.

"Hey, Chief. It's Ricky. Just wondering where you are and if you're okay. It looks like your bike took a hell of a beating last night. We found it in the ditch next to Firehouse Road."

"*I* found it," John said, grabbing the phone. "Are you all right? Where are you?"

"I'm fine," she said. "I could use a ride. I'm at Ben Carson's place. Could you come and get me?"

Ricky had the phone again. He let out a long low whistle of surprise and repeated what she'd said to John. "What are you doing up there?"

"It's a long story. Can either you or John come and get me?"

"Sure," Ricky said. "I'll be right there. Tell them so they don't shoot me at the gate, huh?"

Stella could hear John saying he would go, protesting as Ricky ended the call. It was just as well—her grandfather was coming to check on her and her cell battery was running low. She didn't care which of them came for her.

"You're not leaving us already," Carson said. "I thought you could stay for a tour of the house, give us some time to get to know each other."

"I really need to get back and get my Harley out of the ditch. I appreciate all you've done, but I have a few things I have to check on."

It sounded a little lame. She could hardly tell him she felt overwhelmed by this new family and its obvious relationship problems. She didn't know them well enough to understand their dynamics. She wasn't sure that she wanted to. And she needed to talk to her mother somewhere private on a phone that wasn't about to quit.

"I understand. I don't want to lose you either," he said with a smile. "I have your cell number from your phone. If I call, will you meet me for lunch or whatever time you have?"

It was all still a little new for her, but her mother had wanted her to get to know them. "Sure. That would be fine."

"You know, I would've had someone take you home. You didn't have to call for help. You were never a prisoner here."

"Thanks. They offered—"

Felicity came toward them. "There's a police officer at the gate, Mr. Carson. Shall I tell Bernard it's all right to let him in?"

"That's fine," Ben said. "It sounds like Officer Trump didn't want to waste any time getting up here."

Stella smiled. "He's a good friend."

"Let me know if he becomes *too* much of a good friend. I'll handle it for you."

Her grandfather had issued the proclamation with a steady voice and a ruthless twist to his lips that told Stella he would gladly do exactly as he promised. Maybe this was what had sent her mother packing, never looking back for all these years.

Someone was pounding on the front door—Stella assumed it was John. She smiled at her grandfather. "I'll talk to you later. Thanks again."

It surprised her when he suddenly hugged her, unshed tears glittering in his eyes. "No. Thank *you* for giving me the opportunity to meet you. You don't realize how much it means to me."

Felicity showed Stella to the large double door. John was getting ready to pound on it again. He stopped in midswing, fist raised high. His face immediately changed from anger to concern. "Chief! Stella—are you all right? Do you need to go to the hospital? I can call an ambulance."

"I'm fine." Stella thanked Felicity and took the three

boxes of shoes from her. She handed them to John, who put them in the trunk before opening the passenger-side door of the police car for her. "I don't think I need an ambulance or the hospital."

John closed her door and ran around to the driver's side, sparing a moment to glare up at the big house. "I realize you probably were pressured to say you were fine. It's only me and you now. I'll take you to the Mayo Clinic, if you need to go. Don't let them overwhelm you, Stella."

She was surprised by his attitude *and* his driving as he burned rubber getting away from the house. She would've liked to have had a better look at the place. It was reassuring to her, though, that he and Ricky didn't seem to know about her relationship with the Carson family.

"Have you been taking driving lessons from Ricky?" she asked with a smile.

"Was it Marty, the stepson?" John questioned. "Did he run you off the road? Do you want to press charges?"

"It's not like that," she said.

"The Carson family has gotten away with too much for too long. Say the word and I'll take care of it."

"The word would be that Ben Carson is my grandfather, John. What are *you* talking about?"

Chapter 12

~~~~~~~~~~~~~~~~

John pulled the car over to the side of the road and stepped hard on the brakes. If she needed any further convincing that he didn't know, his face was it.

"Hit me with that again?"

"My mother is Barbara Carson Griffin. Apparently she left Sweet Pepper when she was very young. She never told me that she had family here."

He shook his head and stared out the side window for a few seconds before turning back to her. "So all of this, you getting the job as chief and all, all of it was because Ben Carson needed someplace for you to work while he gets to know you."

Stella didn't like his tone. "I thought that too, at least to begin with. You changed my mind about it. Or at least I thought you did. If you didn't know, maybe no one else knew either."

"Maybe," he scoffed. "I'd be willing to bet next month's salary that the town council knows."

"You might be right. But I didn't know."

He looked skeptical. "The Carsons have run this town from the get-go. Why shouldn't one of them be the fire chief?"

"I understand. You don't like them. Why would my

grandfather go to all the trouble to set this up so I'd stay for three months?"

"Because it would give him a chance to talk you into staying here permanently. He doesn't have a real heir, you know. Marty is Vivian's son from her first marriage. Maybe he wants to keep the money with the blood."

"None of that makes any sense to me." She wasn't happy about defending her position. "I'm still going home when my three months is up. I hope that makes you feel better. Can we go on to the firehouse now so I can get my bike?"

"Yes, ma'am." He looked annoyed.

Stella didn't care. She was annoyed too, and none of it made any sense to her. John had liked her and respected her—at least she'd thought he had—until he found out she was part of the Carson family. Another reason her mother had left Sweet Pepper?

They didn't say another word to each other. John dropped her off at the firehouse, where half of her volunteers were looking at her mangled Harley in the front parking lot.

He left the firehouse the same way as he had the Carson property, giving the car too much gas and leaving a rubber trail behind him.

Everyone turned to greet Stella. Ricky and Tagger were up front as they reached her. "You look better than your bike," Tagger said with a grin. "What the hell happened to you?"

"Never mind that. Anyone can have a wreck. What did you do to *John* to make him drive like that?" Ricky laughed.

"Let's talk about it later," she suggested, hoping everyone wouldn't have John's reaction. She'd worked too hard with this group to lose it all now. "How's my bike?"

"Chief, maybe you should have that head wound looked at," Banyin said. "You probably shouldn't be up and around yet."

"I saw a doctor last night," Stella told her. "I'm okay. Thanks."

She was actually feeling a lot better—until she saw her bike. It had taken months of working every spare moment to

get it up and running again. Now the fenders were messed up
and the crash bar was bent. It would need a new paint job.
Hopefully all that mud, water, and grass hadn't hurt the engine.

"I think she'll be okay with a little work," Ricky said.
"I'll help you get her going again, Chief."

"Thanks," Stella mumbled, her head starting to ache again.

"We'll all help, Chief," Tagger said. "You're looking a
mite pale. Head wounds can be tricky. My best buddy got
shot in the head during the Big One. He didn't even know
it until he fell over dead."

Petey glared at him as she put her arm around Stella.
"Maybe we should take you home for a while, Chief. You
could lie down. We'll spend some time practicing. Don't
worry about a thing. We'll figure out something for you until
your Harley is fixed."

"I'll take her," Ricky volunteered. "You all get started."

Stella got willingly into Ricky's pickup. Standing up for
that long had made her feel dizzy and sick again. She'd had a
concussion before—she knew the drill. "Thanks for the lift."

"Yeah, well, how else was I going to ask you about being
at the Carsons without everyone else butting in?" He started
the old truck. "That's why John was upset, right? He hates
the old man. I suppose he didn't like seeing you there."

"Ben Carson is my grandfather." She told him about her
mother. "Now John thinks I got this job because of them."

He shrugged as the truck hugged the side of the road.
"So what? You probably did. It's not like there was someone
from Sweet Pepper with your kind of knowledge."

"I guess that's true. I wonder how many people know
about my background and hate me for it."

"It won't matter. There probably are some who know.
They won't say anything if the old man told them not to."

It was hard for Stella to imagine that one man could have
that much power—until she thought about all the powerful
men who'd ruled Chicago at one time or another. It was
probably easier here to get everyone on the same page. There
were no unions or other groups to give her grandfather a

hard time. Besides, he employed most of the people in the area. That gave him some leverage.

"Is that why John hates him so much?"

"You could hear this from anyone, but if it comes up, you didn't hear it from me. John's father worked for the old man. He was fired for stealing. He shot himself in the face after it happened. John has some understandably hard feelings about that."

"So he blames my grandfather for his father's death," Stella said, more to herself than to him.

"Yep. That's about the size of it." Ricky stopped the pickup as they reached the cabin. "You need some help getting inside?"

"No. I'll be fine." She faced him. "How about you? How do you feel about me being related to the Carsons?"

He laughed. "I feel pretty good about it. No problems with funding the fire brigade with the old man on the team. In fact, if you'll consider staying on after your three months are up, I'd be proud if you'd agree to marry me."

Stella was stunned—until she realized he was joking. "Marry into the wealthiest family in the area, right?"

"Yes, ma'am. I could get me a new pickup and hang around the mansion all day watching TV and having someone else shine my boots. No more dishes or trash at the diner. I think you should consider it, Chief. I'd be a good, rich husband."

She laughed until tears rolled down her cheeks, which made her head hurt more. "I appreciate the offer. Rich family or not, I have a life and a job to go home to. You'll have to find some other member of the family to marry."

"That's the problem. You and your mama are the only ones left who really sprang from the old man's loins, so to speak. We all know about his pre-nup with Vivian. Who's gonna get all that money if it isn't you?"

Stella got out of the truck, thinking about the two very different reactions from John and Ricky. Whether everyone else hated her or not, when word got around, it would certainly change her status in Sweet Pepper.

She let herself into the cabin and shut off the alarm. The phone call to her mother was going to have to wait until she could get to another phone. She plugged in her cell phone to charge it for the next time she went down the mountain. It seemed she and her mother had plenty to talk about.

In the meantime, there was her laptop. She had Internet service there, though it was spotty at best. She sat down at the table and turned on the computer, waiting impatiently for the welcome screen to come up.

She wasn't sure if she'd find the information she was looking for about her new family, but an Internet search was at least a place to start. She was also thinking she should input her findings on the fire at Tory's house.

Her head almost hurt too much to think, and her bruised ribs ached. She went to the fridge for a Coke. Caffeine would help—along with a few aspirin.

"That stuff isn't good for you," said a now familiar, though still disembodied voice.

Stella took out a can, popped the top, and remembered her security camera setup with the alarm company. "Go away. I have a headache. And when I find out who you are, I'm going to prosecute. Got it?"

Laughter shivered through the cabin. "I don't think that will make any difference to me at this point. Do what you have to do."

"We'll see." She washed down three aspirin with a long swallow of Coke. It took only a few minutes to log in to her site with the alarm company. "I've got you now."

There was nothing there—literally. She'd forgotten to drop off her laptop to have the software installed. She groaned and put her head down on the table.

"Not working?"

"Go away."

"Sorry. I can see you're hurting."

"You need a phone up here, Eric. I guess you must be Eric, right?" She succumbed to the ghostly conversation.

"I guess there was a phone sometime, but it's been a while since you've had a permanent resident."

"That's true. Most people don't like haunted cabins. I wonder what makes you so different."

"I don't know. I'm going to work for a while. Wake me up if I fall asleep, huh?"

There was no reply.

She started entering the information from the folder Tory had given her about her husband's terrible death. Reading through it, Stella could see why the police, and then Fire Chief Eric Gamlyn, didn't press any harder into the idea that Adam's Presley's death was anything but an accident.

What made Tory think he was murdered?

Stella thought back to their conversations on the subject. Tory hadn't been too clear about it either. She'd said it had become an obsession down through the years. There were notes and maps. Tory was sure her husband had quit smoking and wouldn't have smoked behind her back. She also said the cigarette found at the scene, a menthol variety, was not the kind Adam had smoked.

Of course, there was no DNA testing going on back in the 1970s. The police and fire chief had signed off on the dead man being Adam because he was wearing Adam's jewelry and was about the same height, weight, and coloring. There was no mention of having compared dental records.

Stella closed her eyes and saw Tory's face as she'd handed over the folder just hours before she died. She would do what she could to research Tory's claims. The older woman had been a good friend to her, even if only for a short time. Stella couldn't save her, but she could do this for her.

An hour later, Stella got up from the computer and staggered to the sofa near the fireplace. It was a little chilly in the morning, though the afternoons warmed up enough for most people to wear shorts.

"A fire would be nice," she said as she closed her eyes. "Could you do that with your ghostly powers?"

* * *

The wood clock with the carved animals on it was ticking on the mantel. Stella heard that and another sound that she couldn't identify. She knew she'd been asleep for a while. Her head hurt less. She was comfortable on the well-worn sofa.

It was the smell of smoke that brought her upright quickly. There was no other smell like it. In her line of work, it was never a good smell.

Then she realized that the sound she'd heard was the popping of logs burning in the fireplace. That's where the smell had come from too.

And someone had pulled a blanket over her while she'd been asleep.

"I'm either crazy or there really is a ghost here," she said out loud.

"I'm not totally convinced that you're not crazy," he said. "But I've been trying to tell you that you're not alone."

"I think I should go and stay at Flo's place again." Was the old cabin really haunted? No. It wasn't possible—was it? It was crazy. Unreal. Against everything she was brought up to believe.

Well, not exactly.

Her father's Irish heritage included plenty of stories about ghosts and the little people. But those were just stories. At least she'd always thought so.

"That's up to you, of course. I'd rather you didn't. You're the first person I've been able to talk to in forty years."

Stella's eyes roamed around the empty living room. She wasn't sure how to address the whole cabin. "I thought the idea was to scare everyone away. You've done a good job of it for a long time."

The cabin made its familiar sighing sound. "I didn't start out to scare anyone. It just happened. I don't regret it—I didn't want to have a bunch of tourists up here. You're different."

"How?"

"Maybe because we have so much in common. I want you to succeed in bringing the fire brigade back to life. And there's the selfish reason—the sound of your own voice gets old after a while. Before you got here, all I could do was push things around and mess with the electricity. It's different now."

Stella didn't know if she should be happy about that or not. "This is kind of weird. I don't know if I can stay."

"Sorry. I didn't think about it like that. It's been a long time since I had real company. I miss it."

"Why don't you go on into the light or whatever?" She felt stupid even asking. She also felt stupid talking to a ghost in the first place.

"If there's a light to go on into, I haven't seen it. I'm trapped here, I guess."

Stella sighed too. Not only was he a ghost, he was a sad, forlorn-sounding ghost. How could she leave him? It might be another forty years before someone else stayed here long enough to talk to him.

"I only have a few weeks left on my contract with the town," she said, weakening.

"That sounds like a lifetime to me," he replied. "Will you stay?"

Chapter 13

~~~~~~~~~~

Stella heard a car drive up, followed by a rap at the door. "Yes. I'll stay. At least for now. Stay out of the bedroom and the bathroom. That's my personal space. And don't try to change my eating habits. Deal?"

"Deal," he agreed.

She tossed the blanket to the side of the sofa and hoped her hair wasn't sticking out all over or flat on one side from sleeping. The rap at the door came again, and she finally went to answer it.

"Hey, Chief." It was John. He had an unhappy look on his handsome face. His police uniform hat was in his hand. "I hate to bother you, but I need to fill out an accident report on your wreck. I'm sorry if I sounded like I was judging you in the car this morning."

Stella glanced at the kitchen clock. It was after two p.m. She'd been asleep for hours.

"I forgive you." She stepped back from the door. "Come in and sit down. Would you like some coffee?"

"I would." He smiled. "I'll make it. You should be resting. That's why I waited to come up here. I went back to the firehouse to apologize. Ricky said you weren't feeling well and that I was an idiot. I needed some space to take that in."

Stella sat back down on the sofa as John made coffee. The low fire still crackled and put out a little warmth. She decided it was nice to have two men waiting on her—even if one of them was dead.

"I suppose Ricky told you all about my dad and the Carsons." John took coffee cups off the deer-antler rack on the cabinet. "It's hard to get over the feeling that Ben Carson should've just taken a gun and shot my dad. It would've been kinder."

Stella didn't deny that she had talked with Ricky. "I'm sorry about what happened to your father. I'm sure I'd feel the same way. I really had no idea what I was walking into. I haven't been able to hear it from my mother yet. No cell phone."

He smiled. "That's part of the pleasure of living on a mountain. You don't have to talk to people if you don't want to."

Stella thought about her conversation with Eric as John handed her a cup of coffee. "I suppose that's true. If I were going to stay here, I'd have a landline put in."

John sat opposite her in the big chair by the fire. "The heat feels good. You're as good at starting fires as you are putting them out. Can you tell me again what happened last night when you wrecked? I'm afraid my hearing wasn't so good this morning."

Stella went over it again. "That's really all I remember about it. I guess I passed out when I hit my head. I woke up at my grandfather's house."

John wrote down what she said. "How did Marty find you? Tagger called us this morning when it was light. He saw your bike in the ditch. It's dark down there where the road ends."

She shrugged. "Maybe he saw the accident. I'm not sure. I didn't have a chance to ask him about it. To tell you the truth, I wanted to get out of there. It was strange finding out

I have family here—especially that way. I still don't know what to think."

"I can see where that would be unsettling. On the other hand, think of the possibilities. Your mother must not plan to come back. That probably makes you heir to pretty much everything you see around you every day. Don't tell me you've never thought about being rich."

Stella sipped her coffee. "I really *haven't* ever thought about it. I was raised to believe that service to other people was the only thing that mattered. My father's family has lived their lives either as police officers or fire department personnel for generations. We've been lower middle class my whole life. I don't see myself as the heir to anything. I guess my mom must not either since she left. My plan is still to go home in a few weeks."

John put away his notebook. "I think they'll change your mind. They're a very persuasive family. Just think how they've already set your life up the way they wanted it. Without you even knowing anything about it, right?"

She wanted to ask him if he knew anything about what had made her mother leave Sweet Pepper and never look back—never even talk about it. His tone had become angry again, like it had been this morning when he'd dropped her off. It didn't seem like a good time for that discussion.

She was feeling better. Her cell phone was probably charged. All she needed was a ride down the mountain and she could find out for herself.

"Will you wait a few minutes so I can ride back with you?"

"Sure. Oh. I almost forgot to tell you. They sent over the preliminary autopsy results on Tory."

"Yes?"

"She was diabetic, you know. Had been all her life. It seems she injected too much insulin and it caused her to go into a coma. The coroner said there was some smoke in her lungs, not enough to kill her. Cause of death will be the insulin coma. Guess she made a mistake when she administered it."

"After she'd been a diabetic her entire life?" Stella frowned. "Doesn't that seem unlikely?"

"I don't know. Coroner said it happens. People get in a hurry and are careless about the dosage. Anyway—I thought you'd like to know. He's not finished yet, but that's how it looks right now."

"Have you spoken to Tagger about the kerosene at the house?"

"No. Not yet. Other things came up. Petey went to Potter's, and Tommy told her Tagger regularly bought kerosene for Tory there, as well as other items. Maybe Tagger will still be at the firehouse when we get down there and we can both talk to him."

"Thanks, John. I'll only be a few minutes."

"Have you decided to stay here now that you've got the all clear on the snakes?" He glanced around the empty room.

"Yeah. I think it'll be fine now. No more electrical problems."

He smiled. "No more ghosts? Everybody in town will be sorry to hear that. Our spooks give us character."

"I don't know about the ghost. I guess we'll see."

"Good." He ran the brim of his hat between his fingers. "I'm sorry about this thing with the Carsons. I don't hold it against you."

"Thanks." It seemed like an odd thing to say. "I'll be out in a minute."

There were no spooky feelings in the bedroom as Stella changed out of her mother's old, too-tight clothes. She glanced around, wondering if the ghost was watching her as she changed into clean jeans and a Sweet Pepper Festival T-shirt. It was creepy thinking she could be living with someone she couldn't see.

What was that old show on TV she used to watch with her aunt? Oh yes! *The Ghost and Mrs. Muir*! She'd loved that show.

She wore the shoes she'd taken from her grandfather. They were comfortable. Why not?

Maybe that was what John meant about her being corrupted by them.

Stella looked at her scratched and bruised face in the bathroom mirror as she ran a comb through her hair. There wasn't much she could do to make it look any better. Considering that she'd wrecked her bike, she counted her blessings. It could've been much worse.

When she stepped out of the bedroom, John smiled. "That was quick. You're a woman of your word, Stella Griffin. In some ways, I wish you were staying in Sweet Pepper."

"Just not if I'm going to be corrupted by my family name?"

"I guess I shouldn't have said that either." He nodded at the fireplace. "I closed it up for you—no sparks. I wasn't sure if you'd thought about it, being a city girl and all."

"Thanks. That's fine." She picked up one of her many Sweet Pepper Fire Brigade hoodies. "For the record, people in Chicago have fireplaces too. Not to mention that I'm a firefighter and I know about that type of thing."

"I bow to your superior knowledge, ma'am."

Stella could've sworn she heard a *humphing* sound from the cabin. She ignored it. She tried to pull up the zipper on her sweatshirt. She was still cold, probably still feeling the effects of the accident. "I don't know what's wrong with this thing."

John put his hat down on the kitchen cabinet and bent to the task of trying to pull up her zipper. "It might be you instead of the jacket. That looks like a pretty nasty cut on your head."

He managed to manipulate the zipper, pulling it up to her chin. His hand lingered against her throat. He looked down into her face and smiled again but didn't speak.

She swayed a little closer to him, prepared to let something happen, her eyes closing a little.

The security alarm went off, throwing them apart as Stella went to check the control pad. Finally the terrible, blaring noise stopped. She wondered if the ghost she hardly believed in had anything to do with ruining that moment.

"I think we should go." She grabbed her cell phone from its charger and put her laptop into a bag. She could drop it off with Charlie while she was in town. He was only open a few hours on Sunday.

"Looks like it. I'll meet you at the car."

She put the key in the lock, holding the door open until John was off the porch. "I hope this isn't an example of our new spirit of cooperation." She faced the house as she locked the door.

There was no response. She noticed as she and John drove away that the porch light came on. Despite being a little annoyed, she smiled. She might have to talk with Eric about leaving the house when John was there.

"You're not planning on asking Tagger any questions about Tory's kerosene lamps, are you?" John asked as he started the police car.

"You can have that honor, if you want it. As the arson investigator, it's still my job to find out what caused the fire. We might run into each other a few times. Nothing personal."

"Fair enough." He manipulated the sharp turns on Fire-house Road with a smoothness that she wished Ricky would learn.

"You know, Tagger is a nice guy," she remarked. "Why is everyone so protective of him?"

"I don't know. We take care of each other in Sweet Pepper. They say he hasn't really done much since he came back from the Vietnam War. Before that, he was a different person. Like Chief Rogers said, he's a hero. We like that around here."

Stella understood that—unless he had something to do with the fire at Tory's. She hoped he didn't. She didn't want to keep butting heads with Don Rogers all the time.

They arrived at the firehouse to find the volunteers practicing with the three-inch hose. It was difficult for the new-bies to control the larger hose. Tagger was sitting in a lawn chair watching them as Stella and John pulled up.

Petey and Ricky had the hose in hand, but lost their grip when Allen turned and dropped his side. As the barber waved to Stella, the hose went crazy, flopping across the parking lot until Kent turned off the water.

"Why do we even need a bigger hose?" Ricky asked. "It seems to me like the two-inch is enough for the job."

"You all will need that three-inch if the pepper-packing plant catches on fire or one of the hotels goes up," Tagger explained. "That's the commercial size. And from where I'm sitting, we'll lose the plant before you figure out how to hold on to it."

"That's not fair," Ricky complained.

"Tagger's right," Stella added. "You need to practice with all the hoses. You aren't even hooked up to a hydrant here, so the water pressure isn't at full force. You can't get distracted."

The team picked up the big hose again, this time with Allen, Petey, and Kent on it. Ricky went to turn on the water.

"Thanks, Chief," Tagger said with a broad smile. "Between you and me, we'll get them into shape yet."

"I know we will," she agreed.

"Tagger, did Ricky tell you about the kerosene lamps in Tory's basement that made the fire burn hotter?" John asked.

"Sure. I was surprised." Tagger struggled to his feet.

"Why was that?" John replied.

"Because Miss Tory would never keep a kerosene lamp in the house, not even in the basement. She was scared of fire. Her first husband died in a fire, you know. That's one reason she wanted you here so bad, Chief. She thought it was real important to have a strong fire department." Tagger looked at John as though he couldn't believe he had to tell him that last fact.

"Where did she store the kerosene?" John asked.

"In the back shed, with the lawn mower and the gas." Tagger nodded. "It's back away from the house."

"Did she normally keep the lamps back there with the kerosene?" Stella wondered.

"Yes. I kept them filled in case there's a storm and the power goes out." Tagger scratched his head, looking puzzled. "How did those lamps get in the basement? There hasn't been a storm in a while. And she should'a only had one, even if there was a storm."

"That's something we have to find out," Stella answered.

John shrugged and looked at Tagger, obviously hating to ask the next question. "Where were you when the fire happened?"

"I don't know. Probably at the park, helping with the celebration. That's where I was when the chief saw the smoke from Tory's house. You can ask Bob Floyd, if you don't believe me. He was helping me move that big container of potato salad that Lucinda Waxman brought over."

Tagger looked near tears from John's question. Stella put her hand on the old man's arm to steady him. He sobbed and pushed his face into her chest, hugging her tightly. She gasped as the pain in her ribs shot through her.

John glared at her. "So now I'm the bad guy for asking what you wanted to know."

Stella eased Tagger to her right side, which wasn't so painful. "I didn't tell you to accuse him of anything."

He put his hat on with a little extra force. "Thanks a lot."

"Well, now we know." She smiled at him. "We can move on to other suspects you can interrogate for me."

He didn't respond.

Eventually, Tagger stopped crying and wiped his eyes on his sleeve. "Sorry, Chief."

"That's okay," she answered. "Now we know that something unusual happened with the fire. What did Tory store her kerosene in?"

"It was in a red can marked 'kerosene' last time I was at her place," Tagger said.

"We checked in the shed for a container," Stella said. "We didn't find one."

Tagger's eyes widened. "Maybe somebody started that fire with it. I'll be glad to help you look for it, Chief. I know that old house really well."

"We'll talk about that later. Thanks for offering. I have to go into town and make a phone call. Have everyone practice another thirty minutes or so, then clean up."

He nodded with a smile. "You got it, Chief. I know they can learn to use the bigger hoses. Just wait and see."

Stella thanked him for his help with the training, though his role was mostly to cheer on the volunteers from the sidelines. She hated to tell him he shouldn't be there. It seemed to mean so much to him.

John was waiting for her by the police car. He held the door for her as she painfully eased into the passenger seat.

"I would've thought you'd be all over getting that bike of yours back on the road," he said as he started the car.

"Normally, you'd be right. First, I need to have a discussion with my mother about the family she forgot to mention. I can't tell you how much it bothers me, not knowing why she left or why she thought it was important for me to be here. It's not like her to keep things from me." She shrugged. "Or at least I didn't think it was like her. You think you know someone, but I guess everyone has their secrets."

"You really didn't know, did you?"

"I know I was a little woozy this morning when you picked me up, but I think that's what I said. Did you think I was lying?"

"The thought had crossed my mind."

"Why would I lie about it?"

"Beats me. I've seen some strange things on the job. Maybe you wanted us to get to know you and love you before you told us the truth, so we wouldn't hate you."

She stared at him. "And how's that working out, John?"

Chapter 14

~~~~~~~~~

His face turned red as he realized what he'd said. "You know what I mean, Stella. Not love exactly. Infiltrate the masses. Spy on us for the old man."

"In the guise of a mild-mannered fire chief," she teased him.

"Don't make it any worse than it is." He grinned at her. "I'm sorry. I wasn't thinking clearly. Just the idea that you're one of *them*—"

"I know what you mean. Imagine how I felt waking up there—'Sorry you wrecked your bike. We're your new family.' I thought I was in a horror movie. I spoke with my mother briefly before I passed out again. Now I want some real answers."

"I guess I can understand that." He glanced over at her as they got to the "Welcome to Sweet Pepper, Population 5,245" sign. "Ben Carson has a plan, Chief. There's a reason you're here. Don't forget that."

"I won't." Privately she thought he was a little paranoid where the Carsons were concerned. "You could drop me off over there at the café. I might as well have some apple pie and coffee while I talk to my mom."

"I could, but the mayor would have my badge if I don't drop you off right there at town hall where you see that crowd of people standing around the new fire chief's truck."

She looked where he'd nodded. "Are you kidding me?" She saw a large red Cherokee parked half on the sidewalk. There were a lot of people standing in the street and on the sidewalk next to it. "How did they find out already?"

His eyes were tender on her bruised face. "This is Sweet Pepper, darlin', where the peppers are hot and sweet and the gossip flows like moonshine. Enjoy the moment."

John stopped the car. Mayor Wando opened the door for her. "Chief Griffin! We've been waiting for you."

"We heard about your terrible accident." Councilman Nay Albert put his arm carefully around her shoulders. "We were so worried."

"And we're so grateful that you're still among us," Councilman Bob Floyd added.

"We know your motorcycle has been seriously damaged," the mayor continued, "and we would like to offer this replacement. The fire chief needs a vehicle anyway. We were working on it. This little mishap kind of moved our time-table up a bit."

Everyone started moving out of the way, allowing Stella to see the new fire-engine-red truck in front of town hall.

"Have her pull the ribbon off the top so I can get a picture, Mayor," Pat Smith said as she held her camera high. She and her husband, John, ran the *Sweet Pepper Gazette* together. Most people referred to them as "The Smittys" because they were always together. They looked a little alike with their gray hair and rounded bodies. Plus they always wore matching *Gazette* T-shirts.

The mayor and all of the councilmen got in on the pictures. The crowd applauded as Stella pulled off the big red ribbon on the hood.

"There wasn't quite time to get all of the necessary equipment in place," the mayor said. "Ricky Junior can take care of installing the radio and the siren—and whatever else you need."

"Thank you." Stella was overwhelmed by their generosity. She reminded herself that they didn't purchase the vehicle for her specifically. It was for the fire chief, whoever that would be. But it was still a nice gesture—especially since she'd been thinking she'd have to rent a car until the Harley was repaired.

"Say a few words so we have something to write about," Pat Smith said. "We need a nice caption for the front page."

The crowd applauded and then quieted down. Stella looked at the group, spotting all of the volunteers who were supposed to be practicing with the three-inch hose.

She also saw her grandfather in the very back of the crowd and guessed where the money for the SUV had come from. She could only suppose that John hadn't realized yet, since he was as happy as everyone else.

Oh well. He could be cynical later.

"Thank you all so much," she said in a loud voice. "I'm really glad to be here and to work with Sweet Pepper's finest—the volunteer fire brigade."

Applause broke out again. Ben Carson nodded and smiled at her. There was no sign of Vivian or Marty.

Stella was swamped immediately by her volunteers and other citizens of the town wishing her well. Lucille and Ricky Hutchins Sr. handed out ham biscuits to the crowd while a waitress from Scooter's gave out ice cream samples. Valery from the Daily Grind passed around coffee in small cups. The event became a party on the street.

The Smittys coerced Stella into getting in the driver's seat of the SUV so they could take her picture again. As soon as they had finished, her grandfather stopped at the window.

"It's a good-looking vehicle, don't you think? It needs detailing—it should say 'Sweet Pepper Fire Brigade' and maybe have the current fire chief's name on the door."

"That would be the usual procedure," she agreed. "But a waste until there's a more permanent chief."

"You know, there could be a good life for you here, Stella. You seem to fit right in. I know the town council would like you to stay. No point in searching for something you already have."

"I appreciate the offer, but I'm not staying. I have a life already back home."

He smiled and shook his head. "Stubborn as a mule, like your mother. If you won't consider staying on permanently, at least come and stay with me at the estate while you're here. We would have more time to get to know each other, and you wouldn't have to put up with that old haunt."

"Thanks, but he and I are getting along much better now. Excuse me. I have an important phone call to make."

"I meant the cabin. Stella?"

Her grandfather opened the door and she got out of the truck. "Yes?"

"Tell your mother I love her and I wish she'd come down for a visit sometime. It's been too long."

She smiled but didn't respond. Was anything ever private here?

She hoped her mother had some reasonable explanation for keeping this large secret. Maybe finding out what it was would take away some of her uneasiness about the situation.

Everyone from town seemed to be out and about. They all wanted to shake her hand or have a picture taken with her and the Cherokee. Their enthusiasm made her feel jaded. It was only a vehicle, after all. The people of Sweet Pepper had made it into something so much more.

Or maybe that was her injuries from the wreck talking. Or that she'd had to acknowledge that a ghost lived with her and that she had a new family she'd never met—all in the past twenty-four hours.

She reminded herself what a nice gesture it was and kept on smiling.

The crowd also made it difficult for her to reach the café.

When Stella finally sat down at a table, the town's attorney had her sign some documents that included promises that she'd take care of the SUV. He also took her driver's license number for insurance purposes.

When he was finally done and the excitement had dwindled to various café patrons waving and smiling at her across the crowded dining area, Stella ordered some apple pie and coffee. Ricky's mother, who usually didn't wait tables, brought it to her.

"I put some rum sauce on the pie for you." Lucille set down the big piece of pie on a warm plate. "It has a tiny hint of pepper in it. The recipe won the festival award two years running."

"Thanks, Lucille." Stella realized there was no way she was going to have a heart-to-heart with her mother like this. She needed somewhere quiet—that had cell service—where she could be alone. In the meantime, she might as well enjoy her pie.

People continued to stop by her table to shake her hand and introduce their children. She also felt someone staring at her and looked up to see Deputy Chum at the counter. His plate was still full, ignored while he looked at her with curious apprehension.

At least he wasn't running away screaming.

She picked up her plate and coffee to join him at the narrow counter. Maybe she could pump some information out of him.

"Deputy Chum."

"Chief Griffin." His smile didn't reach his eyes. She could see that she still made him nervous. He pushed his plate of fried catfish and hush puppies farther away from her. His hand shook when he picked up a hush puppy and started eating.

"I know we met earlier on the road coming into town," she started. "You called me Abigail."

He swallowed his hush puppy and made a pretense out of washing it down with a large swallow of iced tea. "That's right. Funny that. My old eyes were playing tricks on me, I guess."

"You thought I was Abigail Carson, my grandmother, didn't you?"

"I was mistaken. I mean, you aren't her." He got flustered and red-faced talking about it, obviously wishing she'd go away.

"I saw some old pictures. I look like her." Stella smiled. "I guess that's why you were surprised to see me."

He nodded over the top of his glass. "You do favor her. Even more than your mama did."

"You knew Abigail well?"

"She—I—"

"Were you friends?"

"With Abigail Carson?" he blurted out. "Of *course* not." He wiped his mouth with his napkin. "She died. She was my first death scene when I came on with the sheriff's office. I was the first deputy on the scene that night. It's something you never forget. I never saw a single person dead in my whole life before then—except in a coffin, of course."

"On the scene?" Stella asked. She'd figured Abigail had died from cancer or something. "How did she die?"

"She fell down those long stairs and snapped her neck. Looking at her made a goose run across my grave. She looked like she was still alive. I can see it as clear today as if it was yesterday."

"Was it an accident?"

He stared at her, forgetting for a minute who he was talking to. "Of course it was an accident. She lost her balance, that's all. It was tragic."

Deputy Chum started eating his catfish in earnest, stifling any further conversation between them. Stella was prepared to wait, but Officer Richardson, another Sweet Pepper policeman, asked if she would kindly move the Cherokee as it was blocking people trying to get in and out of town hall.

"It was good talking with you, Deputy," she said before

she left Chum. "I'd like to see someone like you come out and join the fire brigade. We could use all the experienced emergency people we can get."

"I'm about to retire. Thanks for the invite. My wife would kill me if I did anything besides work on the house and help out in the garden."

"I understand." She held out her hand. "Thanks for telling me about Abigail."

He took her hand and leaned close to her. "Some things are better left unsaid," he whispered, staring into her eyes with great intent. "You're leaving here soon. No call for you to get caught up in it."

Deputy Chum glanced around at the rest of the patrons in the diner, then hitched up his pants and walked out.

Stella left too. Maybe she'd only imagined the intensity of his gaze, as though he were issuing a warning. Was there some question about her grandmother's death?

She thought about it as she carefully drove the SUV off the sidewalk and parked it on the street. Was that what had driven her mother away?

She grabbed her computer bag from John's police car and took it down to Charlie Johnson's shop to have the software installed. She was fairly sure at this point that there really *was* a ghost, as crazy as that sounded, but it wouldn't hurt to try one more, logical thing to be certain.

Charlie took the laptop and smiled. "Thought you'd given up and accepted the truth, Chief Griffin. I don't know if a ghost is gonna appear on a surveillance picture."

"Things came up," she said. "I have to investigate every possibility before I can accept the ghost theory."

"Oh yeah." He looked at the bandage on her head. "You wrecked your bike. Sorry to hear that."

"Can we put the security program on my laptop?" Both of the subjects were sore points for her right now.

"Of course! I'll be happy to defrag and tune it up a bit too, if you like. Can't be too careful nowadays."

"Sure," she agreed. "I'll pick it up later."

"Should be ready in about an hour, Chief. Thanks for your business."

Town hall should have been closed since it was Sunday, but since the mayor and town council had been out and about anyway, they'd decided to have a meeting of some sort. Part of the building was always open since the police department was also located there.

Stella walked in and asked the clerk if there was someplace private where she could use her phone. It was time to have that conversation that she hoped would answer some of her questions.

The woman with the beehive hairdo and pink sweater set said, "Of course, Chief Griffin. You just come right this way. You can use the mayor's office. Would you like some coffee? I can put on a new pot."

"Thanks. I had some. I hate to take you from your work—which way is the mayor's office?"

The clerk wouldn't hear of Stella finding her own way. She led Stella down the long corridor past several closed doors with names on them. John didn't have an office, but Don Rogers did.

"Here's the mayor's office. Make yourself at home." The clerk smiled. "I was wondering if we'd meet before you left Sweet Pepper. I'm Sandy Selvy. I grew up here—your mother and I went to school together. I always thought we'd hear something from that side of the family again. I bet Ben Carson is glad to have you back. That man deserves some happiness in his life."

Stella didn't say anything. She didn't know what to say. Maybe it was because of her head injury, or maybe because of the whole weird situation. At least it was nice to hear someone say something pleasant about her grandfather.

Sandy smiled again, blushing a little. "Here I am talking your ear off when you have a phone call to make. I'm going back to take minutes at that meeting."

Stella waited until Sandy was gone, then sat down at the desk in the quiet room. She punched in her mother's number on her cell phone and touched the picture of her laughing face on the screen as she waited for her to pick up.

She felt oddly disconnected and wished she could go home now. Rather than making her want to stay in Sweet Pepper, the Carson legacy made her want to run away.

"Oh, Stella," her mother answered. "I've been so worried. I heard you wrecked your motorcycle from Dad. Are you okay now? I've tried calling you a hundred times."

"Never mind how she is," Stella's father quipped in the background. "How's the Harley? If I would've known you were going to wreck it, I might not have given it to you. That bike is a family heirloom."

"Quiet, Sean," Barbara Griffin said to her husband. "Never mind. I'm going upstairs to talk to Stella."

Stella took this to mean that her father didn't know the whole Sweet Pepper story either. She heard some rustling and the closing of a door on her mother's end. "Mom?"

"It's okay now. I wanted some privacy."

"Sorry about the missed calls. You forgot to tell me that your hometown has hit-or-miss cell phone service too. Kind of like you forgot to tell me anything else about it."

"I'm really sorry about that, honey. I left there so long ago. I didn't want anyone to know. I made up a whole new background for myself."

"I understand that," Stella said. "But you knew I was coming here. I know you didn't want to prejudice me against your family, but come on—a whole, rich family who everyone fears and/or despises? I think you should've mentioned that to me."

Her mother was silent for a moment. Her voice was shaking when she said, "It's hard to explain. I was so afraid he'd find me. I never wanted to see him or Sweet Pepper again."

Chapter 15

~~~~~~~~~~

"What changed your mind?" Stella asked.

"Right after you broke up with Doug, I got a call from Dad. It was the first time I'd talked to him since I left home. I didn't even know what to say. Looking back on it, leaving seems kind of stupid and dramatic. Like something a kid would do, only I'd held on to it all these years."

"You left because your mother died, right?"

"Of course you've heard about it," her mother said. "There's plenty of gossip in Sweet Pepper. Most of it you can't believe."

"So you were devastated by her death and left. Did you blame your father?"

Barbara laughed. "That's my girl. I'm not sure you shouldn't have been a shrink instead of a firefighter. Yes, I blamed him. I thought for a long time that he had killed her."

Stella recalled her talk with Deputy Chum. "What changed your mind? I'm assuming you wouldn't have let me come down here if you still believed that."

"Ha ha. Very funny. No, I would've told you before you left. I realized after I talked to Dad that I was still holding on to all those crazy teenage ideas. I dug out my old scrapbook that I'd brought with me—almost the only thing I brought. The police did a thorough investigation into my mom's death."

"They didn't find anything suspicious," Stella guessed. "Was that because there *wasn't* anything suspicious to find or because they didn't want to charge Ben Carson with a crime? Because I have to tell you that it doesn't seem likely to me that the police would look *too* hard at him as a suspect."

"I know what you mean. I thought the same thing. The police said my mother had been taking sleeping pills and probably lost her balance on those stairs—I take it he still lives there and you know what I'm talking about."

"What made you think your father killed her?"

"They argued a lot. I thought maybe they were arguing and he pushed her. I loved her very much, Stella. We were very close. I knew she and my dad had problems. She thought he was fooling around and that's why he was gone all the time. I guess I hated him for her."

"Did the police take that into consideration?"

"Yes. They questioned Dad. He wasn't even home at the time. There was some emergency at the pepper plant and he was there. Ironically, spending all his time there was one of their biggest problems. In this case, it was also his alibi."

"That wasn't good enough for you?"

"I couldn't look at him. I couldn't stand to be at the house. I had to get out of there." She paused. "That was a long time ago. I wasn't practical and smart like you, honey. It wasn't until I looked at everything again that I realized how silly and selfish I'd been."

"Why selfish, Mom? You had to find yourself and your own answers."

"I was selfish because I left my dad alone with all of that heartache and grief. I could've been there to help him get over it. We could've helped each other. I hope if something happens to me, your father will have you to lean on. There are only the three of us—like my family was."

Stella felt like she was beginning to understand though some details were still unclear. "Did you tell your father about me breaking up with Doug?"

"You mean your grandfather? No. At least not the first time I talked to him."

"So he got all of his personal information about me from you?"

"I guess so. Why? Did you think he'd had you investigated?" Barbara laughed. "Maybe we aren't so different after all."

"Maybe," Stella agreed. "There's still the thing about how Sweet Pepper knew to put that ad in *my* station's newsletter. And, if your dad called you, he's probably known all this time where you were."

"You don't like him."

"I don't know him. I thought *you* didn't like him."

Her mother sighed. "It's not that simple."

"But you want me to like him?" Stella asked.

"I want you to make your own decision. Now you know all about it. You can choose to let the Carsons be part of your family too. Or not."

"What have *you* decided? Are you coming down here for a visit?"

John knocked on the door. He stuck his head in and said, "When you're finished, Stella, come find me. I have something important to tell you."

"Who was that?" her mother asked as Stella nodded to him and he shut the door. "He has a nice voice."

"That was John Trump. Maybe you knew his father, Bobby, or his grandfather, Ray."

"No. Probably not. I was a little sheltered from most of the people in Sweet Pepper. As to me coming down there, I'm considering it."

"You know he's remarried, right? He has a stepson too."

"Yes. He told me. What about you, honey? Are you still coming home?"

"I can't tell you how many people ask me that every

day," Stella said, annoyed. "But, yes, I'll be home before Thanksgiving."

Stella briefly told her mother how everything was going with the new fire brigade. She also told her about Tory Lambert.

Barbara knew that name. "That's terrible. She was a powerful woman. She and Dad had a few run-ins. I think they wanted different things for the town. Do you have any suspects in the case?"

"Not exactly. I'll let you know what happens. Mom, did you ever meet Eric Gamlyn?"

"The name sounds familiar. Didn't he work for the old fire department?"

"Yeah. That's him. People think his ghost haunts the cabin where I'm staying."

"That doesn't surprise me, Stella. There's a teenage girl people swear they see on the old bridge on the way out of town. She's supposed to be a hitchhiking ghost who gets in your car and disappears. Sweet Pepper—well, the whole area—has a lot of folklore."

"Is that what it is?"

"Don't tell me being down there has made you believe in the supernatural?" Her mother laughed. "You never even believed in that stuff when you were a child. Remember those awful ghost stories your father used to tell?"

"Used to?" This time, Stella laughed. It was so good to hear her mother's voice. It really made her homesick too. "Well, I have to go, Mom. I'll talk to you later."

"Okay, honey. I love you. I'm sorry I wasn't able to tell you about this sooner."

"That's okay. I love you too. Don't worry about me."

Stella watched her mother's face disappear from her phone screen. It was hard to picture her as a rich heiress who thought her father might have killed her mother. It was a surprise she never could have imagined when she'd made the decision to come to Sweet Pepper.

She put her phone into the pocket of her jeans and left

the room. At least she knew now where to have a decent phone conversation. She might need to call home more often now. Finding out about the Carsons had changed a lot of things.

Stella went to find John. He wasn't at his desk. She asked Sandy if she knew where he was. "He's in the meeting room with Chief Rogers and everyone else. I'm sure they won't mind if you join them."

Following Sandy's instructions, Stella located the all-purpose meeting room where the town held everything from council meetings to any other official function requiring space for more than a hundred people.

Standing outside the room now reminded her of her arrival in Sweet Pepper, when the council had greeted her here with a big buffet of food from all the restaurants in town.

There had been that one moment when she'd first walked into the room and everyone had done a double-take. They hadn't run away, but they'd stared at her like she was a ghost.

Now she knew why.

Tory had been the first one to come forward and shake her hand. She hadn't seemed to be as affected by Stella's appearance as the others, even though she probably knew the truth about who Stella was. The mayor and the other council members had recovered quickly after that and come to greet her.

At the time, their behavior had seemed odd. Stella had chalked it up to being in a small town. She now realized that they had probably known Abigail Carson and had been surprised by how much Stella looked like her.

Before Stella left Sweet Pepper, she had to take another look at her grandmother's picture at the Carson estate. She'd been too dazed and afraid to get a really good look when she was in her mother's old bedroom.

The door to the meeting room was closed, but she ventured in anyway. All of the Sweet Pepper police officers, most of whom were part-time, were there. The mayor, and

Councilmen Nay Albert and Bob Floyd were all there too. Don Rogers was pacing back and forth in front of them, gesturing at a big white board.

John motioned for her to come down and sit beside him. His action drew Chief Rogers's attention. He looked back and said, "Chief Griffin. Glad you could join us. Since this is partially your case too, I'd like your input."

Skewered on his angry glance, Stella sat down in the empty front row of seats. "I'd be glad to help in any way I can. What's going on?"

Chief Rogers laughed. "You mean your *boyfriend* didn't fill you in?"

There were several snickers from the other officers. John didn't flinch even though everyone knew Chief Rogers was talking about him.

It didn't bother Stella either. "Let's assume he didn't, and you can explain from here."

The chief bowed slightly to her. "Yes, ma'am." He pointed to the white board behind him, where several pictures of Tory and her house were displayed. "I think you were the first one to say Ms. Lambert's death might not be an accident. It seems we've had a murder in Sweet Pepper. You must've brought the crime element with you from Chicago."

Chapter 16

～～～～～

She ignored the crack about bringing crime with her, got up, and examined the photos closely. She'd been so busy looking at John when she first came in that she hadn't paid much attention to them. "What happened?"

"The coroner found bits of silk in the abrasions on Ms. Lambert's neck and wrists. As he completed the autopsy, he also found bruising on her body consistent with a struggle of some kind. Two of her fingernails were broken. From this, he made the decision to declare her death a homicide."

"I thought she died from an insulin overdose," Stella said.

"Well, now, the coroner believes Ms. Lambert was tied up and held against her will while that overdose was delivered. It seems it wasn't a single puncture wound but several, all of them made by someone not as familiar with injecting drugs as your typical diabetic would be."

Stella sat back down. She'd thought something about Tory's death was suspicious, but she'd never guessed it would be this bad. She was tough by most standards—she had to be in her line of work—but knowing that someone had brutally murdered this capable woman made her want to cry.

Chief Rogers continued to stare at her. "Any particular

clues that made you think Ms. Lambert's death wasn't what it seemed to the rest of us, Ms. Griffin? If so, I think now would be a good time to share."

"I think you've got it all down, Chief." Her voice was thick with emotion. She didn't want to play this game with him right now.

"Could you be more explicit?" Chief Rogers continued to harass her. "And speak up, please. We can't hear you."

Stella cleared her throat and forced herself to stand up again, despite her injuries. "Tory—Mrs. Lambert—felt cooler to me than she should have given the amount of time the fire had been burning at the house. That, combined with the marks on her wrists and neck, made me suspicious. I'm not a police officer, but I've seen deaths like this before. This is not the first time that someone has tried to use a fire to cover up a murder."

Chief Rogers nodded. "I'm sure that's true, Ms. Griffin. That makes my next observation important—are we any closer to finding out who started the fire? It seems to me, and apparently to you too, that if we find that person, we find the killer."

Stella told them what she'd learned from Tagger. "It seems to suggest that the kerosene was poured into the lamps and left on the basement table to help get the fire going. We're still missing a key piece of evidence. We haven't found the kerosene container used to fill the lamps. If we can find that, it might provide more information."

"Thank you, Ms. Griffin. You can rely on my officers for anything you need," Chief Rogers said. "To my knowledge, we haven't had a murder here in Sweet Pepper for a very long time—I believe that was when Sarah Morrison was killed by her husband."

"The only relative Ms. Lambert had was Victor," one of the officers said. "Do you want us to talk to him?"

"I think that would be a good idea since we know he stands to inherit everything from his mother," Chief Rogers said. "Officers Richardson and Schneider, the two of you will have a polite conversation with Victor Lambert. I know he's told us that he was at Beau's when the fire occurred. I want details about his alibi and whatever else you think could be pertinent."

"I'll have a talk with the insurance investigator again," Stella said. "Now that we know the fire was set intentionally, he might want to rethink his observations."

"That sounds like a good place to start," Chief Rogers said. "Officer Trump—you will be our liaison with the fire department. I'll rely on you to work with Ms. Griffin. Keep me updated on any progress."

"I was wondering about Tory's first husband," Stella added. "I probably don't have the whole story of what happened, but wasn't he killed in a fire?"

"That's right," Chief Rogers said. "I don't see where that is relevant to this. That was a long time ago."

"I'm sure it was. That fire was ruled an accident, although there were some unanswered questions," Stella continued. "Did that fire happen in the same house?"

Chief Rogers smiled in a condescending manner. "I'm sure Officer Trump can fill you in on all the town history at some time when we aren't looking for a killer. In the meantime, let's keep our eye on the ball."

Stella felt all the eyes in the room on her. Chief Rogers had slapped her down a little, insinuating that he was in charge. She knew better, at least where the fire was concerned.

She didn't respond to him. The group began breaking up and heading out, some to follow through on their chief's directives, others to go back home until it was time for their shift. The men studiously ignored her, even though she knew several of them by name.

Mayor Wando and Councilman Floyd came over right away. "We appreciate your help with this terrible thing that has happened in our town," the mayor said, sounding as if he were running for reelection.

"Yes," Bob Floyd agreed. "Losing Victoria Lambert is

devastating for us. I expect there will be a huge memorial for her. When it's appropriate, of course."

"I'm sorry you had to go through this," Stella said. "I was wondering if either of you remember the fire that killed Tory's first husband. Adam Presley, right?"

Wando and Floyd exchanged looks, obviously wondering if they should relate the information they had to her.

Don Rogers came up and slapped a hand on both men's shoulders, causing them to jump. "It's okay, gentlemen. We certainly have no secrets from our fire chief. I believe his name was Presley. Is that what you recall?"

The mayor responded nervously. "That's right. I'd almost forgotten. It's been so long."

"I remember Adam," Bob said. "He owned the car dealership down on Second Street. He was very successful."

"Of course he was." The mayor smiled. "Tory wouldn't have had him if he wasn't. That woman always knew what she wanted."

Stella wasn't sure if she should be grateful to Don for loosening their tongues or if this was all a game for him. "Thank you. I'll see all of you later."

Whatever information she needed about Adam Presley's death, she could get from other public sources. Not that she felt any of these people would outright lie to her. It was more a question of details not revealed.

Like knowing she was related to Ben Carson. Never once since she'd come to Sweet Pepper had anyone—including Tory—mentioned it. Yet she was fairly sure now that most of them must have known.

"Like I said, Ms. Griffin," Don added, "no point in scaring up old problems when we have an important new one right here in front of us."

"I promise to keep my eye on the ball," she said. "Thanks for your help."

John caught up with her as she was leaving the town hall. "Stella? Do we need to talk about what's next in the arson investigation?"

"I'm not sure right now. I'm going over to Tory's house. I'd like to see what else I can find. There's more there."

"I'm off duty. I'll be glad to go with you."

"Okay. I have to run home and get some things. I'll meet you there in about thirty minutes."

"Sure."

Stella's laptop was ready at the computer shop. Charlie showed her how to get real-time images from the newly updated system.

"You won't be able to see a ghost, mind you," he said. "But anything else should show up."

Stella was a little exasperated with the ghost talk. "Aren't there some programs I could use to see the ghost? That way I could talk to my ghost and also ask Tory Lambert who killed her."

Charlie looked surprised. "I didn't know the police were investigating Tory's death as a murder. How did that happen?"

For once, Stella knew something before everyone else, it seemed. "I don't know yet. She was dead before the fire. Her ghost would probably know it all. Thanks, Charlie."

She felt him staring after her as she left his shop. He probably couldn't believe she had that information. Now he'd have to call everyone else in town to let them know. That had to be how the grapevine worked and she'd just contributed to it.

"Chief Griffin!" Elvita Quick and Theodora Mangrum sang out as they saw her.

The women were dressed in matching pink-and-purple dresses today, with purple hats that sported large pink flowers.

"Ladies." Stella smiled at them. "What can I do for you?"

"It's about the recipe contest," Elvita said. "We were thinking how nice it would be if you had a recipe in one of the other contests."

"Of course, you couldn't have one in the chocolate contest as you're judging that one. It wouldn't be ethical." Theodora shook her head, mindful of her hat.

"Of course." Stella wasn't sure what to say. She wasn't much of a cook and didn't have a recipe to her name.

"So you'll do it!" The two women grinned at each other as they spoke at the same time.

"How wonderful! We'll need a copy of the recipe and a taste of the finished product, of course," Elvita said. "We haven't had a Sweet Pepper fire chief enter the contest for a very long time."

"Since Eric." Theodora looked around as though he might be there beside them.

"Yes." Elvita shuddered. "We look forward to your recipe, Chief Griffin!"

Stella watched the two women disappear into the coffee shop. What had she agreed to?

She got in the new Cherokee to drive to the cabin. It was very large and radically different from her motorcycle. Unlike Ricky, she'd never driven an engine or pumper back home. Before the motorcycle, she'd taken the bus everywhere.

She was going to have to find someone who'd be able to make the repairs on her Harley, and she needed an insurance quote. She knew she'd be faulted for the accident. Without another driver to point to, she had no way to prove she'd been run off the road. There was only her word for what had happened.

She stopped at the firehouse, where Ricky gave her the name of a mechanic friend in Pigeon Forge who could do repairs to the Harley. She called the man at his home and mentioned Ricky's name. He said he'd be willing to come and pick it up for her the next day.

There was so much to think about given everything that was going on. She forgot about her ghostly roommate until she walked into the cabin.

"Nice truck."

She jumped and dropped the flashlight she'd picked up from the counter. "That wasn't funny."

"Tell me about it."

"Seriously. Why are you doing this?"

"Wouldn't you want to talk to the only person in the last forty years who could actually hear you?"

Stella stopped foraging for duct tape and paused to consider his words. "So you were around in the 1970s?"

"That's right. If you mean alive, anyway."

"Did you know Tory Lambert?"

"Lambert?"

"No. Tory Presley. That would've been her name back then, I guess. She was married to Adam Presley. He died in a fire."

"Sure. I knew them both. Adam wasn't my favorite person in the world—typical car salesman type. No one should have to die that way."

"What way?"

"The report said he fell asleep while he was smoking. All I can say is that he didn't die from smoke inhalation."

"So the fire wasn't accidental."

"I didn't think so at the time. I couldn't prove it wasn't an accident, but there were some unusual findings surrounding his death."

She stopped trying to untangle some duct tape. "What kind of findings?"

"Adam had stopped smoking about a year before the fire. I interviewed Tory and all of his friends. No one had seen him smoke in that length of time. Also, he had lighter fluid spilled all over him. It made him like a human torch when the fire hit it. We never found a lighter either. It bothered me that he calmly sat there with lighter fluid all over him and never even moved when he burned."

"That sounds strange. He couldn't have been asleep and burned like that. Why did you drop the case?"

"Why are you so interested in an old fire?"

Stella explained about honoring Tory's wish that she look into it. She located her crowbar and hacksaw. "I guess it sounds kind of lame, as I'm saying it. I don't really see what difference it makes. Just because Adam died in a fire doesn't mean it has anything to do with the fire at Tory's house, I suppose."

"You have a bad feeling about it, don't you?"

"I don't know. I'm getting stonewalled every time I ask about it. It should be old news, right? From what I've read so far in Tory's notes, it sounds like someone may have killed Adam. Now Tory's been murdered and it looks like a fire was set to cover it up. Coincidence?"

"Sounds like an interesting theory."

"I guess." She grabbed her gloves and looked around the empty kitchen. "Look, I don't know if I believe you're real or not. Just a warning. My laptop is now set up to monitor the cabin from the security system. I might be able to see you."

"So either you're standing here talking to yourself in another voice, or I'm real?"

"Maybe." There was humor in his tone that made her smile. "Let's pretend you're real a moment longer. Why did you stop investigating the Presley fire if you thought it might have been set intentionally?"

"Two words: Ben Carson. He didn't want it investigated any further. He said it was bad for the town's image. Adam died a few days before the festival. Murder doesn't bring tourists to the Pepper Festival every year. As you may have noticed, people do what Ben Carson tells them to do."

She was surprised by that. Why wouldn't her grandfather have wanted to know the truth? She was also a little disappointed that Eric had given up because of it. It was probably all that talk about him that made him sound larger than life. She'd expected more from him.

In reality, he'd only been a man who probably would have lost his job and the fire brigade he'd built up, if he'd stood his ground. She certainly understood that he wouldn't have wanted to destroy the group he'd worked so hard on. Stella wanted her little group to do well.

She knew politics were sometimes involved in these

things. There had been some unsavory happenings at home too that had led to a chief resigning last year.

Stella could tell from Eric's voice that he had no love for her grandfather. How would he feel about her if he knew the truth? "Do you know who I am?"

"Stella Griffin? Temporary fire chief? Is this a test?"

She stared into the empty air around her. "Can you see things other people can't see?"

"What kind of things? I can't see further than about fifty feet around the cabin, if that's what you mean. It seems to be my proximity."

"No, I mean ghosts are supposed to know things and see things that living people can't. Do you see things like that?"

He laughed. "I don't know. If I do, I'm not aware of it. Until you came, there were only bits and pieces from the TV or the idiots who tried to live here. I don't think I know anything you don't know—except about Sweet Pepper's past."

"Did you know Barbara Carson?"

"Ben's daughter? A little—in passing. She left town right before I died."

"I'm her daughter. She's Barbara Carson Griffin now."

There was only deep silence after her statement.

"Eric? Do you want to start dragging chains or turning the lights on and off again to get rid of me now?"

"Sorry," came the reply. "I should've known. It's been a long time. You look a lot like Abigail Carson. Not so much like I remember Barbara, but she was much younger the last time I saw her. I bet everyone tells you that."

"Now that I know about it, they do." She explained what had happened. "I walked in blind. I had no idea. My grandfather was out of town when I first got here. Everyone kept it a secret. I'm not sure why. Any ideas?"

"Not really. I'm sure it was something Ben wanted to tell you himself, when he felt the time was right."

"Well, I guess the time was right after his stepson pulled me out of the ditch at the end of the road. It was kind of strange."

"That was a long time for Barbara to hold on to that secret," he said. "I'll bet the old man is happy to see you. I'm surprised you didn't have everything moved to his estate. Or is that still coming up?"

Stella zipped the equipment she'd gathered for her next trek through Tory's house into her backpack. "I told you it was strange. I mean eerie strange—like the twilight zone. I woke up after the wreck to find this man I didn't really know telling me he was my grandfather. I wouldn't have stayed the night except I kept passing out from this stupid head injury."

"I see. Not impressed by the old man's money?"

"Would I be a firefighter if money impressed me?"

"No. I suppose not. I guess it still doesn't pay all that much even forty years later."

Stella liked his voice. She wished she could see him. He hadn't even done the shadow-in-the-chair trick since he'd first appeared to her on the deck.

"How am I going to decide if you're real, Eric? Or if I'm being pranked? Or if I've lost my mind? I'm standing here talking to thin air."

"I don't know what to tell you. I guess you'll have to go with your gut on this too."

She smiled. "Okay. You don't have any of your tried-and-true recipes from Sweet Pepper Festivals long past, do you?" She told him about Elvita and Theodora's request.

"I'll see what I can recall," he promised. "It's been a while."

"Thanks. I'm better with a fire hose than a stove. I'll be back later. Wish me luck finding something important at Tory's house."

"Be safe. That's more important than luck. Whoever killed Tory won't hesitate to kill again to hide their secret."

Chapter 17

~~~~~~~~~~

Stella drove thoughtfully down the road from the cabin. She saw John's patrol car at the firehouse alongside a cute little Italian sports car. John was standing in the parking lot talking to Tagger and Marty. He waved her down, and she pulled in to find out what was going on.

"Chief," Tagger greeted her. "I think you know Marty."

"I do." She shook hands with her ersatz relative. "Is there a problem?"

"Marty wants you to consider him as a volunteer." John's tone expressed his wish that she wouldn't.

"I can speak for myself." Marty smiled at Stella. "It's true. I really want to do this. I would've been here sooner, but we were in Lucerne. It was worth it, though. We'll probably sell a lot of peppers there from now on."

Stella studied him. He was handsomely polished and probably looked good driving down the road in his sports car. He had an appealing way of talking. He was probably used to getting his way too.

She knew John wasn't going to like it, but she had no reason not to give Marty a shot. If he was sincere and willing to work, they could use another volunteer. If not, no harm done.

Did her grandfather have anything to do with Marty showing up here? Maybe some of the things she'd heard about Ben Carson were affecting her. She didn't know Marty well enough to decide if he was his own man or not.

Stella liked that he hadn't brought up the fact that he'd pulled her from the ditch. Not that she would have been embarrassed by it. His not taking credit for the act made her feel like he wasn't trying to trade on that single act.

"Okay. I don't see why not. Tomorrow morning. Come ready to work."

"You won't be sorry, Chief Griffin."

Tagger, John, and Stella watched Marty get into his sports car, which probably cost more than all of their salaries combined, and drive away. She'd been right. He looked good with his hair flying in the breeze.

"I can't believe you're going to let that little Carson weasel be a volunteer," John fumed. "It's a mistake. It's always a mistake to get involved with *them*."

She bristled at his tone. "I guess that includes me too then, huh? I don't think badly of people because of the family they come from. He's not a Carson, really. His mother is married to one, right? He might not actually be a bad person like the rest of us who have that blood."

John was clearly angry that Stella was twisting his words. He got in the police car and slammed the door closed. "I'll meet you at Tory's house. I hope you don't regret this decision about Marty. Someone else's life could be on the line if he doesn't do his job."

Stella watched him peel out of the parking lot again. She seemed to be having a bad influence on him. Maybe it was her Carson blood.

"I think you did the right thing, Chief," Tagger said with a big grin that showed his missing teeth. "Everybody deserves a chance. You did right."

"Thanks. I'm heading over to Tory's house to continue the investigation into the fire. Chief Rogers thinks it's possible whoever killed her started the fire. I guess that means it's up to us to figure out who that was."

"Good luck, Chief. I've got the watch tonight with Kent. If you need any help, give me a call," Tagger said.

Stella thanked him, hoping his offer of help meant he would stay sober. John hadn't questioned the decision to keep Tagger on the crew. Everyone in Sweet Pepper treated him with great respect. Like Don had said, Tagger was a hero and that meant something here.

She knew it wasn't going to be fun working with John after that blowup. She had to make what she felt were the right decisions. Once she was gone, it would be up to the new chief to decide who to take on. Marty might not even make it past tomorrow. That would be on him.

A white-haired woman in a pink jogging suit was walking a white poodle when Stella pulled up in front of the burned house. The little dog looked remarkably like her in a doggy pink jumpsuit. As Stella got out of the pickup with her backpack, the woman came around to see her.

"Good afternoon, Chief Griffin. We are having some lovely fall weather, aren't we? This is my favorite time of year. I don't know if you remember me—I'm Myra Strickland. My husband used to be the mayor of Sweet Pepper. He died, unfortunately. The legacy of the Sweet Pepper Festival still falls on me each year. You might say I'm the chairman of the board."

"I'm glad I'll be here for that this year, Mrs. Strickland. I'm looking forward to it. Is there something I can do for you?"

Myra let out a deep sigh. "Believe me, it pains me that Tory is gone, along with her lovely family home, bless her soul. I don't want you to think less of me, but we really need to have all that mess cleared up before the festival."

"Pardon me?" Stella wasn't quite sure what the other woman meant.

"It's an eyesore now." Myra gazed at the burned house.

"You understand that hundreds of thousands of people come here for our little festival each year. Main Street is a favorite attraction. We must have the house cleaned away before then. Believe me, Tory would be standing here saying the same thing about me if I were dead and this was my house."

Though Stella was surprised, she understood what Myra was trying to say. "I can't make that decision, Mrs. Strickland. I'll try to complete the investigation into what caused the fire as quickly as possible. After that, the town can make arrangements for the property."

Myra's bright red lips stretched into a wide smile. "I knew you'd see it my way, Chief. It's been wonderful talking with you." The little white poodle started barking. "Hush now, Sir Walter. We're going home to have our din-din right now."

John pulled up behind the Cherokee as Stella was watching the other woman walk away. "Problems?" he asked as he approached.

"Not as long as the investigation wraps up before the festival."

"Yeah. I could see that coming."

Stella started walking toward the house. John kept up with her. "I hate saying I'm sorry again," he said. "This whole Carson thing is like fingernails scraping on my own personal chalkboard."

"I could tell. You don't have to keep apologizing. I get it. You don't like them and you don't trust them. That's okay. I'm not sure I do either."

"Then why let that useless idiot on the team? The old man probably made him show up so he could spy on you. Or Vivian wants him to marry you and keep the money in the family."

"I think you might be a little paranoid when it comes to that family." She rounded the corner of the once beautiful house to head back down to the basement. "If he's useless, I'll send him home."

"You don't get it, Stella. They are *never* going to let you leave now that you're here. He'll find some way to own you.

That's the way he works. It's eating me up thinking about you being with them."

Stella stopped at the basement stairs. "I'm a big girl, John. I can take care of myself."

He didn't say anything else about it after they entered the basement. She could still feel the tension between them. She wasn't sure exactly what he wanted from her. She was here until her contract was up. She wasn't leaving because people were afraid of her grandfather. She wasn't staying because of it either.

"What are we looking for?" John asked as they shuffled to the back of the soot-covered basement.

"I'm not sure. I'd like to find that kerosene can. I don't think an arsonist filled these lamps and took it with him. It's probably here someplace."

"What difference does it make?"

"We could get a fingerprint from it if the arsonist wasn't careful enough to wear gloves."

"Is that even possible? Look at this place."

"In some cases, a print can bake into a metal surface. There's also a cold-water rinsing technique that can be used to retrieve prints. It's a long shot, I agree. It might be all we have."

"So you think there could be a print on whatever is left of the kerosene can?"

"If we can find it. If it didn't melt into slag or the arsonist didn't take it with him. A few big 'ifs'."

John walked through the debris, shining his flashlight around the dark basement. "If you were going to start a fire right here and still had the kerosene can, what would you do with it?"

She shrugged. "You can never quite get the last of the kerosene out of the can. I think I'd put it somewhere it could help the fire burn without being obvious. Maybe up from the point of origin, under the stairs."

John took out his crowbar. "Let's get crackin'. We don't want to disappoint Mrs. Strickland."

The walls in the house were old—plaster over wood slats. John and Stella began working up through the burned wall area below the stairs.

"Why is everyone reluctant to talk about the fire that killed Tory's first husband?" Stella's voice was muffled through the mask she wore to keep from breathing in the soot and plaster dust.

"What makes you say that?"

"I think it's obvious. People start running the other way when the topic comes up. I heard the old fire chief wasn't allowed to pursue the possibility that it wasn't an accident."

"I've never heard that. It happened before my time. Does it have anything to do with this fire?"

"I don't know. Probably not. Tory had been investigating the first fire before she died."

"Really? All that time? What did she think happened?"

"She thought Adam Presley was murdered. Where is Tory's second husband—Victor's father?"

"Greg Lambert? He's the plant manager at the pepper factory. You might have met him, if Tory wasn't anywhere around at the time. They hated each other."

"Probably not always. Maybe he got rid of her first husband so he could have her." Stella's crowbar snagged on a piece of wood below the middle stair.

"Maybe. I don't think he killed Tory. They were apart a long time. Why would he want to kill her now?"

"Slow simmer? Maybe something changed in his life. Maybe he regretted killing her first husband?"

"My money would be on Victor for the fire." John added his efforts to hers as they tried to dislodge something caught under the middle stair. The wood around it had been charred but not burned, thanks to the efforts of the fire brigade. "Although I don't think he could have killed Adam Presley."

"You mean since Victor wasn't born yet? He does seem to have the most to gain on this fire," she agreed. "He also has an alibi. Anyone else who might want Tory dead?"

"Probably a few people. She was rich and powerful. Folks like that make enemies. She was very insistent about having her own way. I can't really think of anyone who would go this far. I guess you never know."

With one joint tug, the wood split, sending Stella and John back on the filthy floor. Something else came down with the wood.

"Looks like we found the kerosene can." John rubbed his shoulder, which had hit the concrete. "The fire didn't get it."

Stella looked up into the area where the can had been. "Somebody had to be here for a while to get this into place. Maybe while Tory was out."

John carefully lifted the kerosene can with his gloved hand. It was covered in heavy soot from the fire. "Are you sure we're going to find something on this can under all the soot?"

"It's been done before. Do I need to find an independent lab that can do the tests, or does your department have some-place we can send it?"

"I can send it to the state police lab. The kind of testing you mentioned sounds expensive. I know Don will question the process."

"I'll be glad to take care of Don if you want me to give him the can for testing."

"No. I'll try to sound like I know what I'm talking about. I *am* the police–fire department liaison, after all. I'll do it. Just asking for clarification."

They carefully bagged and tagged the can. Stella took pictures of the area where they'd found it. It was already getting dark as they walked out of the basement, covered in soot again.

"So, do you have any plans for tonight?" John asked as they started toward their vehicles.

"I think a hot shower and a change of clothes are in order." She looked at her cell phone.

"What about after that?"

Stella wasn't sure what to say. Was he asking her out despite her treacherous bloodlines? "I guess a microwave dinner in front of the fireplace. How about you?"

"I was thinking maybe we could have dinner somewhere. I mean, you're still injured from your wreck. Maybe you should eat out." He grinned. "I hope that didn't sound as bad to you as it sounded to me."

"I'd like that. Maybe seven?"

"Okay. That sounds great. I'll pick you up at the firehouse. Or the cabin. Whichever would be best for you."

"Let's make it the firehouse." She thought about the last time they were close at the cabin. "I'll see you then."

Stella went back to the cabin feeling lighthearted for once, despite the investigation. She was looking forward to her dinner with John. Despite his feelings about the Carson family, she sensed they were a lot alike. She had only a few weeks left before she went home, but they could enjoy each other's company until then.

She was going to have to buy clothes if she planned on dating. Or working on the sooty house where she had to change clothes a few times a day. She didn't want to head down to the Wash and Whirl in town every other day.

The easy job she'd planned for had taken an uneasy turn. Between spending time with John outside of work—if that continued—and getting filthy, she'd at least need a few more pairs of jeans. Maybe a sweater or two. Maybe something silly and feminine. She could always have the things that wouldn't fit in her saddlebags shipped back home.

The outside light was on when she arrived at the cabin. It made her think about Eric and then remind herself that there was no such thing as ghosts. She couldn't even imagine what her friends and family would say if she suggested it. Well, except for her father and his family. Maybe.

The door opened when she started to unlock it, and the alarm system turned off. She found it hard not to believe that this particular ghost was real.

Chapter 18

"Find anything useful?" his deep voice asked as she closed the door. "I hope so. You're a mess. Don't tell me you drove home in that brand new truck like that."

"It's a fire scene—what can I tell you." She put her backpack on the kitchen counter. "We found the kerosene can, almost in one piece. I think we might be able to get a print or two off of it. Did they do that kind of thing in your day?"

"You're cheeky this evening. Are you flush with success, or is something else up?"

Stella was surprised he noticed so much. "As a matter of fact, it's a little of both. John invited me out for dinner. We found what we were looking for. My Harley is going to the repair shop tomorrow. A good day."

"All of that sounds really exciting."

She was also surprised at how much she noticed about him. It was odd what you could pick up on from listening to a person's voice, when there were no facial expressions or body language to influence what you were hearing. "I'm sorry. Am I boring you?"

"I'm not sure about dating John Trump. His father was

an abusive alcoholic and he hates your family. Not a good start for a relationship."

"Good thing you're not dating him then. I don't care about his father, and the Carsons are never going to be like family to me. Not to mention, I only have a few weeks left on my contract. I'm just looking to enjoy myself while I'm here—not get married and have kids. Were you always so nosey, Eric?"

"Just looking out for you."

She walked in the bedroom. "I'm going to take a shower and get dressed. You stay on *your* side of the door."

Stella felt a little smug at getting the upper hand with her ghost. She wasn't sure why everyone who'd tried living here before her had run away screaming. Eric wasn't that bad. He just needed boundaries.

She put her sooty clothes in a trash bag—there wasn't enough to save—and got in the shower. Nothing Eric could say about John was going to ruin her night. She deserved a little romance and was happy she'd found someone after her experience with Doug. A thing like that could scar you forever.

Once the soot was gone, she got out and dried off quickly. The hot water tank wasn't very big. That meant the last of every shower was cold. She ran a comb through her hair, thinking she might have to get it trimmed before she went home. The ends of the red strands were starting to look straggly. She didn't want to go back looking like she'd been living in the wilderness for three months.

Sweet Pepper was a nice place. Most of the people were friendly and helpful. She could see where it could be a good place to live. Not for her, but for others.

She rummaged through her drawers looking for some clean underwear. She might have to buy some of that too.

"What do you mean you only have a few weeks on your contract?" Eric asked.

Stella grabbed a fire brigade T-shirt and held it in front of her. "I thought I told you to stay on your side of the door."

"Both sides are actually mine," he said. "Why are you leaving?"

"Because this was only a temporary arrangement to get the fire brigade going. I have a life—friends, family, job—at home in Chicago. Don't worry. The fire brigade will be fine when I'm gone. I'll leave someone I've trained in charge."

"That's not the point," he argued. "You should stay. Even if you leave someone else in charge, it won't last."

She recalled that Flo had said Eric's fire brigade had fallen apart after he died. Of course he was worried that history would repeat itself. "The town is motivated to stay in the business now. The county won't help them anymore. It will be fine. Now, will you please go away so I can get dressed?"

"Since you can't see me, how will you know if I'm gone or not?"

"You're a southern gentleman, Eric. I'm sure I can rely on your honor."

"You may be too trusting, Stella. Did someone tell you I was a gentleman in life?"

"Eric, get out of the bedroom right now or I'm moving down to Flo's. Get it?"

There was no reply. She wasn't sure he was gone, but she had to get dressed, and the bathroom was too small. She found all her clothes and arranged them on the bed before she started dressing. She also turned her back to the bedroom, with a wall directly in front of her.

She thought about Eric being lonely once she was gone. Forty years was a long time to go without talking to anyone. On the other hand, she couldn't live her life for a dead man either. Maybe someone else would move in who could talk to him.

Stella combed her hair again and put on a little makeup so she'd look dressed up in her jeans and fire brigade T-shirt. There wasn't much she could do about the bandage on her forehead.

She checked in on her computer. No one had been in the

house while she was gone. "Say something, Eric. Now's your chance to prove you're real."

"What are you talking about?"

"My laptop is checking for other people in the house." Nothing was registering. Of course, if it was a two-way radio—

But it was too late. She already believed that the cabin was haunted. She grabbed her jacket from the sofa in the living room. She believed Eric Gamlyn's ghost was her roommate.

"Did I pass the test?" he wanted to know. "Am I real?"

"It looks like it. Don't wait up."

"Take a towel with you."

"Excuse me?" She frowned as she looked around the room.

"Dirty truck seat. I'd hate for you not to look your best for your date."

"You know, it would be easier if I could see you. This way, it's hard to know where to throw things so they'll hit you."

He laughed. "Have a good evening. Reconsider leaving Sweet Pepper."

"You sound like my grandfather. He didn't put you up to this, did he?"

"*You* aren't invisible, you know." A pillow floated up off the sofa. "You're an easy target."

She was amazed, watching it fly slowly through the air toward her. "Good night, Eric." She smiled at his banter as the threatening pillow fell back down on the sofa. She took a kitchen towel with her.

The door opened for her to go out and then closed behind her. The porch light came on, but she didn't hear the alarm set. She supposed it didn't really matter anyway. A ghost was probably better than an alarm.

He was right, of course. The towel was filthy after she'd wiped the shiny new seat in the Cherokee. She could at least take care of the vehicle for the next chief—probably Petey or Ricky since John didn't seem to want the position. He would've been her first choice. He seemed happy working for the police department. She didn't want to mess that up for him.

Stella drove down Firehouse Road and parked next to the firehouse. There was light coming from the tiny room where they kept the computers and other communication equipment and from the kitchen. As she got out of the pickup, she could hear music coming from inside—the Beatles' *White Album*. Apparently, Tagger and Kent were fans.

A dark pickup was parked on the other side of the firehouse. A light in the vehicle bay, under the doors, caught her eye. It wasn't the big, overhead lights she might have expected if Tagger were in there. This looked more like a flashlight beam. She passed the smaller door they all went in and out of each day. It was open.

A strong sense of something not being right made her quietly slip in to see what was going on.

Stella could hear Tagger singing Beatles songs in the kitchen as he used the microwave. Smelled like he was making popcorn.

There was something else happening. A flashlight beam was moving around the fire engine and the pumper in the dark bay area

Vandals? Thieves? Could be.

It might be kids exploring. It seemed unlikely that it was anything more serious than that. Standing beside the closed door to the kitchen and communications room, the dark bay beside her, she grabbed an ax from its place near the door and advanced on the drifting light.

Her heartbeat accelerated as she moved through the darkness between the equipment. Once she got far enough away from the music in the communications room—and Tagger's singing—she could hear faint scratching sounds. That made her think it was even more likely that vandals—teenagers, maybe—were marking up her equipment.

She held the ax close to her, hoping she wouldn't round a corner and come face-to-face with someone holding a gun.

It probably would have been smart to call the police and let them handle the situation. She rested her hand on the driver's side of the pumper, following its lines as she walked carefully, still listening to the scratching sounds.

As she got to the front of the pumper, someone dropped something—a heavy tool perhaps—on the floor. The sound ricocheted around the bay. She dropped down and waited to see what happened next. The flashlight beam hadn't found her. It would be as hard for her attacker to see her as it was for her to see him.

Stella heard footsteps coming closer, and clutched the ax, careful not to give away her position by making any noise. Her plan was to catch whoever it was off guard, maybe trip the intruder with the ax. She wasn't sure she had it in her to actually use the weapon on a person.

She waited, quietly and patiently, trying not to breathe too hard and hoping no one could hear her heart pounding.

The footsteps were right in front of her. Faint light from the windows in back showed a shadowy figure. As he went by, she put out the ax and was gratified to hear a muffled curse as the figure tripped and fell. That was no ghost!

She wasn't sure what she was going to do next. This was where it would have been useful to have the police on their way.

At that moment, all the inside lights came on, along with the flashing lights and sirens on the equipment. Both vehicles started up, engines revving loudly in the closed bay. The sound and lights kept her at the front of the pumper. She heard the other person shout and run for the door.

"Not so fast!" She dropped the ax and ran, trying to catch the fleeing vandal.

She tackled him as they reached the parking lot together. He was wearing a hoodie and a mask. All she could tell about him was that he didn't seem in particularly good shape. When she punched him in the stomach, he grunted and kicked at her.

His foot connected with her sore ribs in a lucky shot. She

dropped to her knees, not able to move, trying to catch her breath.

He ran to the pickup at the side of the building and started the engine. Without turning on the headlights, he put the pickup in gear and raced back toward her. The truck's dark form loomed like a wall in front of her, blocking everything out.

"Get up, Stella!"

Stella could have sworn she heard Eric's voice. She clutched her arm to her chest and rolled away from the back of the pickup. The vehicle stopped abruptly, but the driver seemed to have lost his thirst for violence. The pickup screeched out of the parking lot, leaving the stench of burned rubber behind.

With the threat gone, Stella crawled to the side of the building. The engines, lights, and sirens were still flashing and wailing. She groaned. "Eric? Is that you?"

"I don't know anyone else who could do all of that at one time, do you?"

She saw a shadowy image near her, just as she had that night in the hot tub. "But you can't be here. I really have lost it."

"This is the only other place I can be," he said. "I built this place with my own two hands. I can show you where every nail is. It's as much a part of me as the cabin. Do you need an ambulance?"

"I don't think so. But thanks for the diversion."

The lights and sirens suddenly died away, followed by the big engines shutting down. "You took a big chance going in there by yourself, Stella. I can't believe you've worked with a fire department for so long without knowing any better. How many people go into the burning house?"

"Two." She coughed and tried to breathe normally. The sounds of Beatles' music still whispered through the night air. "You're right. It was careless. I didn't think about it until it was too late."

"Back to training for you, Chief Griffin."

"I guess. Of course, *you* can't tell anyone what happened. I don't know if Tagger or Kent even know anything went on. They're both wearing headphones. I think I'm safe on this one."

"Is that old Tagger in there after all these years?" Eric asked. "I thought he'd be dead by now."

"Well, you'd know, right? Don't you guys all know each other? Kind of like firemen's heaven?"

She was left with no reply. She pushed herself up using the side of the building for leverage and went to check on the equipment.

Chapter 19

~~~~~~~~

"Chief?" Tagger said, coming out of the kitchen and blinking rapidly, like an owl wakened in the daylight. "I didn't know you were here. I think you might be a workaholic. I'm worried about you."

She explained briefly about what had just happened outside. "You might need to turn that music down. Someone could sneak up on you."

He laughed. "Now, who'd wanna do that? I know everyone for fifty miles around, and they all know me. No one would want to do old Tagger any harm."

"Maybe not, but let's turn it down a little anyway, okay?" He was supposed to be there to help with communications—not act as a guard dog, still he and Kent might have been having *too* good a time with the Beatles.

Kent came out with the Dalmatian puppy in his arms. "Thought I heard someone else out here. What's up, Chief?"

She told him what was going on. They turned on the lights and took a look around.

Sure enough, the pumper and the engine had been vandalized. Large scratches had been gouged through "Sweet

Pepper Fire Brigade," and the intruder had scrawled "GO HOME STELLA" all over everything.

"What a mess," she said, irritated.

"Don't worry, Chief," Kent said. "I know someone who can take care of it. Old Jack Carriker will make it good as new. He's a whiz. Kind of does handyman work all over the area. I can call him, if you like."

"Sure. That would be great. Thanks, Kent."

"Don't know why anyone would want you to go home, Chief," Tagger said. "I hope you never leave."

"Thanks, Tagger," she said. "I guess we should call the police and report this for the insurance company."

"No need." Tagger held the door open. "The police have come to us!"

John was pulling up in his pickup. He rolled down his window and called, "Doing a late night inspection, Chief?"

Stella walked out to the car. "We had a break-in."

"Somebody wants to get rid of the chief," Tagger said with tears in his old blue eyes. "They marked up the equipment."

Stella started to explain what had happened, but before she could get out the first word, the siren at the top of the firehouse started screaming its warning. Stella's and John's pagers went off, as did Kent's.

Tagger rushed inside and took a look at the computerized warning system. "Fire at Fifth and Main. It's the old Dempsey house."

"So much for dinner," John moaned. "You owe me."

Stella frowned as the pain in her ribs grew more intense. "I think you've got that backward. You invited me, which means you were paying."

"You know you could stay in the truck and monitor the fire," he suggested when he saw her wince. "You've been through a lot in the last twenty-four hours."

"I can handle it," she insisted. "Suit up."

Within five minutes, six volunteers were at the firehouse. Stella noticed that Marty pulled up with everyone else.

"I know I have no training, but I was thinking there might be something I could do."

She was impressed, despite John's sour frown. "Thanks. Hop on. You can see the action anyway and get an idea of what goes on during a run. Stay behind until you can get some practice in, okay?"

Ricky pulled the engine in the lead on the way to Sweet Pepper. Kent was driving the pumper. They might not need the water, but the pumper's ladder or some of the vehicle's other equipment might come in handy.

"You and John sure got there early." Ricky smiled at her. "Were you close by, maybe together?"

"Not that it's any of your business—we were going out for dinner."

"See? I knew it. You and John are perfect for each other. Maybe the two of you could get married and you wouldn't want to go back to Chicago."

"In the next few weeks? I'd been dating my boyfriend back home for two years and we weren't even engaged."

"Tennessee boys work faster."

"I thought you wanted to be chief when I was gone."

"I can always wait until you retire. You're a lot older than me, you know."

"Yeah. Don't hold your breath. Do you think Petey would wait? If she knew we were talking about it, she'd probably run us both down and take over."

He shook his head as he carefully maneuvered the large truck around the corner of Fifth Street, which was barely wide enough to allow the turn. "I know. That woman is driven. I like that. I'm thinking about asking her out."

Stella ignored most of his conversation, focusing instead on where they were going and searching for any signs of smoke. The air was clear—not even a whiff of smoke. She looked at the GPS. They were very close to the address. Maybe they'd caught the fire early.

"It's right up here," she said. "Slow down. I hope it's easy to get into."

"I know where it is. Mr. Dempsey used to be the football coach at the high school. I think he and his wife moved to Florida. There's someone new living there now."

The pumper arrived right behind them. Both trucks fit in the long driveway. A young man and woman, both brown haired and well dressed, were standing out in front of the older brick house.

"Where's the fire?" Stella asked as she got off the truck with her volunteers behind her.

"We feel really stupid about this," the man said. "We didn't check the chimney flue before we tried to start a fire. Now the house is full of smoke.

"We got out right away. We couldn't find Sylvia. We couldn't look around much. The smoke was too thick."

Stella sent Petey and John to put on their breathers and go inside to make sure that there was only smoke and no fire. "Sylvia?" she asked the couple.

"Our dog." The woman started crying. "We got her from a rescue shelter last week. We gave her puppy away, which I told David was probably wrong. I feel so bad that I've abused them this way. They've been through so much."

"We didn't know, Kimmie," her husband consoled her. "It's my fault. I wanted to try the fireplace."

"You were just excited, David," she said. "I hope Sylvia is okay."

Petey and John called out from the doorway of the house. "No sign of fire, Chief," Petey said. "It looks like the logs they tried to use were green. They died out. There's a lot of smoke."

"Check around for a dog," Stella called back. "She's somewhere in the house."

"Okay, Chief," John said. "I'm going to open the flue. We'll open all the windows. That should get the smoke out."

Stella sent the pumper back to the firehouse. It didn't look like they'd need anything from it, including the extra manpower. She stayed behind, waiting to hear about the dog as she and the young couple watched John and Petey go from room to room opening windows.

"We found the dog, Chief," Petey yelled from the downstairs window a few minutes later. "I'm bringing her out now."

David and Kimmie ran to the front door where Petey met them with Sylvia on a leash. At that moment, there were some yelps from the back of the engine. Everyone laughed when the little Dalmatian puppy they'd adopted ran into the yard.

"Who brought the puppy?" Stella asked. No one admitted to it.

The puppy yelped and cried excitedly, jumping all over the couple's older dog. Stella started to apologize to the couple.

Kimmie grabbed the puppy and started kissing him. "It's Sylvia's puppy! Where did he come from?"

David explained breathlessly that they'd sold the puppy to Tory Lambert. He was supposed to be a gift to the fire brigade. "When we heard about the fire and Tory's death, we assumed the worst. No one had seen the puppy. We thought he was dead."

It looked like Tagger had been right about Tory not keeping a pet. "That explains the big red bow he had around his neck when we found him," Stella said with a smile. "I guess he really belongs with us. The station house where my grandfather worked in Chicago always kept a Dalmatian around for good luck. You don't see much of that anymore."

"Does Sylvia need oxygen or mouth-to-mouth?" Kimmie asked as she hugged the dogs.

"She seems fine," Stella answered. "Where did you find her, Petey?"

"She was in the basement." Petey grinned. "I guess she knew it was the best place for her. She is a fire dog, after all."

"We are so grateful to all of you," Kimmie gushed. "You have to keep little Hero. He could be your good luck at the fire station. Tory wanted you to have him."

"Hero?" Stella asked. The puppy ran to her when she said

the name. She picked him up and scratched his neck. "Hero it is."

"And Hero will be providing a community service by helping the fire department." Petey picked up the idea with an appealing smile at Stella.

"I guess we'll have to get him trained to work with us," Stella said.

Ricky scratched the puppy's head. "Somebody is always at the firehouse. We could feed him and take care of him. He could be a guard dog too. He could come with us to fires and stuff."

"I'm going to miss you, Hero." Kimmie hugged the puppy again. "But I know this is the right thing to do now. You were destined to be a true hero."

The firefighters waited to make sure the house was cleared of smoke. There was going to be some minor damage—mostly odor—that might have to be professionally removed.

Marty had been disappointed that the call had been for nothing. "These people could have taken care of this themselves. It was a wasted trip."

"They still needed our help," Stella told him. "Besides, it's better that all calls aren't life-threatening. That would get old really quick."

Kimmie and David thanked Stella again for her help.

"You should spend the night somewhere else and call your insurance company," Stella advised as everyone packed up to go. Petey already had Hero, his food, bowl, and play toys in the back. She admitted that she'd brought the puppy with them.

"Thank you so much for rescuing us, Chief." David shook Stella's hand. "We'll take your advice and come to visit Hero tomorrow. Good night, everyone."

"Thought you didn't think we should keep the puppy, Chief?" Ricky said as they got into the truck.

"Shut up and drive," Stella retorted.

Cleanup of the trucks and equipment seemed to take forever. Stella was ready to go. Her ribs and head hurt. She noticed that Marty went home as soon as they got back. Maybe John had been right about him. Time would tell.

She knew her volunteers could handle getting the work done without her. She stayed because she remembered how nice it was to see Chief Henry standing around the station, working with them and watching. It was somehow reassuring. Besides, she needed to give them an assessment of their performance even though tonight's call hadn't been a major event.

She congratulated all of them on their speed. "We were right there where we needed to be in less time than we have been. You did a great job tonight. I know it might not seem like a lifesaving event, but those people wouldn't have known what to do without you. Good teamwork, guys."

It was nice to have a simple run—nothing dramatic. Or at least she thought so until they were spraying off the pumper. Everyone noticed the graffiti that had been etched into the paint on the engine too.

"Why would anyone do such a thing?" Banyin demanded. "We wouldn't even have a fire brigade without the chief."

"Maybe whoever put Chief Griffin into the ditch on her Harley last night was trying to make a statement," Kent said. "Maybe that wasn't an accident after all."

"People do stupid things sometimes," Stella explained. "You work at the library, Banyin. You know what I'm talking about. How many books come back ripped or written in? This happened at the firehouse. It was only vandalism. We need better locks on our doors."

"What if Kent is right and someone has it in for you?" Ricky said.

"The wreck was an accident," Stella reassured him even though she had doubts about it now too. "Let's finish up here and go home."

She didn't say anything else about it as the volunteers

completed their work and began to drift away from the firehouse.

Ricky was the last one to leave. He took Tagger home while Allen settled into the communications room for the night.

Stella was putting away the last of her gear as John approached her. "I think Kent might be right," he said. "I think you might be in danger."

Chapter 20

"**Y**ou should've told me right away, when you had your first suspicions." John paced the small living room in the cabin. They'd decided to go there so that they wouldn't be overheard. He'd already called in the vandalism, but taking the engine and pumper out had destroyed the crime scene.

"When would that have been? We got the call right after you got to the firehouse. The vandalism had just happened. I didn't think about it until then."

"There's no crime scene now. Any prints or evidence is gone."

"I'm sure it's not the first time the police have had to work with a crime scene that has been messed up." She was getting a little impatient. She thought it might help to tell John about the vandal trying to run her down. If he insisted on mourning the loss of the crime scene, she didn't know how much help he would be. "Besides, what else could I do? We're the fire department. We had to answer that call."

"We didn't even need the pumper," he argued. "It could've stayed behind and been dusted for prints."

"There was no way to know that. We get a call, we don't take chances on what we'll find when we get there."

John finally took a deep breath and sat down. Stella was already sitting back against the sofa, trying to ease the ache in her chest until the pain relievers she'd taken could kick in. She'd made coffee for John when they first arrived. She was sure it was already cold after his twenty-minute rant.

"All right. What's done is done. We'll have to go on from here. I'll talk to Don. We'll have to find a safe house for you and put you into protective custody until we can figure out what's going on." He sipped his cold coffee and frowned.

"First of all, I feel fairly sure that Don isn't going to allocate funds for me to be protected. He'd probably want me to leave now instead of a few weeks from now. I'm not going home until the job is done, and I couldn't do that job in protective custody anyway. We're going to have to figure it out."

"That's plain crazy."

"Maybe. If this person doesn't like me because I'm the fire chief, you'll have to protect Petey when I'm gone."

"You've chosen *her*?" He looked at her in surprise. "I thought it would be Ricky. The two of you always seem pretty tight."

He sounded jealous. Stella kind of liked that. "I would've picked *you*, but I knew you wouldn't quit your job with the police to take the position."

John suddenly seemed to relax. "That's true. I'm flattered that you would've chosen me."

"You're the natural choice since you're mostly trained for it already. Nothing personal."

He moved from the chair by the fireplace to the sofa beside her. "Nothing personal? What about Ricky? Nothing personal there either?"

Stella's heart beat a little faster. Her cheeks felt warm. "Not with Ricky. And I wouldn't let my feelings toward you influence me if you were wrong for the job."

He came closer and ran his fingers through her hair. "What am I going to do without you, Stella Griffin?"

She closed her eyes for his kiss as he leaned nearer. The anticipation was sweet and exciting.

A heavy book from the fireplace mantel dropped to the floor and the door to the deck opened. Chilly air blew across them.

They sprang apart like guilty teenagers. Laughter followed as they looked at each other. John picked up the book and closed the door.

"I think Mother Nature must be telling me not to get frisky with an injured woman," John said.

"I don't think that was Mother Nature." Stella looked around the room, wishing she could see Eric. She'd have to wait until John left to give him a piece of her mind.

"I don't know. We have some light seismic activity from time to time. The wind blows pretty strong off the mountains sometimes too." He moved back to the chair and drank more coffee. "I guess we should be thinking about how we're going to keep you from getting hurt again anyway. We can always resume the hanky-panky later."

"The way I see it, there are only two things that might get someone angry enough to try and kill me," Stella said, not necessarily agreeing about the hanky-panky part. "Re-creating the fire brigade or the investigation into Tory's death. That's all I've done since I've been here. I suppose either of those things could be stepping on someone's toes."

John agreed and took out his battered notebook. "What did you actually see tonight at the firehouse? Could it have been anything to do with the wreck?"

She told him what had happened. "Honestly, that pickup could've been the same vehicle that ran me off the road. I don't know. I wish I'd gotten a better look both times."

He looked at what he'd written. "Either way, it sounds like a threat, Stella. Maybe you should reconsider and go home."

"Changed your mind about wanting my job?" she joked.

"I want you to be safe," he said with a straight face. "We can only do so much to protect you."

"I'll try to stay out of dark places when I'm by myself. For all we know, these are unrelated incidents. If we can't find evidence to the contrary, I don't want to blow them out of proportion."

He put his notebook away, his eyes intent on hers. "Have you considered that someone might also want to get rid of you because you are the only blood heir to the Carson money?"

"You mean after my mother, right? John, everything can't be about that. I know you don't like them but—"

"I know. You can't change who you are." He abruptly got to his feet. "I'd better go. You need some rest. Stay out of trouble."

Stella gritted her teeth as he left without even saying good-bye to her. He was an obstinate, single-minded man.

He was barely out of the house when Eric's voice made his presence known. "Good riddance."

"What was that all about?" She put the dirty coffee mug in the sink. "You had no right to interfere."

"I have an obligation to stop a train wreck before it happens. I know you can't see it, but he isn't right for you."

Stella was outraged. "You don't get to make that decision. Any more outbursts like that and I *will* go and stay with Flo."

"You mean the Mother Nature problem?" He laughed. "That was only the wind and seismic activity. Your *boyfriend* was clear on that."

"I'm going to bed. I don't want to talk about it anymore tonight. You're such a coward anyway—hiding in the shadows. You could at least show yourself. I've watched ghost reality shows. I know you can do it."

She looked around, thinking he might oblige her. There was no sign of him. He didn't say anything else. She went in the bedroom and slammed the door behind her.

Stella fell asleep faster than she'd anticipated. She slept through the night and felt much better in the morning. It was raining when she looked out of the bedroom window. There was also a police car right next to the cabin.

A little thrill went through her as she realized John cared

about her, even though he was angry and hated that she was part Carson. She put on her jacket and shoes and went outside to talk to him. She had some bagels and cream cheese. Maybe they could have breakfast together—outside the perimeter that Eric could visit.

She was disappointed when she tapped on the car window. It was Officer Richardson who smiled and blinked, half-asleep. "Good morning, Chief Griffin. Hope you slept well last night. It was quiet out here."

Well, at least John cared enough to send someone *else* to look out for her. "I'm fine. I'm sorry you had to sleep in the car. Would you like some coffee?"

He came inside the cabin and Stella made a cup for each of them. They ate bagels and stood around talking about the weather and the upcoming Pepper Festival until Officer Richardson had to leave. He thanked her for the coffee and took a brief look around the cabin.

"My dad was good friends with Eric Gamlyn. He still talks about him. Hard to believe this place looks like he built it just yesterday. I wasn't even born yet when he died. There are some tall tales about him around here."

"They say he haunts the cabin."

"I've heard that. I was wondering about it myself. No one has ever been able to stay here as long as you have, Chief Griffin. Maybe it's because you aren't from here. Or maybe old Eric likes you." He laughed. "Thanks for the coffee. Have a nice day."

"He likes you," Stella said when the officer had gone. "Or at least his father did."

Eric didn't reply. Stella took the coffee mug and put it into the dishwasher. She hated to run the machine with so little in it. "Maybe you could have a party while I'm gone today and dirty up some dishes."

Still no reply.

"Hey, I really need a pepper recipe for the contest at the festival. Nothing with chocolate because I'm judging that contest. Do you know anything I could use?"

There was no laughter, no mocking voice. It made her feel a little lonely now that she knew that he was there.

It was silly. It didn't matter to her. It might be better if he decided to be quiet.

She got dressed and left the cabin. At least there would be company at the diner.

John stood in the impressive foyer while he waited for Ben Carson to join him. This visit wasn't his favorite idea, but he thought it was the best way to protect Stella.

"Sorry to keep you waiting, Officer Trump," Ben said as he came down the wide stairs to meet him. "Won't you come into the breakfast room for some juice or coffee?"

John's fingers were tense as he held his hat before him like a shield. "No thanks, Mr. Carson. I'm here about Stella. I assume you realize that someone might be trying to hurt her."

Ben's white brows knit together. "I didn't realize that, Officer. What makes you suspect that anyone would harm my girl?"

The possessive sound of his words put John's teeth on edge. "You know about the wreck. Someone scratched a message on the pumper last night and tried to run her over. Now, I know there's no point in me trying to go through official channels to accuse anyone—where was that stepson of yours during both of those incidents? You might want to look into that."

"Are you accusing Martin of something, Officer?"

"No, sir. I'm not accusing anyone in this family of anything. We both know where that would end up. You and I finally have something in common—we both want Stella to be safe. Not everyone in this family might feel the same, if you get my drift."

Ben nodded. "I appreciate you coming to me with this information."

John put his hat on and turned to go. He'd said what he'd come to say.

"I also hope you realize that I have big plans for my granddaughter. Don't get overly attached to her."

"No, sir." John walked through the front door, which was being held open by one of the housemaids.

When the door closed behind the officer, Ben shouted for Felicity. When she reached him, he said, "Where is Martin?"

She looked bewildered but answered quickly. "He joined the fire brigade. He's training with them this morning. Shall I call him for you?"

"No, thanks. I'll handle it. Go on about your duties."

Ben walked into the breakfast room and found his wife looking through a magazine. "Did you really think I wouldn't notice you throwing your son at Stella?"

Vivian's beautiful face was devoid of emotion. "I don't know what you mean."

"Martin is in *your* will. That's as close as he's getting to my money. He can't have Stella. Whatever you have in mind isn't going to happen."

"I assume you're talking about his interest in volunteer firefighting." She smiled serenely. "That has nothing to do with Stella. Marty has matured. He wants to give back to the community."

"That's bull and we both know it. Keep him away from her. You won't like the consequences if I have to step in."

Chapter 21

Don Rogers joined Stella at the Sweet Pepper Café as she was about to drink a very large glass of vanilla Coke. "Ms. Griffin."

"Chief Rogers." She continued taking the paper off her straw. The waitress brought him a cup of coffee.

"I hear someone might be trying to get rid of you—one way or another. At least that's what John told me after he assigned you police protection twenty-four/seven. Are you sure these events aren't a coincidence?"

"Not at all. John seems to feel there's something more sinister behind what's happened. I don't know if I agree with him. Either way, you don't have to worry. I'm not going anywhere until my contract is over."

He smiled in a patronizing way. "You see, that's exactly what I came to talk to you about. Maybe it would be better for you to leave now. It would be cheaper for the town too. John said you're looking at Petey Stanze to take your place. I'm sure she's as ready as she's going to be. The rest she can learn on the fly. The town saves money. You don't have to worry about your safety. It sounds like a win-win to me."

Stella took a sip of Coke and smiled back at him in an

equally meaningless way. "First of all, you can tell your officers to stop following me around anytime you want to. I'm not worried about my safety. I'm more worried about the fire brigade having the training they'll need to stay together after I'm gone. That means something to me. I'm not leaving Sweet Pepper until then."

Don sipped his coffee and looked around the crowded diner. "I appreciate your honesty, Ms. Griffin. And I'll take your advice. There won't be any officers following you around again. Enjoy your breakfast."

Stella leaned over her Coke and didn't respond. It was cowardly, she knew. She was tired of arguing with him. Thank goodness he was gone. He'd almost ruined the best vanilla Coke she'd ever had. She had a feeling if she stayed on, she and Don would always rub each other the wrong way.

As soon as Don was gone, Elvita Quick and Theodora Mangrum took his seat in the booth, across from her. They wanted to talk to her again about her part in judging the chocolate division of the pepper recipe contest.

"It's very important from here on in not to sample anyone's recipes or give any encouragement to anyone who might be entering your portion of the contest," Elvita said.

"That's right," Theodora agreed. "We're assuming people have asked you to taste this and that. As a judge, it is unethical for you to say yay or nay about their food—until the contest."

Stella agreed not to taste any food offered by potential contestants. She smiled at the two sisters, each wearing large birds on their red hats. "I swear I won't give anyone my opinion until after the festival."

Both sisters were pleased with her promise.

"Now, let's talk about the proper attire for a contest judge. We're assuming you have more than jeans to wear? If not, here is a list of some of Sweet Pepper's most excellent dressmakers," Theodora said.

"And hatmakers too." Elvita smiled and patted her hat.

"They made these hats for us. I'm sure they could whip something up for you too."

"And don't forget about your own recipe," Theodora reminded her. "We'll need to have it soon. What category were you thinking about?"

Stella muttered something she hoped was unintelligible since she had no idea what kind of pepper recipe she could submit, much less cook. She might have to look up a recipe on the Internet if Eric didn't come through for her.

She checked herself. Was she actually depending on a ghostly voice in an old cabin to tell her what to do? Eric wasn't even a whole ghost—only a voice.

Both ladies smiled. Stella thanked them and put their lists in her wallet. They parted company on good terms.

Dozens of people stopped to talk about the fire brigade, her wreck, and the message on the pumper. Word had spread quickly. She finally returned to the Cherokee and drove back to the firehouse.

Marty had arrived to start his training. Even though it was Monday morning, there were also a few other new volunteers. Kimmie and David Spratt had joined, along with their Dalmatian, Sylvia. The couple had tied red neckerchiefs on Sylvia and her puppy, Hero.

A friend of Allen's from the pepper factory, Royce Pope, also wanted to volunteer. He had asked his friend JC Burris to try out too.

Bert Wando was ready to resume training, having gotten a note from his doctor saying that it was okay. Banyin, the librarian, was also there.

Local employers and the high school knew how important this training was and gave special time for practice. The team couldn't keep up if they could only practice on times they were off or on weekends.

They were all standing around talking and drinking coffee. Stella was proud to see the ranks swell with new members. Being in charge was different than being a member of the team. She'd created something here—something that had meaning and would last to serve the people of Sweet Pepper.

She didn't have time to stand there and appreciate it. The new members of the fire brigade needed to start training with the established members.

Stella began by having them climb the stairs to the top of the firehouse, carrying a coiled sixty-pound hose. It was like tag, each volunteer handing off the hose to the next person in line.

There were still enough bunker coats, boots, and other gear to outfit the new people. When the next chief came in, they would have to find a way to raise money for more gear. The old firehouse itself would also need more repairs. There were several holes in the wood floor outside the garage bays.

Tagger sat in a lawn chair beside Stella, watching the trainees' sometimes comical attempts to get up and down the stairs holding the hose. "I remember when Chief Gamlyn used to make us hang from that pole up yonder in the ceiling. He knew how to get everyone ready, that's for sure."

"So what happened to him?" Stella asked as she kept her eyes on the new recruits. Marty was having a hard time going up the stairs in his gear even without holding the hose, but he kept trying. Ahead of him, JC and Royce were running up the stairs with the hose, laughing and encouraging each other, their dark faces gleaming with sweat. They weren't big, but they were fast and strong.

"Don't know for sure. We were fighting a big fire over at one of the grain silos. That baby was hot, let me tell you. One of the men got trapped inside, and the roof was about to collapse. Chief Gamlyn rushed in after him. The man came out. The silo exploded. We never saw the chief again."

"No one went in after the chief?"

"No, ma'am. That roof went down right after Ricky Hutchins Sr. escaped. There was no time to save the chief. We had a good memorial send-off for him. The town put up a nice statue for him in the cemetery. There wasn't another one like him, that's for sure. After that, the county took over and all of us retired from the firefighting business."

"I've heard a lot of stories about Eric Gamlyn," she said. "How can you tell which ones are true?"

Tagger's face became a mass of wrinkles as he grinned widely. "Why, ma'am, they're all true. He was the man all the rest of us wanted to be."

Stella smiled at him and watched him rub his hand across his short hair. "You're a hero too, Tagger. Everyone says so. I'll bet a lot of people look up to you too."

"Not so much. When we came back from Vietnam, people thought we were wrong for fighting and dying over there. Not so much here in Sweet Pepper as other places. Those were some bad times for me. My daddy owned a gristmill that I was gonna take over someday. He died while I was gone and the bank foreclosed. They built Beau's out there on the property. My girl had married someone else. There wasn't much to come home for. I don't think I would've stayed except for Chief Gamlyn and the fire brigade. When both of those were gone too, I didn't know what to do with myself."

"I'm sorry, Tagger. It sounds like it was a hard time for you."

"It's over now. You're here to get the fire brigade back up and running." He leaned a little closer to her. "You know, Chief Gamlyn's ghost haunts this place. I see him sometimes at night when I'm here. He'd want you to stay on. The two of you would've hit it off."

His blue eyes were so sincere, she wondered if he really had seen the old chief. Maybe Eric only showed himself to a select few.

Marty picked that moment to fall down the stairs, creating a domino effect as he cannonballed into Petey and Kent waiting at the bottom.

John came in dressed in his police uniform. Stella had wondered where he was—he never missed practice. Everyone was laughing and trying to coil up the hose again. John ignored all of it and walked straight over to where Stella and Tagger were sitting.

"Could I have a word with you, Chief?" John nodded at Tagger. He walked a few yards away and stopped, waiting for her.

"Sounds important," Tagger said. "You go on. I'll keep these new people straight."

Stella joined John beside the engine. "We got the prints back from the kerosene can we found at Tory's place. It was Victor who started the fire. He paid off that insurance man to cover for him. We arrested him too."

No one would be surprised by that. "You arrested Victor for the arson and Tory's death?"

"We've got Victor for killing Tory," John explained. "His fingerprints were all over Tory's box of insulin. He said he bought it for her at the pharmacy. Don doesn't believe him."

"I suppose that would be easy enough to check," Stella said.

"I think we've got him dead to rights. He admitted setting the fire, even though he claims he didn't mean to kill Tory. Crazy, huh? Of course he wanted to kill her. He says he only wanted to scare her away. He knew she was terrified of fire."

"I guess that's it then."

"I thought you'd be a lot happier about it. Victor was always trying to suck the life out of his mother. He finally got up the courage. We caught him. That's how justice is supposed to work."

She agreed, finally. "You're right. It's a little anticlimactic, I guess. It's good news, John. Thanks for letting me know."

He glanced around. "I'm sorry about last night. I don't know what gets into me sometimes."

"Don't worry about it. I'm sorry you had to miss practice, but you've done a great job finding Tory's killer."

"With your help." He smiled and took her hand in his.

The sirens on the engine went off, startling everyone and causing them to rush over to John and Stella to see what was going on. John let go of Stella's hand and stepped back.

The sirens immediately stopped.

"That was weird," Banyin said. "What were you two doing over here?"

Tagger laughed. "Whatever it was, I don't think the old chief wanted it going on around his firehouse. You two better take it elsewhere."

There was laughter and good-natured joking—everyone had seen John let go of Stella's hand. John left soon after. Drills continued with each of the volunteers taking a turn holding one of the smaller hoses.

The experienced volunteers had the hang of holding the high-pressure hose. A few of the new volunteers confidently picked up the hose but lost it as soon as the water was turned on.

"What am I doing wrong?" Kimmie asked as Sylvia and Hero jumped around barking at her. "It looks like I'm doing what everyone else is doing, but the hose keeps getting away from me."

Stella was about to answer when Petey stepped in. "You have to hunker down. It's like you're wrestling an alligator. At least that's the way I think about it. Grab it with both hands. Kind of squat down, with your feet apart."

She talked Kimmie and David through mastering the hose, much to Stella's delight. Truly, Petey was the right one for the job as chief. Her performance at every turn said so.

No amount of Petey's coaching seemed to help Marty. Again and again, he kept grabbing the hose only to lose it when the water was turned on. Even Royce and JC tried to help him since they got it right away. It was no use.

Finally, when everyone was exhausted, Stella called a halt to the session. "We treat this like we would a fire. Everyone cleans up their gear and the equipment before they leave. Next time we'll be working with getting your gear on quickly and learning to use the mask and breathing apparatus. You all did a great job today. Thanks to the new volunteers for joining and to you old-timers for sticking with it."

"When do we learn to drive the big truck?" Marty asked.

"You don't." Ricky bumped him as he walked by. "I drive the engine. Kent drives the pumper. That's the way it is."

As the other volunteers started back into the firehouse, Stella stooped down to pick up some debris lying in the parking lot. It was a piece of red taillight, probably from the pickup that had tried to run her over last night. Her ribs, which had been silent most of the day, started hurting in response.

Stella heard Hero and Sylvia start barking. She looked up as Kimmie called them back from the road. She was surprised to see her grandfather pull up in a big black Cadillac. A man in a black uniform came around and opened the back passenger-side door for him.

"Stella. It's good to see you. How's that head doing? What's this I hear about someone trying to scare you away from Sweet Pepper?"

No one has any personal secrets here. She pocketed the piece of taillight. "You don't have to worry. I'm not going anywhere until the job is done."

"That's what I like to hear! I'd love to have dinner with you tonight, if you're not busy. Can you come to the house, or would you rather go out?"

She couldn't think of a reason not to eat with him. "Okay. What time?"

"Seven. I could send a driver for you. I'll have the cook whip up something special. What's your favorite food?"

"My favorite is either macaroni and cheese or popcorn, take your pick. Seven sounds fine. At your place? I'll drive."

"Wonderful. Do we know each other well enough now that I could give you another hug?"

"Sure." Stella stood still while he hugged her with enthusiasm. She lightly put her arms around him, feeling awkward.

"Thank you. That meant a lot to me." He released her. "I'll see you later."

She watched him leave as the rollback arrived to take her

Harley to Ricky's friend for repair. The driver shook hands with her. Everyone helped put the battered bike on the truck. Stella hoped it would be ready before her contract was up. She didn't plan to leave it behind.

"Ben really likes you," Marty said after the bike was on the truck. "He talks about you all the time. I've never seen him hug anyone in the whole time I've known him, not even my mother."

"If it makes you feel better, they say I look like my grandmother did at my age. Maybe he's just reliving the past."

"I don't think that's it. I've heard him say he has a future in mind for you. Better watch it—you'll be a Carson yet."

Chapter 22

~~~~~~~~

Stella wasn't worried about being a Carson. She went out and bought a new dress for dinner that night, along with a pair of matching shoes, new boots, and three pairs of jeans. Definitely too much for her saddlebags on the way home, but that's why God had created FedEx.

Eric remained silent while she was at the cabin dressing for dinner. She was glad John didn't show up either. She didn't want to explain where she was going.

She pulled her dark red hair back into a ponytail and pinned it up on her head. She was trying to look a little classier than she normally did with it straight down on her shoulders. She ended up pulling out the ponytail in the truck as she was driving away from the cabin. Maybe she just wasn't a classy kind of person.

The porch light went on as she left. Eric must still be there—just not talking. She wondered what was going on with him.

Stella questioned her motives about buying the new dress and shoes. Surely she wasn't trying to impress her millionaire grandfather. She decided it was more that she wouldn't have worn jeans and a T-shirt to her father's family's house for dinner back home. She wanted to accord Ben Carson at least that much respect.

The gatekeeper smiled from his tiny stone house, opening the gate for her before she had to stop. It was dark, and the property was a fairyland of small lights that showed off the house and grounds.

"Welcome back, Stella." Her grandfather met her at the front door. "I'm so glad you took me up on my invitation. We have so much to talk about."

He led her to a cozy room where a table was set for two near a fireplace. The walls were paneled with dark wood, and the furniture was masculine. There was a large globe on a stand near shelves of books and a rack of antlers above the door.

"Can I get you something to drink?" He pulled out a hidden panel of bottles and glasses. "I have red and white wine, whiskey, rum, and vodka. If something sounds better, I can send someone out for it."

"Red wine is fine, thanks." Stella looked around at all of the different pieces of art he had collected through the years. There was a large portrait of a woman about her age above the fireplace. It grabbed her attention. It was like looking in a mirror. "I guess I do look a lot like Abigail."

He handed her a glass of wine. "She was twenty-five when that was painted. Her hair was dark but otherwise, the two of you could be twins. I would have known you anywhere."

"My mother looks like her too," she remarked. "I guess I got the Irish red hair from my dad."

He smoothed a hand down the side of her hair. "Yes. I love the color. I can imagine Abigail with hair your color." He looked back at the portrait. "She was half of my soul. When she died, most of me died with her."

"How did she die?" Stella sipped her wine.

"I know you've spoken to Barbara by now." He smiled. "What you mean is—did I kill her?"

"Did you?"

"I think, in a way, that I did. That's what your mother picked up on, why she left. I worked too hard, was gone too much. Abigail was alone too often. That was why we argued before I went to the plant on the night she died. That was why we always argued. She wanted to take your mother to Hawaii for a vacation, and she wanted me to go along. It doesn't seem like a lot to ask. I was too busy keeping the factory going and dreaming of wealth to see how important it was to her. The guilt has never left me."

"You kept tabs on my mother after she left, and me, after I was born."

He shrugged. "Wouldn't you? I didn't want your mother to marry some lazy drifter. I was happy with what I learned about your father. I was proud to follow your life, Stella. You're a very accomplished young woman."

A maid and a man Stella assumed was the cook brought in soup and fresh-baked bread.

"I think it's time to eat," Ben said. "I hope you don't mind eating in here. I've never liked the dining room unless there were a lot of people."

"No. This is fine." Stella took a seat as he held the chair for her. "I'm surprised that Marty and Vivian aren't here."

"I thought it would be nice if it was just the two of us. In fact, if you'll come and live with me, be my hostess for parties and whatnot, I'll send Vivian and Marty packing tomorrow."

She was stunned by his careless disregard for his family and quickly tasted the thick pea soup to cover her surprise. She had to assume he was serious. "You know I'm not going to do that. I like being a firefighter. I'm going home when I'm done here."

"I appreciate that. You deserve so much more. I could give it to you—show you the world. What woman your age wouldn't want that?"

"I guess that's me." She broke off a piece of crusty bread, still warm from the oven. "I'm really happy with who I am and what I do. I can't imagine living the life you're talking about."

"That's all right. I want you to know the offer is always there. I told your mother much the same thing and offered to bring her and your father down here to join you."

"I assume you got the same response?"

"For now. I'm relieved to be in communication with Barbara again. She promised that she'd come down for a visit. It's a start." He put his spoon down and rang a small silver bell. "The soup is a little peppery for me. I know that sounds odd since peppers are my life. Having eaten them since I was small, I have a very sensitive palate for them."

The cook rushed in with the next course—salad and cheese. Stella liked the soup and opted to pass on the salad.

"What would it take, hypothetically, to get you to stay in Sweet Pepper? Your own house? Better funding for the fire brigade? Tell me, Stella. We can work out whatever it takes."

At that moment, her pager went off. She looked at it, then apologized as she got up to leave. "I'm sorry. I have to answer this call. Thanks for dinner."

"You'll think about my question, yes? Whatever it takes. Let me know."

"I will," she agreed. "Please don't hold out any hopes that it will happen."

Stella left the estate and headed back down the mountain to the firehouse. She didn't know what to think about her grandfather's comments regarding Abigail's death. She wasn't really sure if her grandmother's death had anything to do with her. It was a long time ago. Her mother had admitted that she'd misunderstood what had happened. The police had cleared the case.

It was drizzling lightly, making the roads slick and glossy. When she reached the firehouse, half of the volunteers were already there, suiting up and pulling out the gear. Banyin had been manning the communications room and told Stella the call had come from the pepper-packing plant. "Not sure yet what the emergency is," she said. "Can I suit up and come too?"

"Much as I'd like to have you there, somebody has to be here to monitor calls. The rookies don't know how to do that yet. I haven't seen Tagger either. If he makes it in, he can take your place."

Banyin frowned. "Okay. I'll look for Tagger. Thanks, Chief."

All of the new volunteers were suited up and ready to go by the time Stella walked over to the engine. Marty was there, looking as smooth and cool in his gear as he did in designer jeans.

Everyone else looked white faced and terrified. There wasn't time to reassure them before they left. She assigned Kimmie and David to ride on the pumper and sent Bert, Marty, and Royce to the engine.

"Let's go," she called out.

"Have you been to the pepper plant yet?" Ricky asked as he turned out of the parking lot. "A lot could go wrong up there. I hope it's not too rough on the newbies. You want me to keep an eye out for them?"

"Everybody needs to keep an eye out for them and each other. You're not much more than a newbie yourself. Watch your back and be careful."

"Aww, Chief. That doesn't sound too good for me taking your place. You've already decided to give the job to Petey, haven't you?"

"I'm not making any decision on that until a few days before I leave. You're still in the running. I have to tell you, Petey is out in front right now."

They drove through town, past the old lady houses on Main Street, then turned onto Pepper Street. The large factory complex was spread out before them, with hundreds of lights illuminating the parking lots and the dozen or so metal buildings. Ricky drove directly to a two-story brick building where, despite the late hour, every light was on.

"This is the main office, which is the address we were given," Ricky explained. "This place has been around since the 1800s when they first decided to start canning peppers."

"Okay. Let's park and get inside."

The factory manager was waiting outside the door in the drizzle with several others. Greg Lambert introduced himself, shaking hands with Stella and then with John, who'd come off the pumper to join them.

Stella gave Greg a subtle once-over. This was Tory's second husband, Vic's father. He was older, with a thick head of gray hair, but still retained some youthful good looks. He appeared to be a determined man with thin lips and a hard chin.

"What's the problem, Mr. Lambert?" Stella asked.

"A couple of times a year, we have an issue with one of the air ducts in the main production building. There's a buildup of dust that catches fire from sparks the canning machine throws out. We get that put out and clean the ductwork, and we're good for a while again."

Stella didn't want to argue with the man—at least not until the possibility of fire was over—but that had to be the worst system she'd ever heard of. She couldn't believe someone hadn't devised something safer given all the years this place had been in business.

"The main building is over there." John pointed toward a large metal building with a giant yellow "1" painted on it.

"Let's get down there," Stella said. "Is there a hydrant?"

"No," Greg said. "In the past, the county fire department has drawn the water from our tank."

"Anybody want to hazard a guess as to what size hose that is?" Ricky asked, obviously trying to show up Petey.

"John, have Kent check it out. Thanks for your help, Mr. Lambert. We'll talk later." Stella signaled everyone to head down to the main building.

About a dozen workers were standing outside the building. JC and Royce both worked at the factory. They explained that the night shift was small, maybe twenty people. Building 1 was used for the packing operation. Most of the others were used for packing, storage, and shipping

There was some smoke coming from inside. It was white and wispy, not much going on yet. Stella held her radio, waiting for a report about the water connection as she walked into the plant with the shift supervisor.

"They always tell us to get out," he said as they walked through the front door. "But really, it's not that bad. It happens all the time when sparks from the pepper-packing machines hit the dust buildup. Not exactly a fire—just kind of smoldering."

Stella went up the ladder at the back of the plant to inspect the duct that was smoking. It was part of the exhaust system. There wasn't a fire, at least not yet. She could see the potential for one in the foot-deep dust that had accumulated in the old ductwork.

When she'd come back down, she asked, "How often is this thing cleaned out?"

The supervisor shrugged. "I don't know. That's not really my call."

"I think they clean it out when this happens," JC said. "It always struck me as something bad waiting to happen. Lambert and, pardon my saying so, your grandfather, always act like it's nothing. Sorry, Chief."

"Don't be sorry. Part of your job as a volunteer firefighter is to notice potential hazards. I'd say this qualifies."

JC exchanged looks with Royce and the supervisor, tension on his dark face. Maybe she wanted to be the one who made a big deal about this, but not them.

John finally called in. "We don't have anything that will fit this connection, Chief. We're bringing the pumper over. Be there in a minute."

It wasn't bad enough that the factory allowed these fire hazards to continue, Stella thought, they weren't even set up to handle a serious fire. What were they thinking? The Carsons had grown rich from this place. They needed to invest some money back into it.

Petey and Ricky, each trying to be the first one to work on the duct, got the smoldering dust pulled out. It dropped to the concrete floor, showering sparks everywhere as it hit. Kent, Allen, and Bert used fire extinguishers to contain the sparks. It was a mess, but the duct was clean and the smoke was gone.

By that time, Stella had lost her temper. "Not only did you have to call us to put out the fire, you got free labor getting your duct cleaned out," she told Greg Lambert. "I'm shutting you down until there can be a complete safety inspection of the plant. And I'm fining you for allowing the safety hazard."

"You can't do that." Lambert looked at John for agreement. "The fire department can't shut us down. I'm calling Chief Rogers and Mr. Carson. You've crossed a line, Chief Griffin. I can't imagine what Mr. Carson is going to say."

Ricky nudged Petey with his elbow. "He must be the only person in Sweet Pepper who doesn't know who the chief is."

Stella didn't have official fire department citations yet, so she wrote what she'd said on a plain sheet of paper and handed it to Lambert. "I'll be back in the morning. I'd better not see any sign of people having worked here until then. Good night, Mr. Lambert."

The night shift started packing up to leave even as Greg Lambert continued his sputtering while trying to punch numbers into his cell phone. Stella ignored him and took her team home.

Chapter 23

Everyone was worried as they cleaned and put away their gear. "She can't just shut down the pepper factory," Royce said. "They won't let her do that."

"I don't think so," JC answered. "She's the law when it comes to fires."

"I'm worried too," Allen confessed. "The old man could disband the fire brigade."

"That's not going to happen." Ricky was still cleaning dust from his boots. "The chief is Carson's granddaughter. He wants her to stay. He'll have to look the other way. Maybe even get that stuff taken care of."

Marty laughed. "He doesn't know how to look the other way—take it from me."

Ricky glared at him. "I don't know what you're doing here, old son, but I'm gonna find out. You've never done an honest day's work in your life. Suddenly, Stella comes to town and you're a Good Samaritan. What are you worried about? Or maybe it's your *mother* that's worried."

There were a few snickers at that remark. No one said anything else about it as Stella finished putting away her gear and looked around.

She'd heard the entire conversation. She didn't plan to get into a discussion of whether or not what she'd done at the factory was right or wrong. She'd never questioned a decision by Chief Henry at home—she expected her volunteers not to question her decisions here—at least not to her face.

She knew she was within her jurisdiction to shut down the factory until repairs could be made. What was going on out there was a disaster waiting to happen, complete with loss of lives and serious property damage. She had to assume the county firefighters had been willing to look the other way since the factory was a large source of tax revenue.

As far as she was concerned, the duct problem and the emergency access to water had to be addressed. She knew she might have to compromise and give her grandfather a time frame in which to address the problem, but shutting the place down would catch everyone's attention.

Not that she had any doubt that people would be pounding on her door by morning.

"Good job out there tonight," she said to everyone before she left the firehouse.

Hero was at her feet, wagging his tail. Sylvia had joined him, waiting for David and Kimmie to finish their cleanup and change clothes. The two dogs sat looking up at her as though they were listening to everything she had to say.

"We'll set up to practice getting in gear and on the trucks tomorrow, about three. Does that work for everyone?"

No one disagreed, and the practice was set for the next day. Stella said good night to her team and patted both dogs on the head before she left.

She was exhausted as she walked to the Cherokee. It had been a rough couple of days. It didn't look very promising for the next few days either. She needed a Coke and a good night's sleep.

The ride up the road to the cabin was accomplished too quickly. Stella sat in the Cherokee for a long time, thinking about everything that had happened.

What would her grandfather think when he heard that

she'd shut down the factory? No doubt, he'd already heard. Had she really crossed some invisible line, taken a step that would taint everything good she'd done here?

Her ribs ached, and her head was pounding. She didn't want to leave the quiet, warm sanctuary of the SUV—she wished she could just sit there until morning, then get on her miraculously repaired bike and go home.

None of that was going to happen. Her father and others had always said she was stubborn. Maybe the actions she'd taken wouldn't look so bad in the morning. There was nothing else to do but wait for it.

Stella finally forced herself out of the vehicle, up the stairs, and to the cabin door. The door opened as she approached, and the inside lights came on. There was a fire crackling in the hearth and coffee perking in the kitchen.

"Wow." She tried to keep her teeth from chattering. "I'd either like to hire or marry you, Eric. You're the best roommate anyone could want—except for spying on me when I'm getting dressed."

"I know you wanted Coke," he said in his husky voice. "But you should have something hot."

"You heard that, huh?"

"Proximity to my space. You should get out of those dusty clothes too."

"You *would* say that."

"It's nice that you still have a sense of humor. You've had a busy night."

Stella didn't care at that point if Eric stood inside the small shower stall with her. She stripped off her clothes and stood in the hot water until all of it was gone.

Shivering in her T-shirt and shorts, a blanket wrapped around her, she went back to the living room to sit in front of the fire.

"I put some brandy in your coffee," Eric said. "I think you need it to ward off a chill."

"You have brandy here somewhere? Bring out the bottle."

She grabbed the coffee from the table, sat down on the comfortable sofa, and leaned back with the cup in her hands.

"I don't think you want a hangover tomorrow morning."

"Maybe not, but a little buzz would feel good tonight. God, my ribs hurt." She sipped the coffee and brandy mixture. He'd put a *lot* of brandy in it. It burned nicely going down.

"Just relax for a while. Stress and exhaustion make injuries hurt more. You'll feel better. Have you eaten?"

"I don't remember." She picked up her laptop and turned it on. She wasn't going to be able to sleep right away. She might as well put more information from Tory's folder into the laptop.

"Damn!" The computer file she'd been using to store that information had gone corrupt. "Now I'll have to start all over again." Probably because of all the glitches. She never had this much trouble with her laptop back home. Maybe it was the mountains that caused the problems she'd been having.

A few minutes later, she smelled bread toasting. "You cook too?"

"A little. I used to love to cook. I thought you knew and that's why you asked about a pepper recipe for the festival."

"It was more like desperation since I don't cook at all." She set down the laptop and went to get her toast. "Thanks. It must be hard for you."

"Being dead?"

"I suppose so." She didn't want to think about what had happened to him when the grain silo fell in on him. It was every firefighter's worst nightmare. "Mostly lonely. Forty years without anyone to talk to is a long time."

"I know."

"Why do you think I can hear you?"

"I can't imagine. I've tried talking to other people. Then one day, you were here."

"And I was naked in the hot tub and I could hear you."

She smiled as she buttered the toast. "Maybe that's the key. Did you try talking to any other women?"

"Yes. No hot tub, though."

"Maybe we can find something on Wikipedia about it." She went back and sat down with her laptop.

"What's that?"

"Just all the information in the world at your fingertips." She typed in "ghost" and got a thousand returns. "It's hard to say what's real and what's not."

"This is a lot of information." His voice was right at her shoulder. He was looking at the laptop too.

Stella read through as much as she could. "I don't know." She put the laptop back down on the table. "I can't focus anymore. I'm sorry. You can keep looking, if you like."

"There may not be an explanation, not a logical one anyway. Take it from me, when I woke up here, I was amazed."

"What was it like? What do you remember?"

"I ran into the grain silo to pull Ricky Hutchins out before the building collapsed. Then I was here. I didn't know what had happened at first. Then slowly, as people stopped coming around and I couldn't leave the cabin or the firehouse, I realized that I must be dead."

All in all, Stella thought it could be worse. She didn't say so. There was a terrible hollow sound to his voice that tugged at her heart. "And what about being able to see you? How does that work?"

"I don't know. There's no guide book."

She saw his shadowy form standing near the door to the deck. "You know, if you get to see me naked, I should get to see you."

"I don't know if that's a good idea. I've thought about what you said, Stella."

"That must be why you were so quiet earlier. I assume this means you've come to a decision."

"I've lived alone for a long time. I didn't want anyone else here. I never dreamed of interacting with anyone again."

"I understand," she muttered sleepily, settling back on

the sofa. "This is different. I think you should go for it. From what I've heard, you weren't exactly a cautious man in life. Why start now?"

"I don't think you *do* understand. I've tried looking in the mirror. I can't see myself. I could be really disgusting. I'm not so old that there weren't horror movies out when I was alive. Nothing compared to what I've seen on TV lately—I don't want to scare you away. I think you should be ready for it. If you say I look like a zombie or something, I can go back to being invisible right away. Can you handle that?"

Stella's head fell to one side. She let out a muffled snore.

"Stella?" He looked down on her. All that preparation had been for nothing. He touched her hair, then left her to sleep. Maybe it was for the best anyway. If he'd been burned in that fire the way people said, what could he expect her reaction to be?

He took her up on her offer of looking at the computer. It might be possible to find out a few things. Google, huh? Funny name.

Ghost appearances. Hmm.

Chapter 24

~~~~~~~~~~

There was a loud pounding going on in Stella's dream. At least she thought it was her dream—until she emerged from her blanket cocoon on the sofa. She realized that not only was someone really pounding on the cabin door, someone was also shouting her name in an angry tone.

"Morning," Eric said. "I hope you're feeling better because I think all hell is about to break loose."

"Yeah." She ran her hand through her hair, which seemed to be standing up all over her head. She wasn't answering the door in the blanket. Whoever it was would have to wait.

"There's still coffee left from last night," Eric told her. "Or Coke in the fridge."

"Hold that thought." She ran into the bedroom and threw on a pair of jeans and a Sweet Pepper T-shirt. She groaned when she saw her new dress from last night was still stuffed into the bag she'd brought home after the fire.

Stella ran a comb through her hair and put on some socks. Then she walked calmly to the door in the kitchen and threw it open. It was barely seven a.m.

"I only want to understand what happened at the plant last night." Ben Carson brushed by her and walked into the cabin. "Did you lose your mind? Did someone pay you to do this? What in the hell is going on?"

"I know you're surprised, but you shouldn't be." She closed the door.

Her grandfather faced her, deep furrows in his forehead. "You shut down my factory, Stella. Several hundred people won't be able to go to work today. I'll lose a fortune being closed. What were you thinking? Why didn't you call me so we could talk about this like rational people?"

She yawned as she poured a glass of Coke. "Would you like some?"

"No, I don't want anything—except an explanation. My blood pressure is probably high enough right now to kill an ox. If you were anyone else, I'd have you fired."

"If *you* were anyone else, you'd either be arrested for these safety violations or you wouldn't be in business anymore."

"I can't believe my own flesh and blood could do something like this. What did they teach you up there in Chicago anyway?"

Stella sat down on the sofa and smiled when she saw the fire had been refreshed. "They taught us that a large corporation, like the pepper-packing plant, has to have its own water source. More important, the fire department has to be able to access it. If that ductwork had produced a serious fire last night, the pumper wouldn't have had enough water to take care of it. You, and your workers, would've been looking at a big pile of ashes this morning."

"You're being melodramatic. We've been handling things this way for a hundred years. It's been fine up until now."

"Maybe it's time for things to be different. I know you had something to do with bringing me here for this job. I did what you hired me to do last night. Every time you let that dust in the ductwork smolder, you take a chance on people's lives. Do you understand *that*?"

He suddenly sat down in the chair near the fire, as though his legs wouldn't hold him any longer. "This is a public relations nightmare. People are expecting me to react in a certain way."

"You mean, people are expecting you to make sure I get fired?"

"That's absolutely true."

"I guess that's your call."

He got to his feet, agitated, and walked around the limited space in the cabin. "I don't want to have you fired. I want this to work out, for both our sakes."

She shrugged, not wanting to get fired either but not willing to neglect what she saw as her job. "What did you have in mind?"

He sat down again, his large, knuckled hands clasped loosely together, elbows on his knees. "A compromise. I admit to neglect in not taking care of the factory the way I should. I pay the fine. You give me thirty days to get the ductwork where it should be."

Stella thought it over. It would be the same with any large employer in Chicago too. There would be a compromise so that the fire hazard would be taken care of and the employer could keep his business running.

It was more than she'd expected of him. He must really want her to stay. "It's a deal—but I need to start seeing progress on the job. I don't want to go down there next time and have to pull bodies out of the factory."

"You might look like your mother and your grandmother, but you're a lot like me. You drive a hard bargain. I'll start work right away on the problem and have a conventional hose connection put on the water tower."

"That sounds good. Thank you." She reached to shake his hand.

His brown eyes twinkled. "Can we seal this bargain with a hug instead?"

Stella couldn't argue with that. He put his arms around her and pulled her close for a moment. She smiled when he stepped back. "I appreciate your cooperation."

"You realize that you haven't called me by name since

we met. I don't expect 'Granddad,' but 'Ben' would be okay. For now."

"Sorry. It's been a little awkward finding out about all of this. Ben, it is."

"That's just fine. If you feel motivated to call me Granddad or Pawpaw, as we do around here, that would tickle me." He looked around the cabin. "Are you sure you won't let me get you a decent place to stay? This is hardly big enough for a dog to turn around and lay down."

"I like it," she told him, seeing something different than he did. "I'm comfortable here."

He shook his head. "Old Chief Gamlyn always liked it too. He and I had a few meaningful conversations here when he was alive. He built this place, you know, and the firehouse. He was an intelligent, resourceful man. We had our run-ins from time to time. He was a lot like you, Stella, a stickler for the rules."

"I'm surprised he didn't make you take care of those ducts forty years ago."

"We'd been discussing that very thing when the county decided to take over the fire service and Chief Gamlyn died. That kind of ended that conversation. The county has been willing to look the other way. I pay a lot in taxes. They respect that."

She wasn't sure if Eric whispered in her ear or she just thought of it, but she remembered her discussion with him about Adam Presley, Tory's first husband.

"In looking through evidence on Tory's death, I noticed her first husband died in a fire too. I understand you and Chief Gamlyn also had some words about that investigation."

"I thought they arrested Victor and that insurance investigator for Tory's death. Why are you interested in what happened to Adam after all these years?"

"I thought it was curious. It said in Chief Gamlyn's . . . notes . . . that you didn't want him to investigate Presley's death."

"If I remember correctly, Adam died from dropping a

cigarette in his lap when he fell asleep watching television. I didn't see what there was to investigate then, and I still don't. How could that possibly tie into Tory's death?"

"I'm not exactly saying it could." She wasn't going to get anywhere if he got upset again. "I was wondering why he cited you particularly in his notes about not wanting an investigation."

"I was probably trying to be conservative with the town's funds. Chief Gamlyn and the police chief at that time, Walt Fenway, were determined that something other than an accident had killed Adam. I didn't see it. There was no point carrying on about it—especially since it was only a few days until the festival. You don't realize how important the festival is to Sweet Pepper. It might have ruined us."

"I see. Thanks, Ben." Stella wasn't willing to fight that battle until she knew a little more about it.

Her grandfather looked relieved. "All right. You're welcome. Let's reschedule that dinner from last night. Maybe next time your volunteers can take care of the problem without you."

She walked him to the door. "We'll do that."

He hugged her again. "I'm glad you're here, Stella. It makes me feel things might still be all right with me and your mother. I can't tell you what that would mean to me. It would be like having part of Abigail back again."

Stella stood on the porch and watched the shiny black Cadillac drive away.

"You believe him?" Eric asked.

"I don't know. I think he'd do or say whatever is best for him, like anyone else." She went back in the bedroom and put on her boots. "I was expecting less honesty about getting rid of me, weren't you? Maybe it really matters to him if I stay or not."

"Maybe." He watched her try to start her laptop. "There may be a problem with that. I tried to use it last night. It kind of died, I think."

"Great." She got her tote bag out and put the laptop in it.

"I think ghosts may be bad for computers. I'll have to take it back to the shop. That man is going to think I'm crazy."

"Sorry. You were right about everything being on that gadget."

She put on her sweatshirt jacket. "Have you thought about a pepper recipe for me?"

"Yes. I'll see if you have the ingredients here. Are you going to eat something before you go?"

Stella grabbed a package of toaster pastries from the cabinet. "Breakfast of champions. See you later, Eric."

"About our conversation last night—seeing me—"

"Oh. Sorry about that. I guess I fell asleep. We'll have to talk later."

"Later." He hoped he didn't sound too disappointed.

Stella munched on her breakfast as she drove the Cherokee to town. She dropped the laptop off with Charlie Johnson again. He shook his head.

"What are you doing with this poor piece of equipment?"

"It wasn't me," she insisted. "The file I was using was corrupted. I lost some information."

"I hope you still have a hard copy, in case it can't be retrieved." He was looking at the laptop with his glasses perched on the edge of his nose.

"I do. I hope I don't have to type all of it back in again."

"I'll see what I can do. What's that file called?"

"Adam Presley. Thanks, Charlie. I think all the ghostly activity might be to blame."

He laughed. "I guess you've finally come around to our way of thinking. I'll call you when this is done."

Stella thanked him and left his shop. Chief Rogers was leaning against her vehicle, waiting for her, when she came out. "I heard you were busy last night. Closed down the pepper plant, huh? I'll bet that went over big with the old man."

"We came to an agreement." She wasn't giving away any information to him. He certainly didn't share with her.

"So, when are you leaving?" he asked with a grin.

"I told you—we worked it out. I'm not going anywhere. Not yet anyway. You're stuck with me for now."

She laughed to herself as she saw the momentary look of complete amazement on his face. He hadn't been expecting that. He frowned and left without another word.

Stella was driving away from the computer shop when she saw John. He was just arriving at town hall in his uniform. She stopped and asked for a minute to talk to him.

He looked surprised when she requested Adam Presley's old police file from the original case. "Do you think that has something to do with what happened to Tory?"

"I don't know. I guess you've got someone in custody for that. I'd like to compare what the police have on file with what Tory gave me that she'd collected. Since it was a death by fire, I'd like to take a look."

He nodded. "Sure. I don't see why not. Would you like to get coffee?"

She wasn't sure if she wanted to go through another round of him trying to get close and then suddenly remembering who she was and running away. Besides, she had work to do.

"I wish I could, but I'm meeting with some people from the festival about contest judging. Maybe later."

"Judging, huh? You should've said no." He smiled to lighten his harsh voice. "I'll look for that file and give you a call.

Stella realized that she'd had no idea what she was letting herself in for when she agreed to judge the chocolate part of the festival's pepper recipe contest.

Elvita and Theodora flagged her down outside town hall. It seemed she wasn't getting ready for the festival fast enough for them. They whisked her away to the dressmaker, a tiny, birdlike woman named Molly Whitehouse. Molly took her measurements and made suggestions for what would look best on her.

"With your coloring and that lovely red hair, I think a nice periwinkle would look wonderful on you." Her announcement brought raptures of agreement from the other two women.

"The theme this year is 'Peppers around the World,'" Elvita explained. "We were thinking your dress could be French in design since you'll be judging pepper and chocolate entries, after all."

"That sounds . . . fine." Stella smiled, not sure about the connection between chocolate and France.

"Molly will whip up a beautiful French gown for you, compliments of the Sweet Pepper Festival Committee. It will be perfect," Theodora promised.

"Vivian Carson will be wearing something Swedish. She'll be judging fish-and-pepper entries," Elvita said. "And Jill Wando, the mayor's wife, will be judging chili recipes. She'll wear a South American dress."

"Not designed by *me*," Molly added. "They both have their own dress designers, thank you very much."

"Ignore them, Molly." Theodora squeezed the little dressmaker. "You're the best."

Elvita sighed. "It's going to be absolutely perfect."

"Except for Tory not being here." Theodora bit her lip and wiped the corner of her eye on her scarf. "You know, she started us all dressing up for the event. Remember the year she dressed up as Amelia Earhart? She even smoked those nasty little cigars. She was so brave—even after Adam's death. I miss her spirit so much, bless her soul."

"Tory told me she thought there was something unusual about Adam's death." Stella put on her jeans and T-shirt now that the fitting was over.

"Now that you mention it," Elvita said, "she did go on about how Adam had stopped smoking months before they'd found him all burned up. She even went around asking questions—went to the state capital."

"Tory took it to Eric Gamlyn, the old fire chief. He said he'd done what he could. The police wouldn't look into it either. After that, the whole thing kind of died out," Theodora explained.

"I can tell you that Tory was more than a mite suspicious." Molly peered over the top of her glasses. "For a while she even thought Greg Lambert, her second husband, might have had something to do with it. There was some bad blood between Greg and Adam."

"You mean because Greg wanted Tory for himself while she was still married." Elvita giggled and blushed. "They tried to keep their affair a secret, but everyone knew."

"That was *before* they got married, after Adam died. She was pregnant with Victor. That child was *not* Adam's baby," Molly continued. "Don't forget, Tory dated Greg in high school before Adam came into the picture. Her father didn't think Greg was good enough for her."

"He didn't think *anyone* was good enough for her," Theodora said.

"Then there was that old flame of hers, the one she'd promised to marry before she married Adam. He joined the Army or something. He threatened Adam several times when he got back because she was married to him. What *was* his name?"

Chapter 25

〰〰〰〰〰

"An old boyfriend?" Stella asked. "Does he still live here?"

"I don't recall," Molly said.

"Don't look at me," Elvita hurriedly said. "I'm too young to remember back then."

"That would be my problem too," Theodora confessed.

"Tagger Reamis!" Molly suddenly remembered. "He came back a war hero. Tory couldn't have cared less. She was beautiful and rich. Adam's business was successful. She was the toast of the town. Tagger tried to get her to run away with him. Adam took care of him, bless his heart."

"What happened?" Stella asked. Were they talking about the same Tagger Reamis she knew?

Elvita sighed. "I heard Adam had his legs broken, or some such."

Molly said, "No. Adam just threatened him. Poor Tagger. He was wounded in the war. Not right in the head. He gave up, of course."

Stella realized she was never going to get the whole story from this group. She told them she had practice at the firehouse later and needed to go to the hat shop before noon.

The ladies were happy to comply, and Molly told them all to come back in tomorrow for a proper fitting.

Though Stella felt sure this was the worst type of gossip, she also thought there might be a kernel of truth in what they were saying. She might find out when she got the report from John.

It was hard to imagine Tagger being in love with Tory, even though it was a long time ago. He might have been a much different man then. Maybe a man who would be willing to kill Tory's husband to be with her, especially since Adam had either hurt or threatened him.

He must not have realized that she was already with someone else on the side, possibly already pregnant with Greg's child.

Tory had really gotten around when she was young. There had been nothing left of that side of her personality by the time Stella met her.

The hatmaker across town was the opposite of Molly Whitehouse. Matilda Storch was a sturdy, buxom woman of strong German stock. Her white hair was pulled tightly back from her pink-and-white face, emphasizing her bright blue eyes and sharp chin.

"Good cheekbones." She examined Stella's head and face. "You should wear a tiny hat to emphasize your features, not hide them."

Matilda looked squarely at the big, overly decorated hats worn by Elvita and Theodora.

"She has to look French," Elvita said. "And the hat must match her periwinkle frock."

"Of course." Matilda measured Stella's head and pushed her hair around her face. "How will you wear your hair that day?"

"I usually wear it like this." Stella looked at herself in the mirror and saw the other three women looking at her reflection too.

"You might want to reconsider," Theodora suggested.

"No. It's fine." Matilda smiled. "I'll create a hat that will be wonderful with your hair just the way it is."

Stella was hungry—the hours had flown with the fittings and gossip. She wasn't looking forward to having lunch with Theodora and Elvita. Happily, she was spared from that by an issue with Elvita's hat that had to be taken care of right away.

"I have to run anyway," she told the other women. "I'll see all of you later. Thanks for being here with me. I'll get that pepper recipe to you very soon."

Matilda reminded her to check back in a day or two so they could make changes to her hat, as needed. Elvita reminded Stella that she'd have to attend judging rehearsal before the festival.

Stella was glad to get away. It was a beautiful day, fresh and crisp with a light wind blowing down from the mountains. She'd miss this kind of weather when she got home. Though she loved Chicago, no breeze would ever smell as sweet there.

When she reached the café, Marty was outside. Had he been waiting for her?

"I've been looking for you, Chief—Stella. I hope that head wound isn't bothering you too much." He gently touched her hair.

That was a little too personal. Stella pulled herself out of her happy fall mood and stepped back. "I'm well, thanks. Everything is going fine."

He didn't seem put off by her movement. "I'm glad to hear it. I was about to go inside. Would you like to have lunch with me?"

"I really have to eat and go," she said.

"Me too. Practice this afternoon, you know."

What could she say? Refusing to eat with him would be rude. He'd found her in the ditch and brought her to safety. She probably should buy him lunch. She was a little wary of him, though. Probably all the things that John had said about him.

Before she could answer, John opened the diner door, irritation plainly written on his face. "Problem out here, Chief Griffin? Is *he* bothering you?"

"Not at all." She felt trapped between the two men. "I think I'll go in and have lunch. Maybe we should all eat together."

Marty didn't like that idea. "You know, I forgot there's something I have to do before practice. Rain check? I'll see you later, Stella."

Stella agreed, mentally chastising herself for acting so weird with him. She couldn't let John's feelings about her family color her ideas about them.

"What was all that about?" John walked in with her and showed her to his table, a tall glass of iced tea at his place.

Stella realized that everyone in the diner had been watching them through the wide plate-glass windows. It made her angry and embarrassed. "Are you waiting for someone?"

"You." He slid the old manila file toward her. "I guess you didn't get my texts or calls about meeting me here for lunch."

"Sorry. I was being properly attired to judge the chocolate and pepper recipe contest at the festival. I guess there was no cell service at the dressmaker or hatmaker shops either." She looked at her phone and found twelve messages from him. "Thanks for waiting."

They ordered lunch, and Stella started looking through the file.

"You didn't answer my question," he said. "Are you and Marty dating or what?"

"Dating?" She didn't remember him asking that question. "I barely know him."

"You looked pretty cozy out there. I wouldn't blame you. You should know that he doesn't get any of the Carson money. Your grandfather made sure of that. Which is probably why he wants you to stay."

She tried to recall that she'd been hungry earlier and that food had sounded good. What was it with John that he always managed to say things that raised her hackles?

"I'll try to remember that." She glanced through a few of the papers in the file. The ink had faded on many of them. "Did you look through this?"

He shrugged. "Sure. I don't see any problem with the investigation Chief Fenway did at the time. People start fires carelessly. You don't need me to tell you that. Why the interest in this?"

Stella thought about telling him that her ghost was interested. After all, they had all been so sure the cabin was haunted, he shouldn't be surprised. Knowing that Eric had spoken only to her, she feared the town's reaction should she confirm his existence. What if they panicked, burned down the cabin or something? She had to keep Eric's presence to herself.

"Like I said, Tory asked me to look into it. I didn't think about it much, until she was killed."

"People want to believe it wasn't their loved one's fault when they die. I'm sure that was how Tory felt. I don't see how this could connect with her death, in any case."

"I don't either." She closed the file. "Like I said, I thought I'd look into it. Kind of a memorial thing, you know."

"I get it. Don't mention it to Chief Rogers, will you? Tory never gave up on it, even when Chief Fenway retired."

"Is he still around?"

"Sure. He lives outside town near Big Bear Springs. I could take you out there, if you like. I'll be at practice this afternoon. We could go from there."

Stella searched John's handsome face. Clearly, he liked her and liked being around her. She liked him too, but she was tired of all the Carson crap.

"That sounds fine—if we can leave the Carson family at their mansion. I'm not my family, John. I didn't have anything to do with the things that have gone on here that you're blaming them for." She stopped short of mentioning his father.

Their food arrived and neither of them said anything for a few moments as they ate.

John wiped his mouth with his napkin. "I know. I feel like an idiot about it, Stella. You could've worn a sign—'Keep out, Carson blood'—to warn me off before I realized how much I like everything about you. It wasn't fair."

She smiled and took his hand. "Life's not fair. We could still salvage what we've got going on between us, if you can get over the Carson stuff."

He leaned across the table and briefly kissed her. A chorus of "oohs" and "aahs" greeted his action, followed by a smattering of applause. "I'm over it."

"Great. Let's go to Big Bear Springs, and we'll see what happens after that."

"Sounds good."

"Have you ever heard anything about Tagger and Tory being a couple?" she asked.

"Are you kidding me?" He laughed. "I don't think so. Can you imagine that?"

Stella felt the same way. She probably needed to ask someone who'd known both of them way back when to find out for sure.

After lunch, she drove out to the firehouse, said hello to Ricky, who was on communications duty that day. She sat down in her small office, no more than a broom closet they'd shoved an old desk and chair into. The cleaning supplies were still stored there.

As she was going through the file, one of the documents floated up and away from her. "Nice trick. Were you looking over my shoulder?"

"This is my report on the fire," Eric said. "I didn't expect to see it again. I can't believe I let myself say what they wanted me to say."

Stella sat back in her chair with the file in her lap. "I've already looked through most of it. I don't see what else you could have said. It looks like an accident. They happen."

"No one sits there after they spill lighter fluid on themselves and calmly lights their cigarette. He didn't fall asleep smoking. Not to mention that there was no lighter anywhere around him."

"I agree that the circumstances are odd. You know sometimes fires are unusual. There is no mention of suspects or motives for someone to have killed Adam."

"Because we didn't have time to investigate since your grandfather closed us down."

Stella wasn't sure about that. "He told me he was trying to save the town some money. John and I are going out to talk to the old police chief after practice today. Maybe he'll have some insights."

"Old Walt Fenway is still alive, huh?" The report that had been hanging in the air fell back to the desk. "He was caught in the middle too. I doubt if he'll have much to say about it."

A quick knock on the door brought Tagger in right behind it. "Chief, most of the volunteers are here. What are you looking at?" He came around to peer over her shoulder.

"An old file." She put the paper back in the folder, feeling a faint *zing* of static electricity as she did so. Possibly something Eric left behind. "Adam Presley's death. Did you know him?"

"Oh sure," Tagger said. "The car salesman. Why are you looking at that?"

"I had a few questions about the fire. I heard that Chief Gamlyn wasn't happy with the investigation. I know Tory didn't believe it was an accident."

Tagger's smile was toothy. "Yeah. The chief had a suspicious nature. He thought everyone was guilty of something."

"You didn't think there was anything unusual about the fire?"

He appeared to be thinking—frowning and puckering up. "I don't really remember. Sorry, Chief. Maybe there was. People don't like car salesmen much, do they?"

Stella put the folder away. "Thanks anyway. I'll be right out."

When Tagger was gone, she said to Eric, "Do you know anything about Tagger dating Tory before she married Adam?"

"Sure. I kind of remember that. Nothing came of it. He went to Vietnam, and when he came back, she was married."

"I heard something about him threatening Adam. Adam beat him up or something."

"I don't remember. Walt might. What are you thinking?"

"I don't know. Firemen are good at starting fires too."

"Not Tagger." Eric defended him. "He was devastated by Tory's rejection, but he didn't kill Adam."

"You're probably right. It bothers me that Tory was so sure her first husband was murdered and then she was murdered too. Even though Tory didn't die in the fire like Adam, both cases involved arson. Tagger was involved with both cases—the first time because he wanted to be with Tory. He was working for her when she died. Maybe he wanted revenge."

"I thought Tory's son started the fire at her house."

"He did, at least it looks like he did."

"I don't think Don Rogers is going to want you to stir the pot after he's made his arrest. You're asking for trouble in the last few weeks you have here."

"I know, but I want to do this for Tory. I probably won't be here for her memorial I've heard people talking about."

"I wish I could be more help. It's been a long time and a lot has happened since then."

She put the folder into her desk drawer. "You can train with us. You could probably use the exercise."

"I'm a little past my prime, but thanks."

She smiled at the laughter in his voice. "You were saying something about being visible last night. I think I passed out. Sorry."

"We'll talk about it later. You'd better go before they come after you. I'm going to try out the pepper recipe."

Hero started barking, tiny, high-pitched sounds, as he came into her office, sniffing at all the corners of the room.

"You didn't tell me you had a puppy." Hero rolled over on his back. Stella guessed Eric was rubbing his tummy.

"It looks like Hero was our last gift from Tory," she said. "He's the fire brigade's new mascot."

"I haven't seen a dog in a long time."

The puppy was wagging his tail and pouncing at something she couldn't see.

Stella left them in her office and went outside. All the volunteers were present—even Marty. She had to admit she was surprised that he kept at it. He didn't seem the type. Again, she cautioned herself on being prejudiced by what John had to say about him.

"There are going to be a lot of times that you only have a few minutes to put on all your gear and pick up what you need for the call," she said to the volunteers.

"Without breaking your ankle." Bert Wando laughed.

"Definitely without injury," Stella agreed. "You can't practice this too much. I know you old-timers think you're as fast as you can get. I guarantee that there's always room for improvement."

With that, Stella took out her stopwatch, whistle, and clipboard. Everyone ran for their gear when she blew the whistle. They were finished when they had reached a spot on either the pumper or the engine.

Marty finished last each time they ran through the drill, though she had to agree that he put in a good effort. He might make a decent firefighter yet.

They moved outside after about an hour and began working with the hoses again. Stella realized she had only three really competent volunteers when it came to using the hoses. The team needed more than that. If Petey, Ricky, or John didn't show up, it might be hard for the brigade to handle a large fire.

The older members were starting to get the hang of it. Royce and Bert were struggling, the hose jumping away from them as soon as there was any pressure in it. Stella encouraged and tried to challenge them as they watched Petey master the hoses.

Royce sat down heavily on the ground and took off his helmet. "I ain't never gonna be able to control that thing. I don't know how she does it."

"You can do it," his friend JC said. "It's taken me a while, but I've almost got it now."

His tough, older face defiant, Royce said, "What difference does it make anyway? The old man won't let us keep doing this. She defied him." He pointed at Stella. "He's gonna come down on all of us like a sack of potatoes."

"You're wrong," Stella said. "Ben Carson and I struck a deal this morning. I've given him some time to get that ductwork cleaned up, the right way this time. He's agreed to replace the connection on the water tower right away. I agreed not to fine him."

Royce stared at her after JC gave him a hand up. "Must be true what they're saying in town. You *must* be kin to the Carsons. The old man would never put up with it otherwise."

"That does bring up an interesting question," Marty said. "If your next fire chief isn't a member of the Carson family, what will happen to the fire brigade?"

Chapter 26

~~~~~~~~~~~~~~~

All the wet volunteers looked around at each other. Stella knew the question had raised doubts in them about what they were doing. They needed their confidence. She didn't think they'd find it thinking about Marty being the fire chief when she left.

Her lips tightened. "I don't think the town only hired me because I'm related to Ben Carson. It's going to be more important that the person who leads you when I'm gone knows what they're doing—a lot more important than who they know."

"Who's that gonna be, Chief?" Banyin asked.

"I'm announcing right now that Ricky Hutchins and Petey Stanze will be assistant chiefs from now on. They'll be working together to take my place. They're the best trained and have done more for the brigade than anyone else."

There was a short round of applause and a lot of backslapping, then the volunteers went to change and put the equipment away.

Marty walked up to her. "I understand your reasoning on this, Stella. I hope you're not sorry. I might be the only person who can keep the fire brigade going."

John was standing behind him. He put his hand on the younger man's shoulder as a warning. "You better watch your mouth, son. I've about had enough of you, Carson or not."

Marty eased John's hand off his shoulder. "Sorry, John. I didn't mean to step on your toes. I know you have feelings for the chief. *Everyone* knows."

John glared at Marty as he saluted him and left. "That boy is wearing a Teflon suit. Nothing sticks to him. I've had him on DUI already and he got off with equipment failure. Nobody around here can top the Carson money."

John's serious face made Stella change the subject. "Are we still on to talk to Walt Fenway?"

"I'll be ready when you are."

Stella was ready before John was done putting away his gear. She filled out reports she needed to send to the state and looked at the proposed budget for the fire brigade.

She heard John telling everyone good-bye and put things away. She was ready to leave when a tall, burly man with dirty clothes and messed-up brown hair stopped her.

"I'm Jack Carriker. Heard you needed some work done on your equipment."

Stella was half expecting some kind of smirk on his face from the way he'd said it. He looked at her with a straight-forward gaze.

"You mean the vandalism on the trucks," she replied. "Yes. I'll show you."

Kent was still there. He came up and shook Jack's hand. "Me and Jack go way back. I used to beat him up at school."

Jack grinned. "You wish!"

Marty came up too. "Jack?"

The older man nodded to him. "Mr. Lawrence."

"Are you volunteering?" Marty's tone left no doubt he thought it was a crazy idea.

"No, sir. Looking after some trucks that need painting and any other odd jobs the chief here might have for me."

Marty patted him on the back. "He does odd jobs at the estate too, don't you, Jack?"

Stella didn't like Marty's patronizing attitude toward the other man. Clearly, Jack wasn't wealthy or well educated, but that was no reason to look down at him.

"Let's check out those trucks," she said. "I'll see you later, Marty. Good job today."

After she showed him the damage on the trucks, Stella also talked to Jack about some other work that still needed to be done at the firehouse. Some of the floorboards were loose, and a few of the doors were warped and needed to be replaced. She had plenty of money in the budget for the work, and she suspected Jack needed the pay.

John came up as she was shaking hands with Jack. She told him to charge what he needed at Potter's Hardware in town.

John and Stella got in the Cherokee. "You're going to let him work here?" he asked.

"I don't see why not. Kent knows him. He seems okay."

John pointed her in the right direction for Big Bear Springs, where Walt Fenway lived. "He's the son of the infamous Shu Carriker. Lives on the family's old farm, or what's left of it, with his mother. Shu was Ben Carson's go-to man years ago. His son took over that position. He also does odd jobs around town. We've never had any problem with him—at least not one we could prove."

"Being a go-to man must not pay as well here as it does where I'm from," she said. "What kind of stuff did his father do for Ben?"

"Kicking people around. Beating them up. Threatening them. That kind of thing."

"And you think Jack does that for my grandfather now?"

"Maybe," John admitted. "Like I said. There's nothing we can prove, but there have been allegations."

The road leading out of town was empty. John was silent
for a few minutes but then explained that there were two
unincorporated towns outside of Sweet Pepper—Big Bear
Springs and Frog Pond.

"Will the fire brigade need to take care of them too?"
Stella asked as they drove through the tiny area that made
up Frog Pond. It looked as though there couldn't have been
more than a few hundred residents.

"We're not clear on that yet. They're talking about starting their own volunteer fire departments. They might need
help getting them going, but that probably won't be for a
while."

She nodded. "Not until I'm gone."

"That's about it."

"I think naming Petey and Ricky as assistant fire chiefs
will work out, don't you?"

"For now. There might have to be only one when you
leave." He glanced at her. "Why Ricky? He's kind of a hotshot. He doesn't seem like leadership material to me. He's
too young to command respect from the older men. For that
matter, so is Petey."

"In other words, you don't like the idea at all."

"I wish *you'd* stay on."

His voice was deep and inviting. She pulled herself back
from trusting him. She wasn't sure where things might lead
with him. As soon as he remembered who her family was,
that would be that.

"I think the group will be in good shape by the time I
leave. Maybe Petey or Ricky won't make it as chief, but
someone will step up." She pointed to the "Big Bear Springs"
sign that was hanging on a pole at the side of the road.
"Where to now?"

"Take a left here."

Stella followed his instructions, and the Cherokee was
immediately on a rough gravel road. The mountains rose up
at the end of it as though there was nowhere to go but into
them.

"Marty won't give up that easy, if he really wants to be fire chief," John mentioned.

She wished he would have stuck with giving directions or talking about the area. She liked him best that way. "He's got a long way to go before he even figures out how to hold on to a hose. He's not taking over my fire brigade unless he's ready."

"I think he wants *you*. The fire brigade is a means to an end." He cleared his throat. "I know you laughed at this before, Stella. I've seen the way he looks at you."

"That's not happening, John. He's not my type." She laughed. "I seem to like bad boy cops with lousy attitudes. Sound familiar?"

"Turn left again at this driveway." He didn't remark on her words.

Stella sighed and left it alone. She was probably better off.

It was hard to tell it was a driveway. There were plants growing through what was left of the gravel, and the rest was a muddy track. If it hadn't been for the mailbox with some kind of animal skull on it, she wouldn't have guessed that the path led to anything at all.

The track went up and down like a roller coaster, with dense trees growing close on either side. Some of them brushed the sides of the Cherokee. Not really used to mountain driving, Stella held the wheel tightly and eased the vehicle through the ruts until a small cabin appeared in a rough clearing.

"Here we are," John said. "I think you might have left indentations in the steering wheel. Don't worry. No one will notice."

Stella turned off the Cherokee and hopped out. "Blue Heaven." She read the inscription on the front door. "Are you sure this is where the ex-police chief lives?"

As if in answer, the front door opened suddenly and a man stepped out. He had a large shotgun pointed at them. "You all just turn around and head back out the way you came. I'm not taking no damn census, and if I won a contest, I don't want to know."

"Whoa! Walt, it's me, John Trump, Bobby's boy. This is the new fire chief, Stella Griffin. We're here to talk to you about one of your old cases."

Walt Fenway lowered his shotgun a little and squinted at his visitors. He was a short man, maybe five feet, with a heavy pelt of yellow-white hair that looked like it hadn't seen a comb in a while. "John? Why didn't you say so, boy? Come on and set down. I finished a batch of hard cider yesterday. You and your lady friend are welcome to help me open the first keg."

The cabin wasn't more than a one-room shack that appeared to be falling down around the old police chief. He put a tap in a wooden keg and let dark yellow apple cider run into three tin cups. "Let's take it out back," Walt said. "It's a fair enough day. Might as well enjoy it before the cold sets in."

Once she saw the breathtaking view from the back of the shack, Stella understood why Walt had decided to live here. Thousands of fir trees swept like a carpet down the side of the mountain, beyond which rose up darker ridges. A large waterfall cascaded from a rocky pinnacle, the frothy water plunging hundreds of feet to a river below.

"What a view." She sat on one of several stumps obviously used for that purpose. In the middle, there was a large fire pit. It looked as though Walt did most of his cooking right here. Red coals still gleamed through the ash in the bottom of the pit.

"So what brings you out this way?" Walt asked after they were seated.

"Adam Presley's death." John sipped the hard cider carefully. "You remember that?"

"Oh yeah." Walt stirred the ashes and added a log to the red coals. "The car salesman. Bad business there."

"You worked with Chief Gamlyn on that case," Stella

said. "I understand he wasn't happy with the outcome of the investigation either."

"Eric Gamlyn." Walt smiled and tossed another log on the fire. "I haven't thought about him in a long time. Many nights that rascal and I sat out here talking and drinking. He was a good man."

"What did the two of you think was wrong about the Presley case?" John tried to refocus the old chief's attention.

"We knew it was all wrong—the whole setup. Nobody douses themselves with lighter fluid, then calmly lights a cigarette."

"Could it have been suicide?" Stella asked.

"Nah. We didn't believe it. Neither did Tory." He glanced at her. "Have you talked to her about it?"

"You haven't heard?" John asked. "Tory was murdered. We thought to begin with that it was arson because her house was set on fire. It looks now like someone tied her up and gave her too much insulin."

Walt swore as he stood up. "Who did it?"

"Right now, it looks to be her son," John explained.

"That little—" Walt threw the rest of his cider into the fire pit, causing the flames to shoot up high. "Sorry. That was a waste of mighty fine cider."

"I didn't know Tory well before she died," Stella admitted. "She told me the day before she died that her first husband had been murdered and asked me to look into it."

"Yeah, she was sure of it. Eric and I knew something was wrong too. We couldn't prove it. Then Old Man Carson started leaning on us. We had to back off or lose our jobs."

"Why do you think Ben Carson was interested in stopping the investigation?" Stella asked.

"I'll tell you why," Walt said. "Because he's a low-down skunk who is more interested in his own gain than in what's right. He knew something was wrong, just like we did. He didn't want his precious festival messed up by it."

Chapter 27

The wood crackled loudly in the silence as the three of them thought about what Walt had said. John certainly wasn't the only person in Sweet Pepper who hated and feared Ben Carson. Stella believed it wasn't unusual for people to feel that way about rich, powerful people.

"Why didn't you go back later and continue the investigation?" she pushed forward. "The festival was over in a few days. There's no statute of limitations on murder."

"I don't know," Walt admitted. "It all fell apart after that. Eric died, and the county took over the fire department. They didn't want to make waves with the old man. He said the DA wouldn't prosecute anyone for Adam's death. I believed him. I guess I was getting old, and I was more interested in my pension."

"Did you question the DA's decision?" Stella asked. "Think about taking it to court?"

"Eric did. He wasn't scared of the old man." Walt laughed at the memory. "I always wondered if it had anything to do with his death."

"I thought he died when a burning building collapsed on

him." Stella glanced at John, who shrugged and finished his cider.

"Yeah, I know. I was there. I can't imagine how the old man could've caused Eric's death, but I felt certain in my bones that he did." Walt offered John more cider. John declined.

Feeling something in your bones wasn't proof of anything. Stella put down her tin cup and stood up. "I'm looking through your file on Adam Presley's death. Is there any hard evidence that could've been overlooked? What about Tagger Reamis as a suspect?"

"Tagger?" Walt shook his head. "He threatened Adam, but we couldn't find anything else there. Seems to me he had an alibi. I can't recall right now. It should be in the file."

"You and Eric didn't like him for it?"

"No. Of course, he was friends with Eric. I don't know. We went over every inch of that case a dozen times. There wasn't anything we could prove beyond some hunches. The old man wanted it left alone. Maybe you should ask Ben Carson about it. I take it he's still alive. They say Satan lets them live a long healthy life once they sign away their souls."

"Thanks for your time." Stella shook his hand. "If we find anything new, we'll give you a call."

John hung back a minute as Stella walked to the Cherokee. He exchanged a few words with Walt, they shook hands, and then he joined her.

"Don't say it," she warned.

"I think Walt nailed the devil perfectly on this one."

"Ben Carson is only one man, John. He can't be responsible for every bad thing that ever happened in this town."

"Maybe you should ask him. You seem to have his good side."

They didn't say much more to each other before they got back to the firehouse. John didn't mention dinner again. Neither did she.

Jack was working in the firehouse with Hero at his feet. They both looked up when Stella walked through on her way to the office. She waved but didn't speak, not in the mood for chitchat.

She sat behind the scarred old desk again and reached in the drawer to get the folder she'd left there. It was gone.

Walking back into the vehicle bay, she asked Jack, "Did you see anyone go in here while I was out?"

He stopped scrubbing. "No, ma'am. I haven't really been looking. But I don't think so."

"Something wrong, Chief?" Petey stepped out of the kitchen area with a can of orange soda. It was her turn to monitor communications.

"I lost a folder." Stella frowned, went back into the office, and closed the door. She was troubled by the loss. Why would anyone want to take that folder? She thought briefly that Eric might have taken it. He didn't respond when she called his name. Obviously he had gone back to the cabin to see about that pepper recipe.

Without the folder, Stella felt like she was wasting her time at the firehouse. She talked to Petey for a few minutes about the next week's duty roster. Petey thanked her profusely for naming her assistant chief. "I won't let you down," she promised.

"I'm sure you won't," Stella said. "You've worked consistently harder than anyone else since I got here. You'll make a fine chief by yourself one day."

Petey pushed a strand of her long brown hair behind her ear. "I get why you had to name Ricky too. I don't think the town would let me run the fire brigade by myself either. I'm just a waitress."

"That's not why I did it, and I don't believe that. I didn't want you and Ricky fighting over it and dividing the volunteers into Team Ricky and Team Petey. I think either one of you would be completely capable of being chief."

"Really?" Petey smiled shyly. "That means a lot to me!"

"Good. I'll see you later. Make sure Jack is out of here by six, and lock up when he's gone."

"Sure. Chief? Do you think Mr. Carson will let me run

the fire brigade when you're gone? A lot of people have been saying he only lets you do it because you're his granddaughter."

Stella frowned. "I think he'll be happy to see the backside of me as I'm leaving. He'll be happy with anyone who can keep it going. Don't forget—the town needs this fire brigade."

"What about Marty?" she said quickly. "He might think his stepson would make a good fire chief."

"I don't know," Stella admitted. "I might be wrong, but I don't think my grandfather particularly cares what Marty does. Just keep doing what you do, Petey. Don't worry about the gossip."

Petey kind of shrugged and said good-bye. It was easy to tell that she wasn't convinced. Stella knew there was no way to guarantee what would happen when she went back home. She wasn't even going to try. She liked Petey and thought she did a great job as a volunteer. She would give the town her recommendation for fire chief and go home with a clear conscience.

Stella drove back up the mountain to the cabin, curious to see if Eric had taken Adam Presley's case folder. She could imagine the old manila folder floating up the side of the mountain. Now that she'd opened her mind enough to allow that there really could be the ghost of an old fire chief living in the cabin, she found it easy to imagine all kinds of things.

Yet she couldn't deny that she thought he was real. She didn't know if it was something in the water that made her believe she was communicating with a dead man or what. So far at least, nothing had happened to convince her otherwise.

There was a silver BMW waiting outside the cabin when she arrived. Stella didn't recognize the car. She knew the woman who stepped gracefully from it. Vivian Carson.

"Vivian." Stella came around the side of the bright red Cherokee. "What can I do for you?"

"You northerners don't have an ounce of manners, do

you?" Though the tone was pleasant, the stiff smile didn't make it to her eyes. She reached into the car and brought out an enormous basket of assorted types of pepper products all with the "Sweet Pepper" label on them. "I realized I'd been negligent in bringing a welcoming gift to you. I wanted to remedy that situation."

Stella took the basket from her, hoping it wasn't going to explode. No doubt that wouldn't be subtle enough for her. "Thank you. I appreciate you coming all the way up here to deliver this."

"I know you don't know any better, so I'll help you out—this is where you invite me in for coffee or tea and we have a friendly conversation."

Stella looked at Vivian's expectant face, momentarily trying to decide if she should ask her in or simply say good-bye. She knew Vivian had a powerful impact on the community. There was no point in stirring up trouble now.

"Of course. You're right, where are my manners? Won't you come in for some coffee? I don't have any tea." Stella tacked a careful smile on her face.

"Yes. I believe I will. I feel that you and I have gotten off to a bad start. Part of that is Ben's fault for not wanting to tell you the truth to begin with. I mean, what could that have been like, waking up at the estate after your accident and learning who you really are?"

Stella kept the smile on her face and led the way to the cabin door. It was open, as usual. She pushed it back the rest of the way and put the heavy basket on the kitchen counter.

"I know you think this is a tiny little place compared to Chicago, and you're right, of course." Vivian followed her in and looked around. "But, honey, we still lock our doors. We don't want something bad to happen."

Stella didn't respond to that. "Coffee?"

Vivian took a seat in the living room. "Yes, please."

Stella made a pot of coffee. It seemed to take forever. She poured them each a cup and put out creamer and sugar on the table.

"You don't have cream?" Vivian asked.

"Sorry," Stella said with a smile that was growing harder to maintain.

"That's perfectly fine." Vivian took the mug Stella had given her. She added a little creamer to it. "I didn't expect you to have much in the way of comfort here. You're only staying for a short time after all."

Stella sat down opposite her guest. She was wondering what Eric thought about Vivian Carson. "I can only imagine that you're here to talk about Marty." No point in beating around that bush any longer than she had to.

"You're very blunt for a woman." Vivian tasted the coffee and made a face. "I appreciate that. Let's get right to the point. Marty must be named fire chief if the fire brigade is going to continue."

"I'm sorry. He's not fit to be chief."

"Because you won't train him."

"Because he hasn't been training long enough. He only started recently."

Vivian laughed, a low tinkling chuckle that sounded to Stella like she'd rehearsed it many times. "Why don't you tell me what your *real* issue is with him?"

Stella took a swallow of coffee and forced it down her throat. She hoped she looked calmer than she felt. "I really don't have any problem with him, Vivian. I do have high standards. Marty doesn't meet them yet. He might someday. Of course, by that time, Petey and Ricky will still have surpassed him in knowledge and experience. I think he's doing a good job right now, but he's been with the fire brigade for only a few days."

"I hope you're not holding your grandfather's decision to surprise you with a family against Marty."

"Not at all. I don't understand all the secrecy. It certainly isn't Marty's fault."

"Then you risk ruining all the work you've put into this group. Once you leave, it will never last. The town council won't support Ricky Hutchins or Patricia Stanze. Who do you think they will turn to when they need someone to take your place? Ben will recommend Marty, and he'll be fire chief. That's the way it's going to be."

"I can't deny it could happen that way. He still won't be *my* choice for chief. I'm sorry he wasn't here to get started when everyone else was. I can't change that."

Vivian put her mug down on the table. "Well, it seems you have your mind set against my son. I guess there's nothing more to say. At least not to you."

"Just out of curiosity," Stella asked, "why do you want him to be chief so badly? Why not go intimidate someone else into giving him a job? Why doesn't my grandfather hire him to run the pepper plant?"

Vivian got to her feet and smiled. "I had so hoped you and I would be friends."

Stella smiled back at her. "I heard you wanted Marty and me to get married so you'd know the Carson money was secure."

"I can't imagine where you heard such a thing. I would never want my son involved with someone like you, bless your heart. I have high hopes for him. Don't worry about the money, Stella. Marty and I have that all taken care of. You enjoy those peppers now. I'll see you later."

Chapter 28

~~~~~~~~

Stella closed the door behind her and waited for the BMW to leave the driveway before she addressed Eric. "Well? What do you think? Does she want me to marry her son or not?"

"I think it's hard to say. I don't trust her."

"What a surprise." Stella sat on the sofa after putting the two cups into the sink. "Is there anyone living or dead in Sweet Pepper who likes or trusts the Carson family?"

"If so, I don't know them. But I've been out of circulation for a while."

"Did you take Adam Presley's file from the firehouse?"

"No. Did you lose it?"

"I'm not sure. I put it in the desk drawer in the office. It wasn't there when I got back."

"Have you considered that Marty might be spying on you for the old man?"

"You know, this infighting is hard to get around. You guys need a scorecard that says who the good guys and bad guys are."

"What did Walt have to say about everything?"

"Not all that much. He told me that the two of you knew something was wrong but didn't work hard enough to get around the terrible Carson family. Was there something more than what I've read in the files so far? Did you leave something out?"

"We might have. It was a long time ago, and I'm a little hazy on that time."

Stella thought he might mean he was hazy about the time when he died. She didn't ask him if he thought, like Walt, that her grandfather was responsible for his death.

"Chief Rogers released Victor today after the DA refused to prosecute him for murder. He'll still stand trial for the arson. He's out on bond now," Eric informed her.

"How do you know that?"

"Chief Rogers came by earlier to see you. He waited around for a while, then got the call from the DA. He was in my proximity."

She smiled. "You're better than a guard dog, you know? You keep people away *and* spy on them. Besides, Walt said you were one of the best people he ever knew."

"Yeah, I liked him too. I'm glad he's still out there. Does he still make that hard cider?"

"Yeah. John and I had some in the backyard, once we got past Walt's shotgun."

Eric laughed. "You're lucky he's older or you wouldn't be telling me about it right now."

Stella glanced at her watch. "I'm supposed to go to town for lessons on how to judge foods made from chocolate and peppers. Do you have a recipe I can pinch?"

"I do." A handwritten recipe floated off the cabinet toward her. "Candied peppers. I entered this one year in the contest. I didn't win. That seems like it was a thousand years ago. I don't think anyone will remember. The secret ingredient is the cardamom in the sugar syrup."

"Hot peppers with candy syrup?" She wrinkled her nose. "Okay. I'll use it. Thanks."

"Like I said, watch your back. You have the Carson target

on it along with any hard feelings from the questions you've been asking about Tory's and Adam's deaths."

"Thanks for worrying about me. Have you thought any more about showing yourself? As enlightening as our conversations are, they'd be better if I could see you."

"I'm still thinking that over. I'll talk to you later."

Stella drove back into town mulling over her encounter with Vivian and wondering if it was possible that Greg Lambert had killed Adam Presley. She also thought about Tagger. It had been a long time, as Eric had said. She couldn't imagine what kind of evidence it would take to get Chief Rogers to reopen the case.

Greg was seeing Tory on the side before Adam had died. Tagger thought he was going to be with Tory when he got back from Vietnam. Both were good suspects. She wondered if Tory had considered the possibility that Tagger had set Adam on fire or if she'd dismissed him, like everyone else.

John talked about Marty being the Teflon man, but she thought Tagger could hold that title too. No matter what he did, people let it slide because he was an old hero. Had that blinded Eric too?

All of the judges were meeting at Myra Strickland's home. Stella wasn't looking forward to seeing the matriarch of the Sweet Pepper Festival. The burned hulk of Tory's house was still a public eyesore. She really didn't think it would be removed from Main Street during the week before the festival.

There were already dozens of people she recognized at the three-story Victorian where the Strickland family had lived for generations. Bill and Lucinda Waxman were there, along with Tommy Potter, Mayor Wando and his wife, Jill, and Hugh Morton, the town attorney.

Elvita and Theodora met Stella at the door, urging her to come in. Stella showed them her recipe for candied peppers, and they were both very pleased. "Just make up a quick batch and we'll be set. This is *so* much fun!"

The two women introduced her to everyone.

"You know," said Pat Smith of the *Sweet Pepper Gazette*, "judging the chocolate and pepper part of the festival recipe contest is probably the most prestigious judging position at the festival."

Pat's husband took Stella's picture. "That's true. I think it might've been the first recipe contest in the festival. What's better than chocolate and peppers?"

The husband and wife editorial pair went on to describe all the various winning ways residents had paired chocolate and peppers in the past. Stella listened as she watched her grandfather and Vivian come in, followed by Greg Lambert and a woman who acted like his wife.

Chief Rogers arrived next. Judging from his unhappy scowl, he'd rather have been anyplace else in the world. Flo, from the Sweet Pepper Bed and Breakfast, joined the group too. It seemed to take a lot of people to judge the recipe contests.

When everyone had small china plates full of snacks and cups of coffee or tea in hand, Myra Strickland climbed up on a chair and clapped her hands to get their attention.

"It's nice you all want to mingle, but let's not forget that this is serious business. We have more than two hundred recipes that have to be judged. Those of you who have done this before know we have strict protocols to follow. We must adhere to our policies if we are going to maintain the good reputation of our festival."

Everyone found a way to juggle their drinks and snacks so they could applaud. Myra's white poodle, dressed in bright red like his owner, jumped and barked around the chair where she stood.

"Now we're going to divide up into small groups—those who have judged before will mentor those who haven't. I have a list of things that need to be said and done during the judging, especially if one of the contestants is present. We don't want to be sued, do we?"

Stella was put in a group with Lucinda Waxman, Tommy Potter, and Vivian. *Bad choice.* The conversation among them was limited—how to handle contestants who didn't win and key words to use when describing the foods they were judging.

"You should never say 'I don't like this.' Instead, say 'This is a good effort,'" Lucinda explained. "And never make a scrunchy face, as my granddaughter does when she eats broccoli. People could take that the wrong way."

"Always fill out your evaluation forms." Vivian held one up. "This is your best way to stay out of trouble. Write down all of your thoughts on the product you're judging. Don't leave anything out, and be sure to sign it. Your contestants will never see your evaluation forms. They are strictly confidential."

"I know now why I've never done this before," Tommy grumbled.

"Your dear wife, Ethel Lou, participated many times in judging and created the most amazing recipes," Lucinda reminded him.

"I know. But I'm not Ethel Lou. I might not be cut out to judge cold pepper dishes. Maybe I could trade with Chief Griffin. I like sweets better." He winked at Stella, who would've been glad to switch categories with him.

"We don't do things that way, Tommy," Vivian said. "Once a judge accepts his or her category for a festival, it is written in stone."

Lucinda solemnly nodded. "It's the way it has been done and shall always be done."

Tommy finished his lemonade. "Whatever. I wish you had something stronger than coffee. Excuse me while I get something real to drink."

Lucinda and Vivian exchanged disturbed glances. Myra seemed to pick up on their difficulties and came to see if everything was all right. Lucinda explained Tommy's problem. Myra immediately headed off in the same direction as the hardware store owner.

"I wouldn't want to be him." Lucinda shuddered. "What category are you judging this year, Vivian?"

"I got stuffed peppers this year." Vivian smiled. "You?"

"Cake, nonchocolate." Lucinda didn't seem pleased with her category either. She looked at Stella. "You did get the best category, Chief Griffin. Although judging the hottest peppers might have been more your forte. I mean, since you are the fire chief and all."

"It's been many years since we've had a fire chief judging recipes in the festival," Myra recalled as she returned. "Eric Gamlyn was always such a good sport, no matter what we asked him to do. And so handsome. The ladies didn't care if they won or not. He had such a charming way of telling them that they had lost."

"I'm sure Chief Griffin will have a similar charm, at least with the menfolk," Vivian said. "The men of Sweet Pepper are already crazy running after her."

Both ladies simpered and stared at Stella like she was a bug under a microscope. Seeing that the small groups were starting to break up, Stella excused herself and went to find a sincerely friendly face.

Flo was sitting at a coffee table with a few other people, none of whom Stella knew. She stood behind them as they looked at an old high school yearbook and talked about the people in the photos.

"Oh, Stella, come and see." Flo drew her into the group and introduced her to everyone. "Here's your mother. Wasn't she beautiful? You look exactly like her, except that her hair was dark. Barbara had hair like her mama. I'll bet she's still knocking them dead."

Stella looked at the black-and-white picture, surprised to find that she *did* look a lot like her mother when her mother was younger. She'd always thought she looked more like her Irish father. Of course, she hadn't known there was another family to look like until recently.

She pulled out her cell phone, which had a recent picture of her mother and father, and passed it around. "I think she's doing all right."

"Is this your daddy?" Flo asked. "He's a handsome devil.

No wonder Barbara stayed up there. If I'd known the men were so good-looking, I'd have gone with her."

Everyone else in the group stopped chattering and stared at someone behind Flo's and Stella's backs. Flo turned around and smiled at Ben Carson. "We were admiring Barbara—then and now. She looked like her mother. Stella could be Miss Abigail's twin, couldn't she?"

Ben didn't reply. He walked away without a word.

Perry Dumont, who owned the local cable TV station, grimaced as he whispered, "Lucky for you the local land-owners can't say 'Off with your head,' Flo, or you'd be walking around without one right now."

His wife, Lacie, crossed herself and shuddered. "Like the ghost on Second Street who lost her head in that carriage accident back in 1820. They never found it. They say she's still looking for it. I think it was last June that Cindy Reynolds saw her."

"That's poppycock," her husband said. "If you can't vid-eotape it, it's not real."

Lacie searched Stella's face. "I heard Abigail haunts the Carson estate. She's looking for justice." Lacie's voice dropped dramatically. "She wants to find the one who killed her."

Perry snorted. "I'd think that would be easy enough since Ben Carson still lives there."

Lacie shushed him. She turned back to look at Stella. "Have you seen her ghost?"

"No." Stella felt uneasy with the conversation. "I've only been there a few times." She thought about Abigail's face in the portrait.

"You should be asking her about Eric Gamlyn's ghost up at the old cabin." Flo changed the subject. "Stella was having such a time with him, she had to spend the night with me."

"That's outrageous," Perry declared, and everyone in the group nodded. "I still don't understand why the town council put someone as important as our fire chief up there when they know what's going on. They need to burn that place down."

"Oh no! It's so beautiful," Stella burst out. "I think I was having a problem adjusting to the silence of the place. It's much noisier back home."

Flo shook her head. "That's enough with the ghosties and ghoulies. Look. It's a picture of Tory." She smiled at Stella. "She was a couple years older than us. I don't know about anyone else, but I wish her ghost would come back and tell us what happened to *her*."

"Yeah, I heard today they let her devil son out of jail," Perry said. "Not enough evidence, the DA said. It's a shame. We all know he killed her."

Pat and Smitty from the *Gazette* joined them as though the merest mention of hard news had drawn them from the other side of the room, away from the buffet table.

"We were there in the courtroom," Pat said. "Baker Lockwood at the pharmacy swore under oath that Tory sent Victor for her insulin all the time. It made sense that his fingerprints were on the box. The DA didn't have anything else."

"Except that he set her house on fire." Myra stuck her head in on the conversation. "He should go to prison for that."

"He probably will," Smitty replied. "They could still charge him with attempted murder, the DA said. After all, he said he didn't know Tory was in the house, but how can we be sure?"

"Well, all I know is that we're no closer to getting that mess cleaned up." Myra glared at Stella. "And here we are just a week from the Sweet Pepper Festival. It doesn't speak well for us as a town."

"It may be inconvenient," Stella said, "but finding out the truth about what happened to Tory is important. I'm sure any of you would want to know we'd done our best finding the truth for you too."

Myra stuck her nose in the air and left the group, cornering Chief Rogers with another request to clean up Tory's house before the festival.

"I think that's all well and good," Lacie said, "but if Victor didn't kill his mother, who did?"

They all looked at Stella. Pat took out her notebook and pen.

"The police don't know yet. They're still looking at all the evidence. I wish there was an easy answer."

"Has anyone talked to Greg Lambert yet?" Perry bluntly asked. "He's a good bet."

"That's crazy talk," Flo said. "Why would Greg want to kill Tory?"

"I don't like to speak ill of the dead," Perry began, "but we all know Tory, bless her soul, was a flirt and a two-timer when she was young. Look how she yanked around Tagger Reamis. Then she married that car salesman and walked out with Greg when he wasn't looking."

"We all know she was pregnant with Greg's baby before Adam died," Flo added.

Perry nodded. "A man can only take so much. She made a fool of every man she ever dated. If Victor didn't kill her, I'd put my money on Greg."

"What about Tagger?" Stella had to ask.

"Oh, he's a hero," Lacie said. "He would never do something like that."

"Greg's another story," Perry added. "He's no hero."

That silenced the conversation for a moment. Some of the group drifted off.

Flo gently rubbed her finger on Tory's picture in the yearbook. "She had a hard life, you know. Her daddy was so mean to her. When she got out from under his roof, she thought it would be okay. Then there were all those fires— her car blew up the day she married Adam Presley. Then he died that terrible way. No wonder she was so happy to have our own fire department again. It didn't help, did it? She still kind of died in a fire. It was like she knew."

Chapter 29

On her way home, Stella thought about everything she'd heard at the event. She wasn't sure any of it was really important to finding Tory's killer. She'd learned a lot about how people felt about things.

Seeing that old picture of her mother had made her homesick. When she went out to the Cherokee, there were two messages on her phone. Her mother must've been feeling the same way. She tried returning those calls as she left Myra's house. She ended up playing phone tag and leaving her own messages. She'd have to try again in the morning.

Stella planned to razz Eric about his legendary charm and good looks. Maybe it was mean taunting a ghost. She hoped he'd show himself to prove how handsome he was. It wasn't that she didn't know what he looked like when he was alive. How would he appear now?

The light was on outside the cabin when she drove up. The door opened as usual, before she could reach the knob. There was an unfamiliar sound when she walked inside. Hero was there, whimpering and whining. He ran right up to her and started licking her boots.

"How did you get here?" Stella bent down and scratched behind his ears. He immediately rolled over and let her rub his soft white tummy. "Eric?"

"He was lonely," the familiar voice said.

"You could've opened the kitchen door at the firehouse and let him in there with Banyin. It would've been easier than bringing him up here."

"Your communications person was asleep."

"It happens. The alert will wake her up if she needs to call everyone."

"That doesn't make the puppy feel any better. Animals need attention."

Hero cuddled up by her foot, as though helping Eric make his point. He put one little paw on her boot and sighed.

"I hope you're prepared to help with cleanup," she said. "I haven't had a pet since I was a kid. My parents took care of it then."

"You're a big girl now. You can handle it."

"We'll see." She moved, and the puppy followed her to the sofa. "They loved the candied pepper recipe. Now I have to make it. Speaking of handling things, I heard an earful tonight at the warm-up for the festival judging. It seems you did a remarkable job 'handling' all the women who entered your contest category."

"What?" He sounded surprised.

"He was so handsome and had such a way with him," she said, badly mimicking Myra's southern accent. "They didn't even care when they lost."

"I'm blushing."

"Let me see. Why not show yourself? Are you afraid you won't live up to all the legendary hype?"

She heard him sigh. The entire cabin sighed with him. "I tried to tell you the other night when you passed out—I'm not sure what that would be like."

"What do you mean?" She asked the question at the same time that her emergency pager went off. "Hold that thought.

And take care of Hero. We'll talk about both of these things when I get back."

When she was gone, Eric appeared next to Hero. "What do you think? Would I scare her away?"

The puppy wagged his tail and barked.

"I wish I knew if that was good or bad."

Most of the volunteers were at the firehouse, in gear and ready to go, by the time Stella arrived. Only one or two were missing.

"Have you seen Hero?" Kimmie asked, brandishing a pryax. "When we got here, Sylvia noticed right away that he was gone. She went crazy trying to find him. David had to put her in the car."

"He's at my place," Stella explained as she put on her boots. "We'll talk about it later."

"Of course. Sorry, Chief." Kimmie looked a little flustered, worried that she had kept the team from something important. She took her pryax and climbed into the engine to wait.

Stella was putting on her helmet and bunker coat as she climbed in beside Ricky. She was surprised when John scooted in next to her, nudging her to the middle of the large seat as he closed the door behind him.

"Remember how we talked about making runs to Frog Pond and Big Bear Springs?"

"Sure. Is that where we're headed?"

He nodded, his mouth a tight line in the dimly lit interior of the cab. "Walt Fenway's place."

They stared at each other without speaking, both thinking the same thing.

"What?" Ricky demanded as they turned out of the parking lot. "What's going on? Who is Walt Fenway? That name sounds familiar but—"

"He used to be the police chief," John explained.

"We questioned him about Adam Presley's death," Stella

added. "This seems like a big coincidence. Word spreads fast in Sweet Pepper. What was someone afraid he'd told us?"

"Maybe it was enough that he talked to us at all," John said. "I haven't told anyone we went out there, have you?"

"No."

"Are you thinking someone in the fire brigade started this fire?" Ricky asked. "That's plain crazy."

"Except that Marty could've heard us talking about going out there," John reminded Stella. "Maybe this thing with Adam Presley affects the Carson interests. Maybe that's why the old man didn't want the fire chief and Walt investigating way back when."

The engine and pumper passed several cars that had pulled off the road to wait. Children waved to them and a few of the volunteers waved back. Ricky pulled the horn. It blared into the evening, scaring a group of chickens that had been roosting next to the road.

Ricky swung the engine onto the old gravel road that led to Walt's house about ten minutes after they'd left the firehouse.

Long before they'd reached the burning cabin, the heavy smoke told her that the fire was fully involved. Given the size of the cabin, it wouldn't take much to make it a complete loss. She hoped the fire hadn't had time to spread to the woods around it and, more important, that Walt had escaped.

She was glad they had a good size group of volunteers. She might need all of them to handle the fire.

There was no point in using the thermal imager—no part of the cabin had escaped the inferno. With no city water in the area, they would have to rely on the water supply in the pumper. She hoped it was enough.

"I know we're outside," she yelled to her volunteers over the roar of the fire. "But wear your breathing apparatus. There are chemicals in the treated wood that could be dangerous. Make sure you can see each other while you're working. No one goes off by themselves."

As she'd feared, the fire had spread to several of the trees, flames eating up the dry fall leaves, making them look like giant torches against the night sky.

She assigned part of the group to preventing the fire from spreading and the rest to putting out the fire in the cabin. John led the group working in the woods since he knew the area so well. Stella didn't want anyone falling off the mountain.

When everyone was engaged in doing their jobs, she walked around the perimeter of the area to look for any sign of Walt. If he was still inside the cabin, he was dead. She hoped he'd managed to escape and was somewhere outside the fire zone. She knew he might need help. The faster she found him, the better.

The smoke was so thick and black, she could hardly make out anything within a hundred yards around the cabin. It didn't help that it was dark and there were no outside lights anywhere close by. They had left the streetlights back on the main road. If Walt was injured, maybe unconscious, it might be impossible to find him.

Just as she considered calling in the sheriff for help in the search, she found Walt. He was sitting on a keg of his hard apple cider, a few hundred yards from the cabin, with a cup in his hands. The orange light from the fire illuminated his face as he watched his home burn. He'd moved in the opposite direction that the wind was blowing so the smoke wasn't affecting him.

"Walt," she called his name. "Are you all right? Do you need medical attention?"

He turned his head to look at her. "Of course I'm not all right. I started building that cabin when I was still Sweet Pepper's police chief so I could retire here. I'm too far from anyplace to get fire insurance I could afford. The only thing I *don't* need is medical attention, Chief Griffin. Thanks for offering anyway."

Stella noticed there were two other barrels of cider around him. They were probably the only possessions that had survived the fire. "Do you know what happened?"

"I believe I do. Someone didn't like me talking to you and John. I went out for supper at the fish house and came back to find this going on. I called 911 myself from the convenience store on the highway."

"At least you weren't injured."

"Yeah. Maybe. Don't it make you wonder what someone was afraid I might *still* say to you?"

"You mean you didn't tell us everything?"

"If I had, there would be no need for this. I think this was a friendly warning. Whoever it was didn't want to kill me or they would've done it while I was asleep. Smell that kerosene? The place was soaked in it."

Stella had smelled it. She'd thought the odor might have come from the chemicals used to treat the lumber in the cabin. "Like Tory's place. It seems hard to believe that Victor would press his luck so soon. He's not crazy. This might be a setup not only to warn you, but also to get him thrown back in jail again."

"We need to speak with Don Rogers when you're done here and I've had some coffee." He sniffed. "I've had a little too much cider sitting around feeling sorry for myself. It takes a lot to sit and watch your home burn down to the ground."

Stella agreed and went to check on her team while Walt got himself together.

"The pumper's running low," Allen yelled at her over the roar of the fire. "I don't think we have enough water to put out the trees and the house."

"Let's give the forest service a call," John suggested. "We could get them to bring Big Bertha. That's the plane that drops the water bombs. This is as much their concern as ours. Nobody wants to see a thousand acres or more burn."

Stella gave him the go-ahead, and John radioed the ranger station farther out in the county. The forest service agreed to send Big Bertha, but it wouldn't be for an hour or more. That was the best they could do.

She gathered everyone together and told them they had

a tough fight ahead of them. "We'll have to keep going, do what we can until the plane gets here. Use whatever you have to and keep the sparks down. Let's get out the shovels and the fire extinguishers. Use your boots if you have to." Stella looked into their tired, soot-blackened faces and wished she had better news before she sent everyone back to work.

The team used the last of the water to douse the flames from the cabin. Petey, Ricky, Kimmie, and David moved in with fire extinguishers and shovels to make sure there were no hidden embers ready to flare up again.

The rest of the team did what they could using fire extinguishers, shovels, and fire-retardant tarps to keep the sparks from lighting anything on the ground even as flames shot from tree to tree above them.

"She's coming in," John finally alerted them to the plane's approach.

"Everyone out of the way," Stella yelled. "Back up to the road."

Walt joined them at the gravel road, less than an eighth of a mile from where the fire burned. He'd enlisted Allen and Marty's help in carrying the remaining kegs of apple cider.

They all huddled together as the pink light of dawn climbed over the tops of the mountains. The large gray plane flew low over the burning trees and dropped thousands of gallons of water across them, some of it splashing back on the weary firefighters, despite the distance.

The water washed down the side of the mountain, dropping like a wave across the trees and the cabin. Some trees cracked under the onslaught and fell to the ground. Hot spots still sizzled in the leaves and peat moss, but there were no visible flames as the plane flew onward.

"They want to know if we need more," John said. "It's a round-trip of at least forty minutes."

"Let's take a quick look," Stella said. "We'll let them know before they get back to their base."

All of the firefighters trooped back into the woods, brandishing shovels, rakes, and whatever else they could find to search for hot spots. Walt marched around too, looking things over. Stella had misgivings about an untrained worker being in the fire zone. She couldn't talk him out of it, and she couldn't argue that he was better trained for emergencies than most of her people.

With the sun starting to peek down on them, the volunteers went over most of the smoking areas and made sure the fire was dead. The long battle showed in their dragging footsteps and exhausted eyes. But they put out every remaining spark.

Stella told John to make the call and tell the forest service they wouldn't need to send Big Bertha out again. "Thank them for us," she said, then turned to her team. "I want everyone who came on the pumper to go back to the firehouse. I know you're tired, but I need you to fill up and clean up. Then go home. You guys have worked hard tonight. Get some rest. Practice is canceled for today."

It warmed her heart that they didn't want to leave the scene before the engine team, but she insisted. "I hope to God nothing else happens in the next twenty-four hours, but we have to be prepared. We'll be leaving soon too. You guys go home."

The pumper team was almost too exhausted to argue the point any further. Stella ignored their halfhearted protests, and, eventually, they were on the pumper and headed back to the firehouse.

Stella worked on her on-scene report while John, Ricky, and the others checked for hot spots one last time. They also looked for anything of Walt's that hadn't been destroyed in the fire, as well as any evidence that might have been left behind by the arsonist.

"We found an empty kerosene can like the one used at Tory's." Ricky held up the can. "They sell these at Potter's Hardware and in Pigeon Forge at the big-box stores. They're a dime a dozen."

"Keep it anyway." She was sitting in the engine and didn't look up from her paperwork. "Get it into an evidence bag and label it. Let's do this right in case we can figure out who's responsible."

There was yellow tape around the area, advising everyone to stay away until the investigation was complete.

John pulled himself up into the truck. "I think we could get some help from the forest service investigating this. There could be extra penalties involved for whoever set the fire since this is part of a national park."

Stella smiled at him. There was a large white space where he'd touched the thick black soot that otherwise covered his face. "Really? What national park are we in?"

"The Great Smoky Mountains National Park, darlin'." He leaned closer to her. "You're laughing at my dirty face, aren't you?" He took one of his fingers and cleared a section of her dirty face. "This is definitely a case of the pot calling the kettle black."

She closed her eyes as his lips touched hers briefly. Then Ricky and the rest of the team returned from putting out the yellow warning tape.

John winked at her as they got back in the truck and Ricky got behind the wheel. Walt had decided to ride in back with his remaining kegs. The engine took off, leaving the blackened area of the forest behind them. It was like a deep wound cut into the side of the mountain, burnt trees like twigs barely standing.

Stella was too surprised by John's display of affection to finish the last part of her paperwork. It hadn't been a big kiss, but sweet and light. Maybe it was the beginning of something more between them. She'd been disappointed before when she'd had that thought. She hoped this time would be different. She really liked John, his common sense and dependability. He had to get over the Carson curse.

With the adrenaline from the fire gone, it was all the team could do to clean up and be ready for the next call. Stella hated to see them so depleted, and recognized the over-whelming exhaustion that was dragging them down. She felt much the same way. Her years of training and previous experience gave her more stamina.

The pumper team came back from filling the vehicle as the team from the engine was storing their gear. There was only one shower at the firehouse. Even though cleaning the soot and smoky odor out their personal vehicles would be a big job later, most of them opted to shower and change at home.

Stella offered a few words of praise before they all left. Walt added his thanks for their efforts as he worked his way through a third cup of coffee. He was calling friends, trying to find a place to stay for a while. Hero was back at the firehouse, to Kimmie and David's amazement. They decided to take the puppy home with them for the day to make Sylvia feel better.

Stella had cleaned her gear and put it away. She showered and washed her hair but her jeans and T-shirt she'd worn under her bunker coat and pants still smelled like the fire and kerosene to her.

She rubbed her tired eyes and tried to concentrate on finishing her report.

"Glad you're safe," Eric whispered from somewhere immediately behind her, though her back was against the wall. "What now?"

Chapter 30

~~~~~~~~

"I don't know," she admitted as she tried to concentrate on her report. It was a lot easier to close the door on living people. Eric wasn't very good at respecting privacy. "Got any ideas?"

"What does Walt know that made someone want to kill him?"

"He thinks whoever started the fire didn't want to kill him. He thinks it was just to scare him off. As soon as everyone gets themselves together, we're going to see Chief Rogers and find out if he can help."

"I heard Walt telling one of the volunteers that he thinks the kerosene signature means Victor Lambert is responsible."

"I don't think anyone is that stupid. Victor got off on one murder charge. He's a little strange, but I don't think he's crazy."

"Who then?"

Stella watched an old baseball fly up and down in the air right off the edge of her desk. She kind of wondered how she'd gotten to this place where she could witness such a thing and not be totally freaked out by it.

"Someone wants us to think it's Victor so we waste our time on him again."

"What did Walt tell you earlier? Did it seem important?"

She shrugged. "We talked about Tory and Greg Lambert. What about *him*?"

"Greg? I guess it's possible he could've killed Adam. Why would he kill Tory now?"

"Maybe he couldn't stand it anymore?" She ran her hand through her hair. "I don't know. Does he have a history with fire?"

"Not that I'm aware of. Tory was the one with that problem."

"I've heard that. I'm almost too tired to think about it right now."

"There's one more thing, Stella. I saw Tagger take your folder with Adam's information out to the trash while you were gone."

"What?" She sat up, wide awake. "Why would he do that?"

"I don't know," Eric admitted. "I can't believe Tagger would have had anything to do with killing Adam. Or Tory. He didn't want you to look at it for some reason."

John knocked on the door. He didn't wait for her to tell him to come in. He entered the office and looked around. "Are you in here alone?"

She heard Eric's soft chuckle. This was something she'd worried about happening. "Yes. Why?"

John inspected the tiny office again then shrugged. "Nothing. If you're finished with the report, I think the three of us should head into town. I have the police car. I'll meet you and Walt at town hall."

"All right. I'll see you there." Stella pushed herself to her feet. She was going to have to make the meeting, smoky-smelling clothes and all.

When John left, Eric said, "Don't forget you have an appointment at the pepper plant to follow up on your citation. That should give you a chance to size up Greg Lambert again."

"Have you been looking at my computer? Can ghosts do that?"

"This ghost can. I love electronics. Talk to you later."

Stella sighed and went to find Walt. He talked nonstop on the way into town. Maybe too much caffeine trying to get rid of the effects of too much cider.

She thought about Tagger, wondering if everyone had misjudged him. Even Eric had admitted there was something off about the other man taking her folder. Was he trying to cover something up?

John had apparently already given Chief Rogers a heads-up on the fire. By the time Stella and Walt walked into town hall, the chief had sent someone out to pick up Victor.

"Chief Rogers." Walt shook his hand. "It's good to see you again. You're doing a decent job, like I knew you would." Walt smiled at Stella. "Don here was the best officer I ever worked with. I was glad he was here when it was time for me to retire."

"It's because I had the best teacher in the world, Chief Fenway," Don said. "I still ask myself, 'What would Walt do?'"

Stella was already tired of their mutual admiration society. She had better things to do than listen to them congratulate each other. "I hear you brought in Victor Lambert."

"You bet. John told me the house was torched with kerosene. I think that warrants a conversation with him, don't you, Walt?" Chief Rogers smiled smugly at Stella as he said it. "Did you have someone else in mind?"

"No," she admitted. "Don't you think that's a little obvious? Anyone can get kerosene, and everyone knows Victor used it on Tory's house."

Chief Rogers burst out laughing. "Walt, don't you just love our fire chief? She's got some spunk, I'll say that for her."

Walt was less condescending. "She did a bang-up job out there at my place last night, Don. I've heard she's done a good job overall while she's been here. That's about all we can expect from a Yankee."

They both laughed at that. Stella was definitely not in the mood for it. "I have an appointment at the pepper plant. I'm sure you gentlemen can interrogate Victor without me. Let me know if he cracks and tells you all the details. I'll see you both later."

She passed John on his way into the office. "Where are you going? I thought you wanted to be here for this."

"Not really. I have to go out to the pepper plant and start checking on their progress in dealing with the citation. I don't think I'm really needed here."

John smiled. "Don't let the chiefs get to you. You're a chief too. You have a right to be here."

She drew him away from the door and the empty town clerk's desk. "I don't believe Victor had anything to do with the fire last night. Chief Rogers seems sure of it. I think we're missing the big picture. There's something else going on."

"Okay. I'll fill you in when you get back. Not that you have to worry overly much about the old man not working with you to clean up the ducts. You seem to have him eating out of your hand. Do what you think is right, Stella." He put his hand on her arm. "I know it's still early—what about lunch?"

She searched his face, trying to decide if he was sincere. With the kiss from early that morning still fresh, she decided that he was. "Sure. Want to meet somewhere?"

"No. I'll call you around that time. I don't want to eat at the café. Maybe we can find someplace a little more private."

She agreed and left town hall with a pleasant warmth filling her tired brain. She drove to the Sweet Pepper packing plant with her checklist on her clipboard, thinking again about what Walt had said about Greg and Tory.

They were seeing each other before Adam died. They were together long enough to produce a child who'd turned into a man most people didn't like. Victor had torched his own house hoping it would scare his mother away.

She couldn't add Victor's poor judgment to the list of Greg's sins.

It didn't make much sense that Greg would suddenly want Tory dead. They'd been divorced for years. What would he gain by it now?

The same could be said about Tagger, she supposed. It had been forty years since Tory had rejected him. Why would he kill her now?

On the other hand, both men looked like good suspects for Adam Presley's death.

Could Tory's continued investigation into Adam's death be the answer? Had she found out something that had suddenly made her the target? That could put Tagger and Greg back on the suspect list for Tory's death.

The pepper plant parking lot was filled with hundreds of cars during the day shift. Trucks pulled in and out, delivering the jars of peppers that kept the town going. Stella parked near the front door of the old brick office building and found Greg waiting for her with a clipboard of his own.

"Good morning, Chief Griffin. I'm sorry we got off to such a bad start at the duct fire. I've been instructed to assist you in any way I can. Where would you like to start?"

Stella wanted to see the new connection to the plant water tower. Greg took her to a golf cart, and the two of them rode to the site. The grounds of the factory were much larger than she'd appreciated at night. The original red brick building was like a doorway to the huge metal buildings where most of the work went on.

"Have you started work on the ducts?" she asked Greg.

"We've contacted an engineering firm that is drawing up plans for the change. We want to make sure it gets done right so it's all good for a long time into the future."

Stella made a note of it and the date. "That sounds fine, Greg. I'd like to see those diagrams in the next few weeks. I need a timetable for the work to be done as well."

His lips compressed a little. Clearly he wasn't used to anyone except Ben Carson questioning his authority. He got through it, though, and made a note on his own clipboard when they reached the water tower.

True to his word, Ben had replaced the connection so that the fire brigade would be able to access what they needed in case of a fire at the facility.

Stella wondered, as she made a show of examining the connection, how she could ask Greg about Tory. She decided to approach it by bringing up the fire last night at Walt's place, and his son's possible involvement.

"I'm sorry about what happened with your son this morning." She hoped she looked sympathetic and not just sooty and tired after the long night.

"What did Victor do now?" Greg demanded.

"Chief Rogers thinks he may have started the fire at Walt Fenway's place. He picked him up for questioning. You didn't know?"

"No. I didn't know." Greg scratched his head. "Fenway? Isn't he the retired police chief? I didn't even know he was still alive."

"The fire was started with kerosene—similar to the fire started at your ex-wife's home." She watched his face for any sign of what he was thinking. If there was a change in his expression, she didn't see it.

"I gave that boy my name, but I washed my hands of him many years ago. He was born evil, pure and simple. Tory and I broke up because of him. I couldn't live with the devil any longer. I don't know how she stood him for so long."

"He's still your son. Arson seems to run in the family." She was tired of beating around the bush. She needed some real answers.

"It doesn't run in *my* family." His chin came up, and his mouth became a thin line. "It seemed to run in Tory's life, what with her first husband's tragic accident. It followed her after that when our car caught fire as we were leaving our wedding. It dogged us through our years of marriage."

"Are you saying Tory was responsible for those fires?"

"No, of course not. She was terrified that she would die in a fire—like Adam. After a while, I was scared too. It seemed like there were hundreds of little fires popping up.

The shed caught on fire. A fire started in the yard. The microwave blew up. It was always something."

Stella was beginning to think that Greg might be what was wrong with his son. "Who do you think started all those fires?"

"Evil begets evil." Greg's face turned a livid shade of red. "Don't you see? It wasn't really the boy's fault. I shouldn't have married Tory knowing she'd been unfaithful to Adam."

That was almost too pompous to be believed. "She was unfaithful to Adam with *you*, Greg. While that may not be a perfect way to live, it's not evil to have a child out of wedlock. Besides, you got married as soon as Adam was dead. I guess you were lucky he died, huh?"

"You can call it luck if you want to, Chief Griffin. Tory was cursed for what happened to Adam. Did it occur to you that she might have killed him herself to get rid of him?"

That surprised her, but it gave her a chance to speak plainly. "No. It occurred to me that *you* might have killed him."

He seemed dumbfounded, and spluttered before he could speak clearly. "I would never do such a thing! What Tory and I did was wrong. I know that now. I wouldn't have killed Adam for her."

His outrage was hard not to take sincerely. Or perhaps he was simply a very good liar.

"I'm sorry for how things turned out for you and Tory," she said. "Were you angry enough about your marriage failing and Vic being different than you wanted to kill her now?"

He made a gurgling noise that sounded like muted laughter. "Take her life? I loved her, despite everything. God help me. I wish every day that the two of us were still together. When I heard that Victor killed her, a part of me died too. I would never have left her if she'd agreed to leave here and get away from him."

Chapter 31

~~~~~~~~~~

"Victor's lawyer showed up before we could ask him anything," John explained over lunch. "We had nothing to hold him on, and the chief had to let him go."

Stella was pleased when they ended up at the VFW Park, sitting at a picnic table, eating box lunches from the café. It was a clever way of spending time alone together since they were the only ones in the park.

She told him about her conversation with Greg. "He's carrying around a lot of guilt for sleeping with Tory before she was divorced. He hates his son for it."

"Tory was good at keeping secrets. I suppose she made Greg good at it too."

"Anyway, I don't think he was involved. Besides the fact that he sounds like he's still in love with Tory, apparently he was at the plant when she was killed. There was some kind of problem with the pepper-packing line."

John crunched a pickle. "So that leaves us with Tagger? I'm not crazy about that."

"I know. He's a hero." Stella finished her sandwich and yawned. "Sorry. I suppose we're all walking around yawning today."

"You should go home and get some rest," he advised. "You never know what's gonna come up next."

"That sounds great, but I have to go and try on my dress and hat for the festival. I'm going to be French, you know."

He smiled. "Like a French-maid kind of thing?"

"I think it might be more like a French woman from a Monet painting. I'm worried about the hat."

"You even look good in a fireman's helmet, Stella. I can't imagine that anything they'd find for you to wear could make you look bad."

He kissed her lightly again, and she wondered what had ramped up their budding relationship. They'd managed to go almost a whole day without him looking at her in disgust because her grandfather was Ben Carson. Of course, some of that time was spent fighting a fire. She wasn't sure that counted.

Whatever it was, she wasn't going to ask him about it. They walked hand in hand back to the café where they'd both left their vehicles. It was nice. She hoped it would continue.

They said good-bye—no kiss in front of the crowded café. Stella felt the speculative gazes on them anyway as she left him there and headed out to Molly Whitehouse's dress-making shop.

It was easier this time, without Elvita and Theodora there, especially since she had to try on the rough version of the dress. It was nicer than she'd expected. The long gown—a walking gown, Molly had called it—was a polite shade of periwinkle that complimented Stella's hair and eyes. It was a little too low cut in the bodice. Molly said she could fix that.

"Let me know about the hat," she said. "I could still add a matching color to the dress if you need it. I'm making a shawl to go with it in case it's chilly that day. Last year, we had snow. You never know what to expect."

Stella yawned and thanked her for her hard work. She went to visit the hatmaker right away, hoping she'd stay awake while she tried on the new creation.

Up and down Main Street, town officials had begun

diverting traffic to make way for the festival. Tents and booths were popping up in every color imaginable. Carpenters were building stages and platforms. Even the big pepper-shaped water tower was being freshly painted.

She'd been in Sweet Pepper long enough to know that the town did a good tourist business from the overflow of visitors to Sevierville and Pigeon Forge. The town also labeled itself as the gateway to the Great Smoky Mountains. This festival was the big event for them. She hadn't noticed until that moment, but all the shops were decorated. There were welcome banners everywhere. Mayor Wando waved as he zipped by in his Sweet Pepper golf cart.

The committee had sent an email and text telling her that she'd receive her supersecret list of contestants and recipes before the end of the day. Her recipe for candied peppers would be among them. There was another reminder that she needed to make samples for the judge.

She hoped she was up to the task. They seemed to have high expectations. It was strange being such a public figure here. She'd be glad to go back to being an anonymous firefighter when she got home.

Home!

She sat down at one of the tables in front of the Daily Grind Coffee Shop and called her mother before she forgot again. While she waited for her mother to pick up, Stella watched the clouds, which were starting to look threatening as they came down from the mountains. She hoped there would be good weather for the festival. It lasted three days. Surely one of those days would be clear.

"Mom?"

"Stella! Thank goodness. I've been trying to get in touch with you."

"I know. Sorry. I've either been busy or out of cell phone range."

"How are you and your grandfather getting along?"

"Okay." She told her about shutting down the pepper plant. "We reached a compromise."

"That's amazing. The years must have mellowed him. I remember that fire chief, the one you were talking about, threatening Dad about the same thing. Dad shut *him* down instead. He wouldn't stand for criticism back then."

"Eric Gamlyn?" Stella smiled, and a woman passing by smiled back and waved. "He's the ghost haunting the cabin where I'm staying."

Barbara laughed. "I'm glad you're enjoying the folklore. Has your grandfather convinced you to stay? Don't bother putting a pretty face on it. I know he wants to steal you away."

"That's not going to happen, Mom. The fire brigade is doing okay. A few more volunteers have joined. I've named two assistant chiefs to take my place. The Sweet Pepper Festival judging committee is dressing me up like some kind of French lady to judge the chocolate and pepper recipe contest. I think I'll be ready to come home very soon."

"Good. It sounds like you have your hands full. Do Myra Strickland and her husband still run the festival?"

"Myra does," Stella replied. "Apparently Mayor Strickland died a few years ago."

"I'm sure a lot has changed since I left." Barbara sighed for the memories of the life she'd left behind. "I miss you, honey. Chief Henry called to ask how you were doing and when you were coming back to work. Doug called too, more than once."

"Doug?" Stella couldn't believe it. "No, Mom. I don't want to talk to him. I don't even want to *think* about him."

"You might be interested to know that he broke up with Chloe. I think it was a stupid mistake. He said he still loves you."

"He had a funny way of showing it."

"Wait until you come back. You and Doug were happy together. You've known each other your whole lives. You may want to give him another chance."

"So in other words, you don't want me to come home."

"What are you saying? Of course I want you to come back. I don't want you to live down there. Sweet Pepper seems like the friendliest little town in the world, but maybe you've noticed, it has a dark underbelly."

Stella shook her head at the idea that Sweet Pepper could have a dark anything compared to Chicago. "Well, let's leave Doug out of the equation, and I should be back home in a couple of weeks."

"What about the Harley?" Stella heard her father yell in the background.

"I've got it all put into boxes," she told her mother, who relayed the joke back to her father. "I'm sending it back to you."

Her father had a few choice words to say that he shouted back at her. Stella promised him she wasn't coming home without it and she thought it would be back on the road in the next few days.

"I have to go and look at my judge's hat," she told her mother. "I'll talk to you guys later. Love to both of you."

Deciding she could wait a few more minutes to visit the hatmaker, Stella ordered a double-shot espresso from Valery, then sat at a sidewalk table drinking it. The Sweet Pepper High School Cougar Marching Band was rehearsing out on the street. They would be performing, along with the award-winning Cougar cheer team, while the festival was going on.

Charlie Johnson from the computer and security service store saw her sitting there and came across the street to speak to her. "Hey there, pretty lady. Just wondering if you were ready to get your laptop back. I think I've fixed those glitches for you."

With everything going on, Stella had totally forgotten about it. She walked back across the street with him to pick it up.

"Hey, I heard about that big fire outside of town last night. Anyone hurt out there? Was old Walt Fenway all right?"

"It was more property damage than anything else." She signed the slip for him to be paid by the town and took the laptop back. She smiled, though. If Eric kept using it, she might need more help with it in the future.

"Well, that's a good thing." Charlie smiled in return and nodded. "You know, this town is gonna miss you when you're gone. I hear you're one of the judges in the Sweet Pepper Festival. I bet you're looking forward to that, huh? Lots of good food."

"Yes. Or at least that's what I've heard. Have you ever been a judge?"

"Who me?" He laughed. "I'm a newbie like you. This is my first festival. Looks like a lot of work. They could rebuild the whole town for what they're putting into this."

"I'm sure you're right." Stella didn't want to stay and gossip. "I'm sorry, but I'm late for an appointment. I'll talk to you later."

"Right. Don't eat too much food and get sick now. See you later."

Stella put the laptop into the Cherokee and walked to Matilda Storch's hat shop. A bell jingled as she pushed the door open.

"Oh, Chief Griffin. I'm so glad to see you. Come and take a look. I know you're going to love it."

The hat, one of many waiting to be picked up, was exactly the right size for Stella's head. It was large and the same shade of periwinkle as her dress. It was also festooned with ribbons, flowers, and a bird or two. When Stella tried it on, she felt like her head was going to fall over.

Matilda frowned when she saw the look on Stella's face. "What's wrong? The color is perfect and it's just right for you."

"Could you take off some of the stuff?" Stella made a circle around the hat with her hand. "It's a little . . . overpowering."

"Of course—if that's what you want." Matilda drew herself up stiffly, not liking the criticism. "It's one of my best. But if you hate it—"

"I don't *hate* it." Stella didn't want to hurt her feelings, but she knew she wouldn't wear the hat if it weighed more than her fire helmet. "I have an old . . . neck injury. I'm afraid this weight, even though it's very nice, might make it worse."

"Oh, well, why didn't you say so?" Matilda ran to get a

pair of scissors and some pins. "We can make it lighter. It will go better with your dress anyway."

Stella sat there for a few minutes as the scissors clicked away on top of her head. She sat very still, mindful of them and their gleaming sharpness, until Matilda was finished.

"How's that look?" Matilda asked.

"Much better," Stella said. "It's more comfortable now. Thanks."

Matilda bit her lip as she removed the hat from Stella's head. "Maybe a little extra ribbon? No flowers or birds."

"Sure. That would be fine."

"Good. Come back tomorrow and we should be ready. And not a moment too soon."

Stella thanked her again and was greeted by Lucinda Waxman and her granddaughter, Foster, who was the Sweet Pepper Festival Queen this year.

"You know I was the Sweet Pepper Festival Queen when I was seventeen." Lucinda beamed at her pretty granddaughter. "I guess it runs in the family."

"Who is the Sweet Pepper King?" Stella asked.

Lucinda was clearly shocked that Stella would even ask such a thing. "Foster will be escorted by Bertie Wando, the mayor's son. We don't call him 'king.'"

Foster smiled and shook her head. "Then we'd have to have a contest for them too, Chief Griffin. What kind of talent would Bertie have besides catching a football and looking good in his tuxedo at the Sweet Pepper Festival dance?"

All three ladies laughed at the very idea. Stella laughed a little to show that she understood. She excused herself then and left the shop.

Exhausted and ready to take a long nap to make up for the night before, Stella drove the Cherokee back to the cabin. She felt like crying when she saw that she had a visitor. Walt Fenway was sitting on the tailgate of his old pickup. He waved as she parked her vehicle.

"This day is never going to be over," she muttered to herself before she got out of the truck. She put a smile on her face as she greeted him. "Walt! What brings you up here?"

"Don't pretend like you're glad to see me after all that mess last night. I have something to say to you that should've been said a long time ago. I think it's what the arsonist was worried I might tell you."

"Okay. Why didn't you tell Chief Rogers?"

"He isn't interested if it's not Victor. He made that real clear at the office." He looked at the cabin behind him. "It's been a lot of years since I was inside. You got any coffee?"

"I do," she said. "Excuse me if I don't join you. I need about a gallon of Coke. I don't think I can make it much longer without it. If I start snoring while you're telling me what I need to know, nudge me."

He laughed. "I wish you were permanent here, Stella. You would give old Ben Carson a run for his money. I'd like to see it."

The door to the cabin was open as usual. Stella did her best to make it look like she'd opened it, but it was kind of obvious she hadn't. Even more odd was the coffeepot already brewing on the counter. She didn't know how to explain that. Maybe she could say she had a timer that was set for whenever she pulled up.

Walt looked around the cabin as she sorted through her options while taking down coffee mugs from the antlers. "You know, you don't have to pretend with me, Stella. I know this place is haunted. Before the town took it over, I used to come up here all the time. I felt closer to Eric. It's still his place, isn't it?"

"I guess so." She was relieved not to have to come up with an explanation. "I didn't know what was going on at first. Things moved around all the time. Lights came on, and the alarm didn't seem to work. Then one night he talked to me."

Walt stared at her. "Talked to you? You can *hear* him?"

Stella cleared her throat. Maybe she had crossed some line of believability. Maybe now he thought she'd lost it. "The house makes sounds. Sometimes I think I hear voices."

"Coward," Eric said. "You don't have to worry. He can handle it."

"Oh." Walt started walking around the living room. "Is he here now? Can you talk to him now?"

She wasn't sure what to say. She finished making the coffee and handed Walt a cup. "I don't know. Eric says you can handle it. Can you?"

Walt started laughing so hard he had to put down the cup. "Are you kidding me? What I wouldn't give to talk to my old friend. Eric? You son of a gun! After all these years, you're still here."

Eric was laughing too. "Tell him it's good to see him again too and that I appreciated his visits after I died."

Stella told Walt what Eric had said. She was uneasy about this whole medium-type role she'd suddenly been pushed into. She sipped her Coke and waited.

"I can't tell you how much it means to know he's okay," Walt said. "So this is what happens to you when you die, huh? What about me? My place is burned out. What will happen to me when I die?"

"Tell him he'd better get busy rebuilding," Eric said. "Then he has to be ready to get rid of squatters who want to take up his space."

Walt laughed again when Stella relayed the message. "So that's why no one has been able to live here. Except for you, Chief. Why are *you* different?"

"He said it's because I can hear him and I'm rebuilding his fire brigade," she explained. "We had a few problems to begin with, but it's better than snakes in the wiring."

"I'll bet you've had some problems." Walt sobered when he looked at her. "First of all, you're a fine-looking woman. Eric always liked the ladies."

"He's just jealous," Eric said.

"Second of all, you're a Carson and he never cared for the old man."

"I haven't had that problem with him," Stella said. "I have with a few others."

Walt sipped his coffee and shook his head. "Wish we had something a little stronger. This will have to do for now. Eric, I'm glad you're here. You're the only other soul who might realize the truth about Adam Presley's death. I think Tory had half an idea. The problem was none of us could put it all together. Until now. I think I get it now."

"Go ahead, Walt," Eric said.

Stella didn't relay the message. Walt got up and faced the fireplace. "It wasn't Adam that died that night."

Chapter 32

〜〜〜〜〜〜〜〜〜

"What makes you say that?" Stella asked. Was this what Tory was looking for?

"Eric and I examined the body," Walt explained. "The dead man was wearing Adam's clothes and shoes. He was the same approximate height and weight as Adam. The man's face and midsection were mostly gone. You know the kind of destruction I'm talking about."

"Yes. I do. What was it that made you suspicious? Obviously it wasn't something that struck everyone else like it did you."

He ran his hand around his neck. "We were uneasy with the circumstances. I mean, a man doesn't spill lighter fluid all over himself and not get up and change clothes. He especially doesn't sit there and light up after he does it, then lose the lighter."

"You signed off on the investigation," she reminded him. "You and Eric both said it was an accidental death."

"You don't understand the circumstances surrounding the death," Eric said. "I couldn't even remember until right now."

"It was the circumstances." Walt echoed what Eric had said to Stella. "It was two days before the festival. The old man didn't want us dragging it around while the visitors were here. He said it was too expensive for the town to keep investigating. Eric and I argued until we were blue in the face. The mayor threatened to fire both of us. In the end, it was what Ben Carson wanted."

Stella thought it over and shook her head. "I guess I understand why he wanted you to stop, Walt. It's not much to go on. An expensive investigation, especially at that time, based solely on Adam Presley's reaction to spilling lighter fluid on himself, isn't very conclusive. What if he was smoking first? He was half-asleep and spilled the lighter fluid. He might not have even been aware of it happening."

"Let him finish," Eric said. "There's more. It takes him forever to get it all out."

"There's more," Walt echoed again. "Eric noticed that Adam was wearing his expensive watch that he was so proud of. One of the car manufacturers gave it to him for top sales or some such. We'd all seen it a million times. He was also wearing his wedding band—"

"His diamond high school ring was gone." Eric finished before Walt could. Their words came almost at the same time. "I remember now!"

"Adam loved that ring," Walt said. "He never took it off. We couldn't prove it since there wasn't enough skin left on his finger to see if there was a white band where it should've been. The coroner actually argued that the ring had melted. No one ever found the ring—or the metal either."

"People take things that matter to them out of their houses before they set them on fire for the insurance money," Eric said.

"I know," she answered him. She looked at Walt. "Eric reminded me about people not wanting to lose their important things when they torch their houses."

"Exactly," Walt shouted. "You've still got it going on, buddy."

It was funny watching Walt dance around the living room, pumping his fists into the air and staring at the ceiling.

"Tory noticed too, but the old man told the DA it wasn't enough to investigate, and the DA agreed." Eric sounded like he was right beside her. Stella jumped, and he laughed at her. *Too much caffeine.*

"Was he telling you that everything else was perfect?" Walt stopped his victory dance. "There was only that flaw and some testimony from Tory and her friends that Adam had stopped smoking months before."

"Tory also said that it was the wrong type of cigarette," Stella added. "It sounds like it was worth looking into with that extra evidence."

"You haven't been here long enough to really cross the old man or see him in action with someone else," Eric explained. "When he shuts something down, it stays down. Like the investigation into your grandmother's death."

Stella watched Walt finish his coffee. She'd heard so much about this. "Was there something odd, beyond the tragedy, about my grandmother's death at the estate?"

"Not according to Ben Carson." Walt sat down heavily on the chair. "I guess Eric told you about that, huh? I wish I could hear him too. I wonder why you can."

"I don't know," Stella said. "What about Abigail Carson?"

"Another case of no proof. Some of the people who worked at the estate said Ben and Abigail were arguing right before she fell down the stairs."

"Including my mother." Stella wondered if anyone knew the truth. "She told me she found out later that Ben had left and was working at the pepper plant when it happened."

Walt shrugged. "If he was, nobody saw him there but the old manager, Shu Carriker. He swore up and down that the old man was at the plant taking apart a broken machine."

Stella took a deep breath. *Jack's father. The one John said had once been Ben's go-to man.* "He counts, right?"

"He did," Eric agreed. "Before he took off for places

unknown right after. No one ever saw him again, which meant no one could follow up."

"Not that this isn't interesting." Stella tried to get back on topic. "Right now, I guess we need to stick with what happened to Adam Presley and whether that had any impact on Tory's death."

"I think it's obvious," Walt said. "The man killed in the fire on Second Street *wasn't* Adam Presley. I believe now that Adam set that fire up to cover him getting away from Tory. He probably left town. He had to get away from the butt-kicking he knew her father would give him for making her look bad, even if she was unfaithful."

"I thought this afternoon that either Tagger or Greg Lambert might have killed Adam. It had taken Tory all these years to gather enough evidence to make her dangerous. What if Adam is back?" Stella asked. "What if he didn't like Tory continuing to try and prove it wasn't him that died in that fire? He went to a lot of trouble to disappear."

"I suppose that's possible," Eric said. "Although it seems like folks would know him right away. He grew up here."

"If he's back, no one might recognize him after all these years." Walt grinned and looked at the ceiling. "I bet I look a lot different now than I did when you passed."

"He looks the same to me," Eric said. "Older, yes. I would've still known him."

"What does Eric look like now?" Walt wondered.

Stella admitted that she hadn't actually seen him. "I think it may be more difficult to see a ghost than to hear one. Adam could also have had plastic surgery. Don't forget, he had to be looking over his shoulder for the last forty years. He probably doesn't look like he did at all."

"Well, that scares the bejesus out of me," Walt said. "If this is true, it could explain the fire at my place. Heck, maybe it even explains who ran you off the road, Stella. Tory left you to walk around asking questions about Adam's death all over town. Maybe that got him riled up."

"He could be right," Eric said. "Not sure how we could prove any of this."

"Eric isn't sure how we can prove it." Stella got to her feet and walked to the big windows that overlooked the deck.

"I don't know if we should try," Walt said. "I'm retired and homeless. Eric is dead. It could be bad for you, Stella. Are you sure you want to press your luck with this?"

"Maybe there's a way to trap him into giving himself away," Stella continued, caught up in the idea. "I'd like to leave Sweet Pepper knowing this was resolved."

Walt seemed to weigh his involvement in the project. "I was too scared of my position when Adam died. I thought about it last night. I don't have much to lose now. What the heck?"

Stella outlined her plan to flush Adam Presley out into the open. Adam's father was still alive. She thought they might be able to use him to help locate Adam. It was a long shot, but Walt agreed that it could work.

Together, she and Walt got everything together that they'd need over the next few days. Technically, Stella would have been required to have Don Rogers's approval to approach Adam Presley's father about exhuming his son's body. She was banking on the fact that Adam's father wouldn't know that.

If he did, and spoke to Chief Rogers, the worst that could happen would be that the police chief would be angry when he found out. Since he was angry all the time anyway, she decided to go ahead with her plan without consulting him.

When everything was in place, Stella and Walt knocked on Joe Presley's front door. It was the day before the festival. The little white house he lived in seemed barely big enough for a person. It was more like a child's playhouse.

Joe came to the door, leaning heavily on his walker. He looked every year of his ninety-two birthdays. He'd once been a warehouse manager at the pepper plant and had taken care of his wife and son on that salary for many years.

"Yes?"

"Joe? It's Walt Fenway. Remember me?"

Lucky for them, Joe not only remembered Walt, he also thought he was still the police chief.

"We need to exhume your son's body," Stella explained after telling him who she was.

Joe looked confused. "Where's that other fella who took care of the fires?"

"Eric Gamlyn? He retired," Walt said. "Chief Griffin is taking his place."

"What is it you want Adam for?" Joe asked.

"We need to talk to you about him," Walt said.

Had Joe forgotten that Adam was dead? Stella wondered.

"Oh. Well, I haven't heard from him for a few years, not since his mama died in 1992." Joe scratched his head, still not understanding.

Stella and Walt exchanged hopeful looks. *That's a surprise.* Maybe they were on the right trail.

"Has Adam sent you anything lately? Checks? Letters?" Walt asked him.

Joe shook his head. "Not in years, sir. He tries to do what's right. He sent his mama a postcard right before she died. It's from California. Imagine going all that way. No one else in our family has ever gone that far from Sweet Pepper."

They went back inside with Joe, who sat down in a ragged chair near the TV.

Stella hadn't been expecting this. She thought they'd have the old man sign the fake document and that would be it. They could take it to the newspaper and pretend they were going to exhume Adam's body. That was supposed to bring Adam out to stop them from finding out that he wasn't in his coffin.

She hadn't thought that Joe knew his son was alive. "Do you have the postcard, Mr. Presley?"

"Sure. I'll show you." Joe got to his feet with great difficulty.

Stella and Walt watched the man hobble into the next room.

"Can we use that as proof that Adam is still alive?" Stella whispered.

"Possibly. All depends on when it's from and if someone believes it."

"You mean Chief Rogers."

"We'd need him to present it to the DA. And we couldn't have worse timing. No one is gonna want to know about this during the festival. It's like the last time."

Stella knew he was right. Maybe the timing was bad, but as Walt and Eric had admitted, if they'd continued pushing the last time, Tory might still be alive.

She looked around the tiny living room, barely big enough for a TV and a chair. The kitchen area looked the same, with a miniature stove, refrigerator, and sink. That left a small bedroom where Joe had gone for the postcard, and a closet-sized bathroom.

She thought her apartment back home was small.

"He must not remember that Adam supposedly died in the fire all those years ago."

"Or Adam told his parents he was moving on and they never said anything," Walt replied. "It happens. Nobody keeps your secrets better than family."

"Or turns you in faster, for your own good," she quipped.

"Yeah." He smiled. "One way or the other."

Joe slowly returned with the postcard in his hand. "See? He was visiting the orange groves in California when his mama took sick and passed. He couldn't come home for the funeral. His mama would've understood. She didn't want him to live with that woman a minute longer than he had to. She was eating him alive."

Stella realized they had at least the start of an explanation as to why Adam had decided to fake his own death. There were a lot more questions—the biggest one being, where had he found a dead man to take his place for the fire?

She and Walt looked at the faded postcard. It was dated March 1992.

"Guess he was alive then," Walt muttered. "Damn Ben Carson. I knew we should've pushed harder."

"Never mind." She handed the postcard back to Joe. "You still have a chance to set it right."

They both thanked Joe for his help.

"You're entirely welcome," he replied. "If you see my son, would you tell him I wish he'd stop in. I'm not so young anymore. I'd like to see him one more time before I join my Lula."

Walt put his hand on the confused old man's shoulder. When he spoke, his voice was ragged. "If I see him, sir, I'll be sure to tell him he should visit you. I'll do my best to get him here."

They walked out of the tiny house together. Stella felt guilty getting the information from the old man who couldn't even recall that his son was supposed to be dead.

"That was awful." She rested her hands on the steering wheel.

"Never mind." Walt slammed his door shut. "We did what we had to do and it worked—at least the part about finding out that Adam didn't die in the fire. Now what? The plan was to go to the *Gazette* and scare Adam out when he saw in the paper that we were going to exhume him. Now I'd be afraid Adam might go after the Smittys if they say they have a postcard that proves he's alive. We need to find out who he is."

"We stick to the plan." Stella buckled her seat belt. "The Smittys won't look too closely at the document. They know you and trust you. They publish the exhumation plan and we draw Adam out."

"Well, as long as you know what the plan is, Stella. I'm only along for backup. I wish Eric could be here too." He glanced at her. "He's not, is he?"

She started the engine. "I think the only two places he can go are the cabin and the firehouse. He said he thinks it's because he built them."

"I guess I better get started quick on rebuilding my old place. I want to have somewhere to haunt too. I hope some pretty woman like you moves in and wants to live with me. For a dead man, Eric has it made."

Stella wasn't so sure about that. What was going to happen to Eric when she left? She'd promised herself she wouldn't think about it.

The plan included going to the *Sweet Pepper Gazette* with intent faces to tell the Smittys that Stella had plans to exhume Adam's body. She and Walt had already looked up where he was buried in the Sweet Pepper Cemetery so they could make it more convincing.

It was a bald-faced lie. It would take a lot more than a fake court order with Joe Presley's name on it to make that happen. Walt had said it was a difficult and lengthy process that was nearly impossible to get a judge to sign off on.

The Smittys didn't know that. Both reporters (publishers, photographers, owners, and delivery people) sat with rapt expressions on their faces, almost unable to write, so amazed that this could happen.

"You realize that this is the day before the festival starts, right?" Pat asked in shocked disbelief.

"That's right," Walt said, still raw on the subject. "Maybe we'll parade what's left of him down Main Street for everyone to see."

Stella cleared her throat, and Walt sat back, frowning. She gave the Smittys enough information to whet their curiosity. She explained how Tory had believed her first husband was still alive and had passed that information along before she'd died. They didn't ask to see the exhumation document.

"Do you think it's possible that Adam Presley killed Tory because of this?" Pat asked.

"Yes, I do," Stella confirmed. "I think he was worried

about her figuring out that he'd faked his own death. I think she was getting close. We should know in a few days."

Of course, they wouldn't know anything if Adam had left Sweet Pepper right after Tory's death or if he decided not to take the bait. It was a chance they had to take.

Walt stayed silent, letting Stella answer the barrage of questions the Smittys put to her. After it was over, they walked out into the sunshine together. The sounds of hammering, sawing, and microphone checks from the festival setup filled the air.

"Well, that's that," Walt concluded. "The fat is really in the fire now."

Chapter 33

~~~~~~~~~

Friday was the opening morning of the Sweet Pepper Festival. The weather was perfect. The booths and tents were all up, hues of red, blue, orange, and green dotting Main Street. The roads through town were already blocked off by police barricades, and the smell of cooking food wafted up from the town toward the mountains.

The only problem beneath the cloudless blue sky was the front page article in the *Sweet Pepper Gazette*. Residents who had seen it, especially those who had anything to do with the festival, had already lodged complaints with Police Chief Don Rogers.

Stella was up early too, not because of the article in the *Gazette*. She was in the kitchen with Eric, who was coaching her on how to make candied peppers. Following his instructions, she cut the peppers into small slices while he made his secret candy syrup of sugar, water, and cardamom. When the syrup was ready, she would dunk the peppers into it, then place them on a baking sheet and cook them on a low temperature until they were crispy.

Stella smiled as pots, ingredients, and spoons whizzed around the kitchen. Hero whined as he watched it happen.

When the peppers were finally in the oven, Eric took Hero outside, staying within his fifty-foot perimeter.

He was calling the puppy up to the cabin. Eric had admitted as much. He enjoyed seeing Hero, and the puppy seemed to like him. Stella didn't say anything about it.

She tasted the bright red peppers when they were done. They were sweet at first, then hot on her tongue. "These are good." She was as surprised as she sounded. She hadn't baked anything since she and her mother made box pizzas when she was a kid.

"What did you expect?" Eric asked. "We might win the contest."

Stella went through her contestants and their recipes from the email sent out to all the judges. She wouldn't actually taste the food until later that day. The ribbons would be given out on the last day of the event.

"This is too dangerous," Eric repeated again. He'd been saying it since she'd arrived at the cabin the night before after a long practice with the volunteers at the firehouse. "You're setting yourself up to be the target of a desperate man."

"It's the only way to catch him." She didn't disagree that there might be some risk to the plan. "I'll be careful."

"I don't think you're listening. Or you don't realize how bad this could be," he continued. "You aren't a police officer, Stella. You're brave, but you're foolhardy." He paused in his rant and listened. "And here's Officer Trump to tell you the same thing. Should I make a large pot of coffee for all the visitors you're about to have?"

She took a deep breath. It wasn't like she hadn't expected it. She had so much to do before the festival started at nine a.m. "If you could be quiet for a while, I could get done with this fairly quickly. Is that too much to ask?"

"Let me help."

Stella knew he was close but didn't know how close until her laptop screen filled with static and the whole thing went down. "Eric! It's not cheap getting this fixed when you do that. I needed that information."

"I thought that way the computer could shut up instead of me. You've already looked at the information dozens of times. It hasn't changed."

"I didn't tell you to shut up," she said as John knocked on the door. "You're too sensitive. I have a lot on my plate right now."

"Everything, except common sense."

Stella put on a smile, despite her annoyance, as she opened the door for John. "Good morning. What brings you out this early?" *As if I don't know.*

He didn't wait to be invited in—a fact that drew some criticism from Eric despite the fact that he knew John would champion his cause once he'd heard Stella's plan.

"Why do you think I'm here?" John slapped the morning edition of the *Gazette* on the table. "The chief is furious. He's threatening to arrest you for putting out false information to the press, because you're a public figure."

"Is that a real charge you can make against someone?" she asked as she closed the door.

"I don't know. People are so angry, they might make a new law for you. What were you thinking? The festival is important to the town. To have this story on the front page while thousands of tourists are here . . . it's not good."

Stella couldn't believe it. "You sound like my grandfather. Tory would probably still be alive right now if he'd let Walt and Eric figure out what happened to Adam forty years ago. That's the same excuse he used to stop the investigation then."

"What are you talking about? There's nothing in the file I gave you about that."

"That's what Walt was trying to tell us. That's why his house was burned down. Walt and Eric had issues with Adam Presley's death. They had doubts about the body being his. They couldn't pursue the truth because of the stupid festival. No one wanted to hear it."

John was briefly taken aback by the information. He regrouped and continued his attack. "You have no real proof that Presley is still alive. You sure don't have a court order to have his body exhumed. It was stupid and irresponsible for you, as the fire chief, to say such things."

"I have proof that Adam was alive in 1992. That's almost twenty years after his supposed death. Maybe I don't have a court order, but Adam doesn't know that—if he's still here."

"You should've brought it to the chief, Stella. You aren't a member of the police. You could've brought it to me if you didn't want to go to Don."

"Don made it clear that he was only interested in Victor. What was the point?"

John sat down at the kitchen table. "What are you trying to do?"

She laid out her plan to trap Adam Presley.

"Are you kidding me? That's the stupidest idea I've ever heard. Not to mention the most dangerous."

"Exactly what I've been saying," Eric agreed.

"You're setting yourself up for Adam to come after you, even though you think he's killed at least one other person."

Stella poured them both a cup of coffee, now that the preliminaries were over. She sat down at the table with him to explain. It would be nice to have him on their side.

"Walt came to me with his story about the minimal investigation that went on involving Adam's death. He believes Adam tried to kill him to keep his suspicions quiet. It could be the same reason Tory is dead. That file you gave me about the police investigation was only half the size of the one she gave me only a few hours before she was killed."

John shook his head. "I can't believe Walt would be a party to all this. He was the police chief. It goes against everything."

"I feel the same way," Eric added. "Two heads aren't always better than one."

"It's done." Stella started on her fifth cup of coffee. She was out of Coke and hadn't wanted to go out, for obvious reasons. Really, the coffee was kind of addictive. She'd never had as much of it before.

"I'm going to get dressed, go to the festival, judge my

contest, and see what happens. You can come along if you're worried."

"I'd like to, believe me," John replied. "The chief would never assign me to help you with that—especially if I told him what you and Walt are trying to do. He's a stickler about citizens taking the law into their own hands. He'd probably put all of us in jail. Maybe that's what should happen. At least you'd be safe there."

"First of all, as you pointed out before, I'm not just a citizen. I'm the duly appointed fire chief of Sweet Pepper, and this crime involves a homicide by fire."

"Stella—"

"Not to mention that I can't let everyone down like that, John. Walt is meeting me at the festival. He has a gun. If Adam tries anything, he'll be there. If Adam tips his hand, then we'll know what happened to Tory."

She didn't tell him that Eric had already said that he dared Adam, or anyone else, to try to burn down his cabin. He didn't let snakes or scorpions in. He sure wasn't going to let a human do anything to it.

"You are the most single-minded woman I've ever met. It's against my better judgment, but I'll do what I can to help."

"Not you too," Eric mourned. "Is everyone in Sweet Pepper crazy nowadays?"

"You'll be in a crowded area. That should help some, *if* he makes his move today," John said. "I can't be there the whole time, but I'll look in, and I'll have a few other officers check in as they walk around the festival. Walt will be there." He was obviously still trying to convince himself that this could work.

"That's right." She got up from the table, with a decent caffeine buzz. "I have to get dressed and figure out how this hat is going to stay on my head. Then I have to take my laptop to Charlie Johnson—again. I'll have to look at the recipes again later after the tasting today. All the recipes I saw before my laptop crashed met the qualifications for peppers and chocolate."

John could see she was already drifting away from the topic of drawing Adam out. "Stella?" He took her in his arms and kissed her hard on the mouth. "Be careful."

She stared at him in surprise and slowly smiled. "I will. Don't worry. This will work."

"Why didn't I think of that?" Eric muttered to himself, angry and jealous.

Stella wandered into the bedroom to change, leaving John to find his own way out.

"I wish this place really was haunted," John said with a sigh. "Any haunt worth his salt could keep her from leaving today."

Eric watched him leave. He agreed, partially, and he *could* keep Stella from leaving the cabin. She'd be safe, but she'd also be angry. He was torn about what he should do.

He knew he was going to lose her in a few weeks. He wanted to protect her. He wouldn't be able to stand it if she left angry at him.

He went out on the deck to sit and look at the mountains. He tried not to think what his existence would be like when she was gone.

By the time Stella had dropped off her laptop with Charlie, she was beginning to understand how difficult life was for women in the 1800s. The periwinkle gown was pretty but made it difficult to walk and even more difficult to drive the Cherokee. She had to hike the skirt up and secure it under the seat belt. The hat was a whole other matter.

"What are you doing up there that keeps frying your laptop?" Charlie asked. "Not that I'm complaining. You're my best customer. Maybe you need a surge protector."

"I think it's something to do with the mountain. Too much strange energy."

"Maybe," he agreed. "I saw the story in the *Gazette* today. Are you really going to dig up some man who's been dead since before you were born? Is that even legal? What could you hope to find?"

Stella had decided to answer all the questions she was asked about the situation. If she wanted to drag Adam Presley out of hiding, he'd better think it was bad enough to take a chance on getting caught.

"They couldn't do DNA testing when he was killed. They can now. As soon as they bring the body up, they'll know right away if it's really Adam Presley. His father is still alive, so we have a good sample to compare. It won't take more than a few days, and then we'll know the truth."

Charlie looked doubtful. "Sounds expensive. Why bother now?"

"Because I think the real Adam is living here again. He killed Tory to keep his secret. I won't let him get away with that."

It might have been too much, from the horrified expression on Charlie's face. Certainly the process would take a lot longer, even if she *really* had the authorization to do it.

She felt certain when she left the computer store that the story would filter around town quickly, following on the heels of the *Gazette* article. It couldn't be too soon for her.

Theodora and Elvita were anxiously waiting for her at the booth where she would judge the pepper and chocolate contest. Stella had removed her large hat because the breeze from the mountains kept threatening to blow it away. As much as she might like that, she didn't want everyone to be disappointed with her performance.

Too late.

"Where's your hat?" Elvita asked. "The costume is very important. Hundreds, if not thousands, of visitors will come through here today. Decorum is as important as the actual judging process."

Stella firmly planted her hat back on her head. Elvita quickly swooped in to securely attach it with a large, dangerous-looking hat pin.

"Now these are your entries." Theodora pointed out the food samples. They were carefully labeled in separate plastic packages. "Each recipe you were sent has been made precisely according to the ingredients. You have some samples of other recipes, older ones, you can give out as people stop by."

There was a large plastic container. Stella couldn't tell what was inside it.

"You have read all the recipes and verified that they meet the correct specifications, haven't you?" Theodora continued with a stern expression on her face.

Stella wondered what the other woman would say if she told her about Eric not wanting her to continue reading. "Yes, I have. I'm ready."

Both women started laughing. "You can never be ready for the festival. You'll find out. Good luck. If you need help, send someone for us. *Never* leave your booth."

Stella, in turn, gave them her pepper contest entry. They smiled and commented on the bright color, then took it to the correct judge.

Walt laughed from behind Stella as the two women left the judging booth. "You're a raw recruit to them. They'll probably enjoy talking about this for months. It will keep them warm this winter thinking about it. Didn't anyone warn you?"

"I'm definitely out of my element here," she admitted. "On the other hand, I don't think either of them could run up and down stairs with a sixty-pound hose either. We all have our places in the world."

"I'd like to see 'em try. Great idea for next year's festival. Some kind of fireman-policeman contest. I'll bet people would get a kick out of it."

"I hope I don't have to run to catch Adam today. It's all I can do to walk in this dress."

"You look real pretty though. Are you all set to taste some good Sweet Pepper cooking? Best in the world. I hope there are extras. It's the only reason I agreed to do this."

"As ready as I'll ever be." She whispered, "You brought your gun, right?"

He nodded and pulled a large pistol out of his jacket. "This will take care of anyone who's looking for trouble—even men who are supposed to be dead."

"Thanks. John was at my place first thing this morning. I didn't have to wait that long to hear what Eric had to say about the plan."

"I got a call at the hotel bright and early from Don. He said he thought we should both go to jail for putting that in the paper. I told him to go fly a kite. If he's not careful, I might come out of retirement and run against him in the next election."

He and Stella talked for half an hour. She was beginning to wonder if the newspaper story had kept everyone at home.

Then it was like someone opened the floodgates on a dam. People were everywhere. They wanted to see the food and taste it. They wanted to know how Stella got ready for the tasting. How did she decide which recipe was best?

Walt was right. She wasn't prepared. She answered the questions the best she could. When she didn't know the answer, she gave the questioner food.

The recipes had to be tasted and judged as the committee members walked around the booths where the judges waited. Someone had to be there to make sure she tasted everything, then wrote down her scores and comments. She was supposed to take a sip of water between each food to cleanse her palate.

The water was a lifesaver because some of the food was really spicy. There were two types of pepper brownies. Each was good, but the one with a chewy center was better. Then there were chocolate-covered peppers, which Stella was reluctant to try. She finally closed her eyes and took a bite. They were surprisingly good, with a snappy aftertaste.

Some of the chocolate pepper foods were very imaginative. There was a chocolate pudding cake with pepper garnish and bits of pepper inside. Another recipe was hot chocolate with pepper garnish. She didn't really care for that. Valery's mocha coffee from the Daily Grind, with pepper-whipped cream, was better.

Flo's chocolate cookies she recognized right away. They were basically the same as the ones she'd tasted at the bed-and-breakfast, but these had walnuts as their secret new ingredient.

Each time Stella tasted one of the foods, the worried cook was there watching. She tried not to give away how she felt, but there were a few times—chocolate-covered pepper pizza—that she couldn't hide her reaction.

The result was tears from the woman who worked at the post office. Stella couldn't remember her name, but she knew she'd remember the terrible disappointment on her face. No wonder the festival committee had a hard time finding judges.

When her part of the contest was over, Stella slumped down in her chair and covered her eyes with her hands. "I never want to do this again."

Walt had brought a thermos of hard cider. He saluted her with it. "You did fine. Now you only have to write everything up and pick your winner. Bear in mind that whoever loses will hate you forever."

"Thanks. You're a big help."

Her emergency pager went off. There was only a weird scrambled message on it. "Great. What a time for an emergency. I hope we don't have to try and get the engine down Main Street. Myra is lucky I'm not staying on as fire chief or we'd have to have a few words about how dangerous this is."

She called the firehouse to see what was going on. Tagger was on duty. "Where is the call?"

"It's a mess, Chief. I can't tell what's going on. I tried to call everyone. You're the only one who got the page, I guess. You might have to come down and sort this out."

"Okay. I'm on my way. Keep trying to call everyone in case we need them."

Chapter 34

~~~~~~~~~~

Stella explained the emergency to Walt. "It's probably nothing. Tagger gets a little confused sometimes."

"And he has a problem with the bottle other times. Say no more."

"Do you think you can handle the booth if I sneak off to the firehouse for a few minutes? If it takes more than that, there really is an emergency and it will have to take priority over chocolate-pepper judging."

"Those are fighting words, my girl. But I've got your back. Go on. Get Tagger off the radio. If someone from the committee comes by, I'll tell them you had female problems."

"Thanks . . . I think. Is that a good enough excuse to leave my appointed booth?"

He shrugged. "Beats me. You better get moving before we find out."

Stella hoped she'd run into one of the other volunteers who could go to the firehouse and handle the problem. No such luck. She knew it was probably just another case of Tagger screwing around with the computer. She couldn't take that chance. If a real emergency came up, there would be no way to notify everyone.

She hiked up her skirt and made the best time she could getting to the makeshift festival parking lot. The hat was another story. Elvita had done a great job making it stay on. She wasn't sure it was ever coming off. She finally gave up and got in the Cherokee with it still on her head. She felt like her neck was going to break when it smashed against the ceiling. She gritted her teeth and started the truck. There was nothing else to do.

There was no traffic going out of town. It was bumper-to-bumper coming in. She wished those latecomers good luck finding someplace to park. She hoped her space was still there when she got back.

It was quiet out at the firehouse. Traffic had died out a few miles back. It looked like everyone was at the festival. Even Beau's bar was empty and closed.

She tried calling Tagger again as she turned into the parking lot. There was no answer. At least the loudspeaker wasn't playing old Beatles music.

Stella walked into the firehouse and went through the kitchen into the communications room. There was no sign of Tagger, until she opened the door. He was sitting very still, staring at her, his face white and pasty.

"Tagger?" She rushed into the little room and put her fingers on his pulse. He was cool to the touch, but his heart was still beating. He must have had a heart attack or stroke. She reached for the landline, and the door closed behind her.

There was a small window in the old metal door. She looked out of it—and saw Charlie Johnson's face looking back at her.

"I'm glad to see you," she shouted. She knew it was hard to hear through the heavy door. "Can you let us out? Something is wrong with Tagger."

"Insulin. I had some left over. You couldn't leave it alone, could you? You had to keep putting that information on your laptop. I'd erase it and you'd do it again. I'd hoped you'd forget about it. Tory had a stake in it. You didn't. Why didn't you drop it?"

Stella tried the door as he spoke. It was jammed from outside. She still had the phone in the office. She could call for help. What was he thinking?

It was suddenly obvious that Charlie Johnson was Adam Presley. The good news was her plan was working. The bad news was that she wasn't prepared for it to work so well. He wasn't supposed to be at the firehouse. She wasn't supposed to be alone.

She locked the door from the inside and stepped back to the desk. No help there. All the communication lines were cut. She reached for her cell phone, which would normally have been in her pocket. She didn't have a pocket—or her cell phone—in the periwinkle gown. She'd left it in the SUV.

"Sorry, Stella." Charlie/Adam pressed his face against the window. "This old shack should've been burned down years ago. I think I'll take care of the job now."

She smelled the gas long before the smoke started flowing under and around the old door. She ripped off some of her large petticoat and stuffed it into the cracks the best she could.

She couldn't page her volunteers or use any other normal outlet to call for help. She thought about screaming for Eric. It seemed absurd to call a ghost to help her, yet it appeared to be her only hope.

John poked his head inside Stella's booth at the festival. Walt was drinking cider and helping himself to some chocolate and pepper cookies.

"Are you supposed to be eating those?" He grinned as Walt jumped.

"Oh, it's you. I thought you were one of those festival ladies."

"Where's Stella?" John asked, looking around.

"There was an emergency at the firehouse. Old Tagger was at it again. He said he couldn't reach any of the other volunteers."

John looked at his pager. There were no messages, not even partials that might indicate a problem with communications. His heart started pounding, adrenaline kicking in. "How long?"

Walt's face grew serious as he staggered to his feet. "You don't think—"

"Let's go. I'll call for help on the way."

The communications room was heating up fast. Adam had started the fire right outside the door. Stella had moved Tagger to the concrete floor. He was still unresponsive. If he didn't get help soon, she knew he could die.

Of course, if they didn't get out of the firehouse, he'd die a lot sooner.

She'd screamed until her throat was raw. She could see the flames spreading through the old wood as she looked through the window in the door.

Where is Eric?

Or was this what happened when you believed you were talking to a ghost and it wasn't real? All this time, she'd convinced herself that Eric existed. Now was a bad time to find out he didn't.

The office was filled with heavy smoke. Charlie/Adam had doused the firehouse in gasoline, a much faster- and hotter-burning accelerant than the kerosene Victor had used at Tory's. The irony was that the volunteers would have nothing to fight the fire with even if they got there in time.

As she lay on the concrete, trying to breath, Stella wondered how long it would be before the flames reached the engine and pumper.

She gave up calling for Eric. She closed her eyes and prayed as she had rarely prayed in the past. It wasn't that she hadn't considered that she could die in a fire—it was a hazard that went with the job.

Stella was suddenly afraid that she was going to die far from home, alone, the victim of a crazy arsonist. She was angry enough to beat on the metal door with her fists, if she could have stood up. She was having a hard time breathing, rapidly losing consciousness.

She thought it was a trick of desperation her brain was playing on her when the metal door swung open, bouncing back hard against the wall. She realized it wasn't when she saw someone enter the office and bend over her.

"Stella? Can you walk?"

She didn't recognize the face in the smoke, but she knew the voice. She coughed and nodded. "Get Tagger out of here. He can't do it alone."

Eric picked up the unconscious man and helped Stella to her feet. "The back door is open. Stay low. Move as fast as you can. The walls won't make it much longer."

Stella followed Eric through the kitchen. The flames were eating all the new appliances the town had purchased for the fire brigade. She focused on getting out, keeping her head down, and moving as fast as she could.

She could hardly think, but the one thought that consumed her was that Eric was *real*. He'd come to save her.

The door leading into the back parking lot was open. She could see the trees and the sunlight, the mountains, dark in the distance. The flames around them were hot, making it even harder to breathe. She was near the end of her strength. She'd felt that way before, when she'd been trapped inside a burning house a few months after she'd joined the fire department back home.

Home.

Stella started thinking about home. She could see her mother and father. She saw herself playing ball in the street when she was a kid. The heat she felt was from the summer sun high up in the sky. Her mom needed to turn on the sprinkler so she could cool down. Everything would be fine.

Eric put Tagger down on the rough asphalt. Stella had been right behind him. She'd faltered inside the doorway, the place most people died during a fire, inches away from being saved.

He ran back for her. The smoke and flames made it difficult to see, even for him.

She was leaning back against a smoldering wall. He grabbed her and put her across his shoulders, then headed back outside within the fifty-foot proximity that seemed to be allotted to him.

Vehicles were pulling up at the front of what was left of the firehouse. The volunteers had arrived. It was time for him to go.

Stella only told Walt what had really happened at the firehouse. She didn't think anyone else would believe that a dead hero had rescued her and Tagger from the fire. She waited impatiently to see Eric again for three days, while visitors came and went and balloons and flowers filled her room at the hospital.

Tagger was okay. He wandered up and down the hospital corridors telling people about his brush with death. He believed Stella had saved both of them—the story John had told when he'd come around the back of the firehouse and found both of them unconscious.

He'd even confessed to taking Adam Presley's folder from her desk. "I didn't want you to keep investigating, Chief. I thought you might get hurt. I didn't know Adam was still alive. Please don't fire me."

Stella thanked him and assured him that she wouldn't fire him. Maybe he really was a hero.

She took the praise from the mayor, the town council members, and the newspaper with a heavy heart. Eric deserved the honors and awards they'd promised her before she went back home. The only thing she could do was to relay the sentiments when she talked to him again.

The festival ladies brought her samples of all the winning foods from the festival and forgave her for leaving before the judging took place. "We've never had anything so exciting happen to one of our judges," Elvita said. "Why it was all over the TV news that one of our judges solved a murder. It was wonderful publicity!"

Not enough for Eric's candied peppers to win the festival prize, but there was a consolation green ribbon for their recipe.

The only one who didn't compliment her was Chief Rogers. He criticized her foolhardiness, as he called it. "Here you are—a victim of your own crazy schemes, lucky to be alive. You almost killed Tagger too. I know everyone else thinks you're a hero. I think you and I know the truth."

Don and his officers had caught up with Adam, and he was in the county jail awaiting arraignment. He wasn't talking about his fake death or how he'd pulled that off, but he had confessed to killing Tory. "That crazy woman didn't know when to leave well enough alone," he'd complained, according to Don. "Neither did the fire chief. Why couldn't they just let me be?"

Adam said he'd come back to Sweet Pepper two years before, when he'd read an article in the *Sweet Pepper Gazette* about Tory trying to prove he hadn't died in the fire forty years ago. He'd almost taken care of Tory right then. He'd left her alone when people seemed to ignore her story about him.

He'd stayed to help his father, who had Alzheimer's, and couldn't even remember him.

Adam admitted that he'd followed John and Stella to Walt's place and knew Walt might get them started on the same path Tory had taken, trying to figure it all out. He'd meant to kill Walt, though. The fire hadn't been meant as a warning at all.

John came by at a bad time—Marty and her grandfather were both visiting her. They'd brought an elaborate flower display that was almost too large to wheel into the room. John brought a handful of daisies he'd bought at the grocery store on the way from Sweet Pepper.

The three men stood and glared at each other before John dropped his bouquet on the bedside table and left. Marty and Ben stayed for a while, Ben talking about Stella's future in Tennessee politics after her heroism.

Marty casually held her hand and sat on the side of her bed. When they were ready to go, he lightly kissed her cheek. There was nothing improper about it, but it made Stella uneasy.

It had taken a while to remember that night at the mansion, after her wreck on the motorcycle. Now that she did, she felt certain it was Marty and Vivian standing beside her bed, talking about her like she was a piece of meat. She still wasn't sure what they were talking about that night, but she was beginning to think John was right about the two of them having it in for her.

She might never know why Marty had saved her that night either. Could it have been to get close to her? Is that why he'd joined the fire brigade too?

Stella was more than ready to leave the hospital. John drove her back to Sweet Pepper in the red Cherokee. She wished John would drive faster, almost wishing Ricky had picked her up. She couldn't wait to get back to the cabin and assure herself that Eric was still there. She planned to demand that he show himself as he had at the firehouse.

Or was that a trick of the smoke and the fire? Maybe he *couldn't* appear to her.

Mostly she wanted to understand how any of it was possible. He'd saved her life. She could still hardly believe it.

"Well, this is it." Stella started to get out of the Cherokee when they reached the cabin. "Thanks for the ride."

"Are you sure you're okay? You've been really quiet all the way back. Would you like me to stay awhile? Do you need anything from the store or something?"

"I'm fine." She glanced at the cabin. The outside light was on. Her heart did a little somersault. "I'm tired. I thought I might go in and lie down. Maybe I'll see you tomorrow."

He smiled and kissed her very gently on the forehead. "I'll come back later and check on you. We're starting work on the firehouse. All that old timber has to be torn down so we can rebuild. Lucky thing how the pumper and engine rolled right through the bay doors. They're in good shape. Just need a new paint job. The science teacher over at the high school said the trucks moving that way had something to do with the heat in the bay doing something to the tires. I don't know, but it was lucky for us."

Stella wasn't surprised. After being pulled from the fire by a ghost, she couldn't imagine being surprised by anything ever again.

She said good-bye to John and walked up the familiar stairs to the cabin. The door opened before she could reach it. She took a deep breath. "Eric?"

"Out here."

She walked out to the porch and sat in a rocking chair beside him. He was completely visible, from his long blond hair tied back with a leather thong to his red Sweet Pepper Fire Brigade T-shirt and hiking boots. He was a tall, handsome man with a broad chest and wide shoulders. She would have recognized him anywhere from the picture in the firehouse.

He had to have been strong in life, Stella thought, to be able to lift her and Tagger after being dead for forty years. Maybe all those Paul Bunyan–sounding legends about him were true.

"I'm glad you're back," he said. "I'm sorry I couldn't come and visit."

"Me too. Thank you for getting me out of there. I know Tagger thanks you too. You managed to get the trucks out too, didn't you?"

"They were in my proximity. I'm sorry I couldn't get all the gear out." For the first time since she'd sat down, he looked at her. His eyes were a stunning blue. "I'm sorry it took me so long to get there. I should've known about the fire right away. I don't understand what happened. Usually, I can hear a mouse run through there. I think I was too wrapped up feeling sorry for myself."

"It doesn't matter. You were amazing. I don't understand how it happened, but I'm glad you were there. Walt was completely calm and understanding about it when I told him. Everyone else thinks I got us out."

"That's the way it should be—except for your plan. I hope you never try anything like that again. You're a firefighter, not an undercover cop. You should act like one."

She was a little surprised at his criticism. "It worked. Adam is in custody. I hope I can get my laptop back since his shop is probably closed."

"Stella—"

There was frantic knocking at her door. "Hold that thought. I'll be right back."

It was John. He had a terror-stricken look on his face, like a kid seeing a monster movie for the first time. "I'm sorry. I know you're trying to rest—you have to come with me. There's something at the firehouse you have to see."

Stella glanced at the deck. She couldn't see Eric anymore. "What's wrong?"

"Just come with me. It's impossible to describe."

Reluctantly, she left the cabin with John. "What is it?"

"You have to see it. No one is going to believe it."

John raced down Firehouse Road like the devil was chasing him. He pulled into the parking lot, which was filled with her volunteers, and a large group of people she didn't know. A coroner's car was pulling up as they got out of the pickup.

For a minute, Stella thought it was some kind of surprise party—except for the coroner. Everyone shook her hand, said they were happy to see her. They all mourned the loss of the firehouse.

Petey and Kimmie managed to hug her very carefully.

John brushed them all aside as he led Stella into what was left of the garage bay area. Most of the walls were gutted. She saw sledgehammers and crowbars ready to take out the rest. The beautiful wood beams were gone forever. The mayor had already described the red brick building the town planned to put up in its place.

"We were starting the demolition," John explained as they approached the back wall of the bay. "I hit it with the sledgehammer and a piece of sheet metal fell out. I couldn't believe what was behind it."

Stella looked into the wall cavity. There were dried bones. It looked like a complete skeleton, the skull staring back with empty sockets. Covering parts of the upper torso were bits of red fabric.

She felt like she'd been hit by the sledgehammer. "Who is it?"

"I took this out." John held up a sealed plastic bag with a badge in it that said "Chief Eric Gamlyn, Sweet Pepper Fire Brigade."

"I think this is what's left of him. I don't know how it got here."

Stella looked at the badge as the coroner knelt in front of the skeleton in the wall. Had someone brought Eric here after the fire that had killed him?

The coroner, a jolly, gray-haired man who seemed more likely to play Santa than look at dead bodies, took the skull out of the wall. "Not sure who this poor fella was, but here's your cause of death." He stuck his gloved finger into a hole in the back of the skull. "He was shot. Probably died quick. Any idea when this happened?"

Stella saw Eric standing in the blackened ruin of the firehouse. He was staring at the skeleton with a look of disbelief and horror on his face.

Then he disappeared.

"I think we can safely say this is a murder case," the coroner said. "It's been here awhile. Might be hard to figure out exactly what happened."

Stella staggered out of the firehouse and sat down at the

old picnic table that had survived the fire. How was this possible? People saw Eric die in the grain silo fire. How would they ever figure out what had really happened?

There was only one thing to do. Eric had saved her life. It didn't take long for her to make a decision.

She called her mother while she still had cell phone service. "Mom, it looks like I'm staying in Sweet Pepper a little longer than we planned."

The Sweet
Pepper Difference

~~~~~~~~~~~~~~~~~~~~~~~~~~~~

Sweet Pepper, Tennessee, grows the hottest, sweetest peppers in the world! It's a combination of our soil and our proximity to the Smoky Mountains that makes our jalapeño peppers superior. Sweet, but with a bite that makes your eyes open. Not too hot—not too tame either.

These are some of the award-winning recipes from our annual pepper festival. Try a few, or some of your own, with our peppers. We're sure you'll agree that our peppers are the best! Enjoy!

Know Your Peppers

Because knowing the strength and taste of the peppers you use can make or break your meal, it's best to know your peppers! This time, we'll talk about the jalapeño.

The Jalapeño
The jalapeño is one of the most commonly used peppers in the United States. It is spicy but not overpowering. Jalapeños

are usually red or green and are about two to three inches long. Their Scoville Heat Index (pepper ranking from hottest to mildest) is 5,000, which is somewhere in the midrange. These peppers can be added for an extra zing without offending the palate.

Recipes

〜〜〜〜

ERIC AND STELLA'S CANDIED
HOT PEPPERS

*These are good on their own or as a garnish for
everything from ice cream to chocolate cake!*

1 cup water
1 cup sugar
¼ teaspoon ground cardamom
2 large mild or medium-hot red chili peppers

Preheat oven to 325° F.

In a small saucepan, mix together the water, sugar, and
cardamom. Bring the mixture to a simmer over very low
heat and let cook for about 5 minutes. Remove the seeds
and membranes from the peppers. Thinly slice the peppers
horizontally into rings. Add the pepper slices to the syrup
and cook on low for about 15 minutes. Drain the syrup and
put the peppers on a baking tray lined with parchment paper.
Cook in an oven on low for about 30 minutes or until the
peppers are crisp.

These store well in a covered container for a long time. They are spicy and sweet with just the right amount of bite!

SWEET STUFFED PEPPERS

12 jalapeño peppers
1 pound ricotta cheese
1 cup sugar
¼ cup semisweet chocolate chips or candied fruit
1 teaspoon vanilla
Chocolate syrup

If using fresh peppers, wash them and cut off the tops about ½ inch down from the base of the stem. Clean out the seeds and ribs. (You can buy our peppers already prepared in this way in some produce sections.)

For the filling: In a large bowl, mix together the ricotta cheese, sugar, and chocolate chips or candied fruit. Stir in the vanilla. Fill the peppers with the ricotta mixture—it's best to use a pastry bag for this.

Swirl chocolate syrup over the filled peppers and enjoy!

SPICY BROWNIES

½ cup butter
⅔ cup semisweet chocolate chips
4 large eggs
½ teaspoon salt
2 cups sugar
1 teaspoon vanilla
1 ¼ cups all-purpose flour
¼ cup unsweetened cocoa powder
5 jalapeño peppers

Preheat oven to 350° F. Grease a 9-inch cake pan with nonstick cooking spray or vegetable oil.

Melt the butter and chocolate chips together in a microwave safe bowl, stirring occasionally, about 1 minute. Blend all the ingredients together. Dice the peppers and fold them into the batter. Pour the melted butter and chocolate into a large bowl and add the remaining ingredients. Stir well. Put the batter into the greased pan.

Bake for about 30 minutes or until the top is firm to the touch.

SWEET JALAPEÑO RELISH

This is a dish best served cold.

5 jalapeño peppers, chopped, with seeds removed
1 cup chopped sweet green peppers
1 large onion, chopped
1 cup white vinegar
1 cup sugar
1 6-ounce bottle of fruit pectin, such as Sure-Jell Certo

Combine all the ingredients in a bowl and mix thoroughly. Add the fruit pectin, to thicken the mixture. Allow it to cool for at least one hour. Serve as you would any type of garnish.

Someone wants to bake a killing.

FROM *NEW YORK TIMES* BESTSELLING AUTHOR

JENN MCKINLAY

RED VELVET REVENGE

A Cupcake Bakery Mystery

It may be summertime, but sales at Fairy Tale Cupcakes are below zero—and owners Melanie Cooper and Angie DeLaura are willing to try anything to heat things up. So when local legend Slim Hazard offers them the chance to sell cupcakes at the annual Juniper Pass Rodeo, they're determined to rope in a pretty payday!

But not everyone at Juniper Pass is as sweet for Fairy Tale Cupcakes as Slim—including star bull-rider Ty Stokes. Mel and Angie try to steer clear of the cowboy's short fuse, but when his dead body is found facedown in the hay, it's a whole different rodeo...

INCLUDES SCRUMPTIOUS RECIPES!

"I gobbled it up."
—Julie Hyzy, bestselling author of the
White House Chef Mysteries

facebook.com/TheCrimeSceneBooks
penguin.com